SACRED
ALARM
CLOCK

ALSO BY

JOHN T. BIGGS

OWL DREAMS

POPSICLE STYX

CHEROKEE ICE

SHINERS

CLEMENTINE: A SONG FOR THE END OF THE WORLD

SACRED ALARM CLOCK

JOHN T. BIGGS

FLEET

OGHMA CREATIVE MEDIA

www.oghmacreative.com

ISBN: 978-1-63373-353-4

Interior Design by Casey W. Cowan
Editing by Gordon Bonnet & Gil Miller

Fleet Press
Oghma Creative Media
Bentonville, Arkansas
www.oghmacreative.com

SACRED ALARM CLOCK is not your average novel. In fact, it isn't a novel at all. It is a collection of short stories that stand alone but also carry a common narrative from the beginning to the end with the same characters. It is just the kind of experimental fiction that scares publishers away as soon as they see it coming.

In addition to having an experimental structure, the book takes on the topics of racism and homophobia while throwing in a bit of contemporary indigenous culture. There is something in it to offend practically everyone if they are so inclined. Then there is the problem of previous publication. All but one of these stories has appeared in anthologies or magazines that varied from young adult speculative fiction to literary fiction.

Needless to say, it took a courageous publisher to bring this linked collection to print. Casey Cowan took on the project when he was putting Oghma Creative Media together. He found a pair of excellent writers, Gordon Bonnet and Gil Miller who took time away from their own projects to edit *Sacred Alarm Clock*. Without their efforts, this book would not have been possible. Thank you Gordon and Gil.

And thank you Casey Cowan. Thank you most of all.

TABLE OF CONTENTS

END TIMES
CONFUSION

MONA'S MOTHER SAID THE WORLD would come to an end pretty soon. Maybe not today or tomorrow, but in a year or two. That's why girls from good Choctaw families were turning into lesbians.

"End times confusion," she told Mona. "I heard it on the radio." There weren't many Choctaw lesbians yet, but by the time Gabriel dusted off his horn there'd be truckloads of Indian girls doing lesbian things with other Indian girls.

"I just hope Jesus understands."

When Mona asked which exact passage in the Bible condemned girls loving girls, Mom told her, "The Hebrew language had no nasty words, so all the lesbian verses were written between the lines."

Mom explained how all the important biblical women were either whores or wives when they quit being virgins. And if that wasn't proof enough, Mona ought to read the part about being fruitful and replenishing the earth.

"Hate the sin but love the sinner," Mom said. "Especially when she's your daughter." Mona's parents wouldn't throw her out, or refuse to speak to her, but they felt duty bound to disapprove.

The worst thing was the sad way Mom and Dad looked at her. The way Mom introduced her to suitable men. The way Dad pretended she'd forget all this sexual foolishness in a few years.

He said she had the right kind of hips for making babies—blushed when he said it. Choctaw fathers don't talk about their daughters that way, even when the girls were natural beauties like Mona. Her long black hair looked like it had been coated with gelatin, her deep brown eyes could swallow a man's self control, and the way she walked made young men turn their heads.

"I see them watching you," Dad said.

Mona couldn't tell if that made him proud or angry. A little of both, she decided. Her dad was a man, after all. A better man than most; he'd provide for her, and protect her. He'd step in front of a bullet or a charging bull, or a runaway train if it came to that, but he couldn't wrap his mind around the idea of lesbian love.

"You're a pretty girl." Dad held up one finger like he was counting up her assets. Like he was describing a prize mule he had for sale, but Mona was more complicated than livestock.

"A really pretty girl." He held up a second finger to keep the first one company.

"A really, really pretty girl." He held up a third finger. Three good reasons for Mona to get married and start having babies instead of letting her ovaries fall to earth like overripe apples.

"You've got it all," her father said. "You're beautiful, desirable, practically Miss America. Why can't you love a man?"

"Why can't you?" Mona knew Dad would never get it. She'd seen herself in the mirror; she knew how attractive she was to men, but those features made some women want her too. Her legs, her breasts, her narrow waste, her bubble butt, and especially her face. According to her best friend Chris, Mona's looks made her a lipstick lesbian who didn't need lipstick.

Dad knew what she was thinking; Dad always knew what she was thinking.

"Chris is almost a man," he said. "But she ain't made it all the way."

Choctaw knew about women with warrior spirits. A cosmic mistake made by Chitokaka, The Great One, before the Europeans came and convinced him to be a Baptist. Mona wasn't one of those warrior women. She didn't like hunting or fishing. Her muscles weren't strong. She couldn't fight. And most especially, Mona wanted to have babies; she just didn't want a man to be part of the process.

It was all very confusing, and depressing, especially a few days before her period, when her body reminded her she was a woman by making her cry for the slightest reason. Maybe girls like Mona were a sign of the last days, like Mom said.

Maybe the end of the world would be Mona's fault, somehow, and "God made me this way," wouldn't be an acceptable excuse.

Chris told her to toughen up, or lighten up, or cheer up, depending on the route Mona's depression took and how Chris was feeling at the moment. Chris couldn't understand because she was one of those women with a warrior's spirit. She'd never understand the baby-wanting part. All Mona could do was think about her mixed up life, and cry. Women are never free of men, even women like Mona who don't want men for lovers, or women like Chris who walk and talk like men and take a man's first name, and get their hair cut in men's barber shops.

Men are rough. Men are crude. Men want to do disgusting things that give a woman not one ounce of pleasure. They'll slap girls on the bottom and pinch them in soft places, and tell them, "You like it, don't you sugar britches."

"The only reason women put up with men is having babies," Mona told Chris. "We can't do it without them. Sex with a man is the price we have to pay."

"Toughen up." Chris's snapped just like a man.

"That's the way things are." But Chris had a solution. Girls like Chris— and men—always have solutions.

"Turkey baster babies," she explained. All they needed was a few tablespoons of sperm and a way to squirt it inside of Mona at exactly the right time.

"You are even more disgusting than a man," Mona told her.

"Just trying to help," Chris said.

Men were always eager to help when it came to nasty things, but Chris' suggestion gave Mona an idea. There was a fertility clinic in Tulsa, where a girl could go and get a tablespoon full of sperm put inside her at exactly the right time with a special instrument that looked nothing like a penis. A female doctor would put it there. She might not be a lesbian, but at least she was a woman. At least she wouldn't tell Mona that the end of the world was coming and that's why girls liked girls. All Mona needed was a negative HIV test and $350.

"Comes complete with an ovulation test kit and an anonymous sperm donor with a college education," She told Chris.

"What kind of man donates his sperm?" Chris asked.

"Men leave their sperm all over the world," Mona said. "In the back seats of cars, in public restrooms and hotel rooms, inside of vaginas that never wanted it. Why wouldn't a perfectly ordinary man donate his sperm to a good cause?"

"Like blood," Chris said.

"Or corneas," Mona said.

"I still don't like it." Chris thought a turkey baster and a couple of gay male friends of hers might be better.

"They have lots of sperm," she said. "And they'd do it free anytime we want."

—

ARTIFICIAL INSEMINATION COST THREE HUNDRED and fifty dollars for each attempt, but the doctors were careful, and generous with their anonymous college educated sperm, and Mona got pregnant on the very first try.

When she finally got around to telling Mom and Dad, she pretended the baby had been started in the normal way.

"Let them think I'm a fallen woman," she told Chris. Mom and Dad would be happy to believe she'd slipped and landed on her back in the appropriate position to make a baby. That kind of thing happened all the time and they'd feel better about premarital sex that they would about artificial insemination. Much better.

Chris kept on about gay friends and turkey basters and how she felt left out of the whole process, especially since Mona didn't even let her come to the fertility clinic, "When the deed was done."

"The deed." Mona didn't like the way Chris looked at her belly, like there was some alien creature inside of her that had nothing to do with Chris, or love, or even the end of the world. Maybe it had something to do with the fact that Mona hadn't told her she was pregnant until people started wondering how she got so plump, and if she'd found a breast enlargement lotion that really worked.

"This baby will have two mothers," she told Chris. "A little girl," Mona was sure of it, "with two mommies." She could already picture her daughter in dresses and ribbons, a miniature lipstick lesbian just like momma.

If Chris had baby fantasies, she didn't say, but Mona was determined her daughter wouldn't be anything like Chris. No butch haircut or men's clothes, or fistfights. She'd be strong and self-sufficient, but in a feminine way, and she'd be pretty like Mona, and smart like her college educated anonymous father. She'd have enough Choctaw blood to qualify for the roles, but enough white blood that banks would give her credit.

"Left out," Chris said. "That's how I feel."

And that feeling got worse as the weeks rolled by and Mona looked less like Miss America and more like a pumpkin with legs. She got florid stretch marks in spite of the cocoa butter. Her face filled up with hormone-enriched fluids. Her emotions teetered on bipolar disorder, and she urinated sixteen times a day.

"Stretch marks fade," she told Chris. "Fluid retention goes away. Hormone levels recede to pre-flood levels. Everything will get back to normal except we'll have a darling little girl."

"Darling." Chris didn't say that word very often.

"Getting back to normal." She didn't say that often either, because there was nothing normal about Chris and Mona—not in Choctaw country anyway—and having a darling little girl around would make things even less normal than before.

"I don't think things are working out," Chris said, talking like a man again.

"I think we should start seeing other people. You need some Mona time. It's not you, it's me." Only a butch-lesbian like Chris could get away with so many cross-gender clichés.

"You're leaving me," Mona said, already crying, already feeling the baby's feet against her ribs, already needing to visit the bathroom for the third time in an hour.

Chris' sense of timing was perfectly masculine. She looked at her watch with its studded leather band and said, "I've got to go right now."

She headed for the front door of the little frame house that Mona couldn't afford to rent without her. She stopped long enough to say, "I'll be back for my things later. See ya."

Wouldn't want to be ya.

Mona knew Mom and Dad would help her if they could, but they couldn't help her very long. And she'd have to listen to them tell her everything happened for the best, except for her passing lesbian phase. They'd talk to her about paternity tests, because they didn't know about the anonymous college educated sperm donor. They'd talk to her about Aid to Dependent Children, and tribal money, and Mom would talk about the end of the world, which was still on the way but might have been pushed back another year or two thanks to Mona's miraculous pregnancy.

It really was miraculous, because Mona was pregnant, but still a virgin.

Maybe this baby would be the second coming of Jesus, like the Bible predicted, only this time the Messiah would be a lipstick lesbian.

End times really were confusing.

INCONCLUSIVE
GIRL

THE TECH POINTED TO HER nametag instead of introducing herself.

"Sylvia Anoli," Mona Beaver read aloud. "Choctaw name."

"Means messenger." Mona thought the name was perfect for someone who did sonograms. She wanted to talk about it, but the tech's expression killed the conversation.

"One sonogram's all the Nation pays for," Sylvia Anoli crossed her arms and waited for an argument.

"You want another, you have to write a letter." The tech's white skin and blond hair didn't match the Indian name. Lots of white women married Choctaw men in this part of Oklahoma. Most of them looked happier about it than Sylvia. A bad marriage explained everything: the name, the frown, why the technician hated Indians.

"One is all I need," Mona said. A girl didn't feel like arguing when she wore a hospital gown that barely covered her important parts. Especially an unmarried Choctaw girl who was getting her one and only free sonogram. Most especially a lesbian Choctaw girl who'd spent her last dollar for artificial insemination at a Tulsa fertility clinic and didn't want to talk about it.

The technician draped a paper apron over the chair beside Mona's hospital bed, an amenity supplied by the Choctaw Nation, so girls weren't quite so naked. Mona looked at the apron but Sylvia Anoli didn't take the hint. Maybe an unmarried, pregnant, lesbian, Choctaw girl who wanted modesty had to write a letter.

Dear Indian Agent:

May I please have a paper apron and a friendly technician now that the buffalo are gone?

Sincerely,
Mona Beaver

The technician put her gloves on with a snap that sounded like a slap across the face.

"Latex okay?" she asked. "Lots of girls your age seem to be allergic to rubber."

"Latex is fine."

Mona wanted to tell the tech, "I'm still a virgin, at least in the most important heterosexual way," but that would take too much explaining.

"The daddy isn't here?" Sylvia Anoli wanted a juicy story she could talk about over lunch but the details of Mona's pregnancy were practically juice-free.

"Away at college."

A convenient lie that might be true. The sperm donor was supposed to be a healthy college student with a high IQ, but Mona had her doubts. The clinic sent their donors into a quiet room with dirty magazines and a check for twenty dollars. Mona didn't think they took IQ tests in there, but lesbians can't be choosers.

Mona could have told Sylvia about her room mate Chris, who looked like she could be a 'baby daddy', but Sylvia Anoli already had a frown on her face as she walked toward Mona with a dollop of ice cold lubricant.

"Away at college." It sounded more reasonable when Mona said it the second time; the most reasonable thing about her pregnancy. Just ask Chris, the nearly baby-daddy. Just ask any anonymous college student sitting in a private room with a stack of dirty magazines—take your pick. Just ask Mom and Dad, who were happy to think the father was a private in the National Guard, whose name Mona couldn't quite remember.

Sinners didn't reform all at once, according to Mom. They moved up the hierarchy of bad acts from felonies to misdemeanors until they settled on one that wouldn't keep them out of heaven. Casual sex fell somewhere between shoplifting and swearing. Mona would get there yet.

The sonogram wand felt softer than Sylvia Anoli's hand. Mona asked about the funny noise.

"Beyond the range of human hearing," Sylvia insisted. Only dogs and pregnant unmarried Choctaw girls could hear it.

"Maybe it's the air conditioning." Mona waited for Sylvia to agree.

One Mississippi, two Mississippi. The longest river in America took exactly one second to name. Plenty of time for a friendly comment.

Three Mississippi, four Mississippi.

"It's really cold in here."

Five Mississippi, six Mississippi.

"I guess it keeps the flies off of the Indians." Mona waited for a smile. It might take Sylvia a few more seconds to find one among her regular expressions.

There it was.

The corners of the technician's lips turned up. A little racial slur was all it took. But she didn't look at Mona. Sylvia Anoli's eyes locked onto a television screen that showed an almost believable image of Mona's baby.

"Don't see a penis," Sylvia Anoli said. "Position's not too good."

The picture moved in and out of focus. A leg, a head, the whole body turned sideways for a moment.

"Probably a girl. Can't be sure." Sylvia Anoli looked at her watch. The allotted time for Mona Beaver's free sonogram was over. Quicker than a rollercoaster ride at the McCurtain County Fair. Quicker than an anonymous male college student earns twenty dollars in a Tulsa fertility clinic.

"A girl?" Of course Mona wanted a girl. Didn't every unmarried pregnant woman want a little girl, to dress up like a life size doll, so everyone would say she looked, "Just like an Angel on the top of a Christmas tree?"

Mona picked out a name already—Leah, which meant delicate according to *Five Hundred Baby Names.* She put her hand onto her belly before she thought about the slick goop slathered there by the technician who didn't like Indians.

"Inconclusive," Sylvia Anoli said.

An inconclusive girl.

Just like her mother.

"You want another sonogram, you'll have to write a letter." Sylvia Anoli pointed to the restroom where Mona had changed into her hospital gown.

"Wash the slime off in there," she said. "Picture's printing. They'll have it for you at the front desk when you check out."

"You're welcome," Sylvia added before Mona had a chance to say anything.

"Thanks," she said to Sylvia's back. "Thanks for the inconclusive girl."

—

MOST OF THE WOMEN'S CLINIC NURSES were as white as Sylvia Anoli. Some had Choctaw last names, but none of them hated Indians. A different one greeted Mona each time she came for prenatal care, interchangeable middle aged women with kind faces, and first names that ended in the letter "Y."

Hi, my name is—Cindy, Nancy, Tammy, Stacy. They wore green scrubs, and smiles they couldn't hide behind surgical masks.

This nurse asked, "Anybody with you today?"

Mona supposed nurses got lots of smile-practice in a birthing center, keeping mothers' spirits up while their contractions got closer together and their baby daddies got further and further away.

"Let me guess," Mona said. "The Nation will only pay for one baby. If I want another one I have to write a letter."

The nurse's smile increased its curvature. "I'll bet you met Sylvia Anoli."

"How'd you guess?" Mona stayed busy trying concentrate on something besides the next contraction.

"Bless her heart." The nurse propped up Mona's knees lifted her gown and touched her in the places doctors had been touching on a regular basis since the pregnancy achieved sure-thing status.

"Six centimeters," the nurse said. "You're well on your way."

The birthing room had everything a mother-to-be needed, except for a support system. Mona didn't want her mother around during labor and delivery. She especially didn't want her Dad. She might say something she'd regret during transition. That's what the birthing class instructor told her. Mona might say things everyone would regret for a long time.

"Will the father be coming later?"

"Can't make it, bless her heart." The contraction raised Mona's voice an octave or two, so the nurse probably thought the *her* part was a mistake.

Mona supposed the *her* part was a mistake—at least *this* her. Chris, the sort-of baby daddy, brought Mona to the hospital, but she waved goodbye as soon as the wheel chair arrived. She wouldn't come inside with her pretty, pregnant girlfriend even though she'd made a pinky swear.

Mona knew something bad was coming when Chris pulled into the parking lot and turned off the radio because the music made her too confused to talk. Chris wanted to say something but she couldn't. She'd probably tape a note to the refrigerator, or send an email or leave a message on the answering machine. Chris was so much like a man in all the most the important ways.

Chris said, "Later," then she climbed into her worn out Jeep Cherokee and drove away. Maybe she waved one last time to Mona's reflection in the rearview mirror.

Or maybe not.

"Objects may be closer than they appear," Mona said.

"Ain't it the truth," the nurse said.

"My name is Stacy Daniels. I'll be here for the next twelve hours." She showed Mona how to use the call button.

"I'm all yours," Nurse Stacy said. "Anything you need."

Bought and paid for like a prostitute. Compliments of the Choctaw Nation.

———

NATURAL CHILDBIRTH DIDN'T SEEM SO natural after all.

"Not a good time to start an epidural," Nurse Stacy said.

"Seems like a pretty good time to me." Mona had already let out a string of curses that would embarrass the ghosts of her Choctaw ancestors a thousand years back.

"A little pentazocine will take the edge off." Nurse Stacy had the hypodermic inserted into the IV line before Mona could ask questions.

"Helps you rest between contractions," nurse Stacy said. "Dulls the pain. Helps you forget about the world."

According to Mona's mother, everyone would be forgetting about the world pretty soon, because the *Last Days*, were finally here, as advertised in the *Book of Revelation*.

"It works fast," nurse Stacy said.

"Mom says . . ." Mona tried to tell nurse Stacy things she never understood until this moment, but most of her useful words vaporized in the burst of pentazocine clarity.

"Wow." The world slid into oblivion and Mona didn't come back until the next contraction. Then she remembered everything—about Chris, about the clinic in Tulsa, about nurse Stacy and baby Leah, who would be here any minute because the doctor magically appeared and told her to push.

Pain came at her from a great distance, getting closer all the time. It felt like someone else was hurting; someone Mona barely knew having a baby girl whose name meant 'delicate'.

"Just like baby Leah," Mona told the masked man who ordered her to, "Push harder please!"

So polite. The Doctor's name was Surrender Nanda. He came to Durant, Oklahoma from India to deliver American Indian babies. Nurse Stacy told Mona all about him just before the last contraction.

"Nice," Nurse Stacy said. "And competent, even if he talks funny."

Surrender Nanda. Good name for an Indian—East or West. But not as good as Leah. That name came from the Chosen Tribe. Leah was a Biblical name, like Rebecca, or Mary, or Caleb, or Joseph.

No one had to tell Mona to push when the final contraction came. Every part of her pushed at once until it felt like she turned inside out, then presto-chango, Dr. Surrender Nanda pulled a baby out of Mona the way a magician pulls a rabbit from a hat.

"There's a little stranger in the room." Surrender Nanda's voice ran up and down the scale like preparation for a music recital.

"Have you thought of a name for him yet, Mona." They were on a first name basis now. Why not, after all they'd been through?

"His fingers are nice and pink," Surrender Nanda said. "His pulse and respiration are good. His Apgar score is 8."

His?

The doctor placed Mona's baby on her chest and listened to her heart.

My baby boy?

Ecstatic tears dripped from Mona's chin onto the baby whose name could not be Leah. Nurse Stacy cried too. Even Surrender Nanda dabbed at his eyes. The only one in the birthing room who didn't cry was baby—what's his name?

"Joseph," Mona told Nurse Stacy and Surrender Nanda, like she'd picked a boy's name just in case.

"A Biblical name, because childbirth is a blessed event." That's what Mona's mom had told her, and she got it absolutely right; even if Mona and Joseph were in this thing alone; even if Joseph's father was an anonymous college student with a high IQ; Even if Mona's baby wasn't a delicate, inconclusive girl.

SACRED
ALARM CLOCK

FOSTER MOM HAS SO MANY complaints they stick in the back of her throat. Her lips move without sound, the way a fish prays to be thrown back in the water. I cup my hands behind my ears so I'll be ready when the first words break free.

Listening with the biggest possible ears. Listening the way Apaches always do when white people speak.

I wiggle my fingers so *The Fosters* know I'm trying hard, but it doesn't help. Dad squeezes his fingers into a ball, holding his anger so it can't get away. Mom tells me, "Stop acting crazy, Wylie."

She takes my right hand in hers like a fortuneteller who sees bad things in my future. Foster Mom is looking for spray paint. Foster Dad looks too, but from a distance, the way he checks a rental car for scratches before he gives the company his credit card.

"Not all Indians huff paint." I talk slow, so my good luck key stays underneath my tongue. Talking slow is good for hiding secrets. Not talking is better, but that reminds *The Fosters* about Indian ways, and that reminds them of my Apache mom and they wonder if I'm huffing paint all over again—the way she did before they saved my life. Before they gave me a chance to grow up like the white son that never happened.

Before things didn't work out like they planned.

My good luck key clicks against my teeth the way it does sometimes. My tongue pushes it underneath again, but it's too late. Foster Mom heard the click.

She looks at Foster Dad like he should be able to fix me, like maybe I have a loose part he can fasten with SuperGlue. *The Fosters* cross their arms and squint like they're inspecting cracks in the foundation of the house they let me live in.

Like I am their real son.

Like I am really a white boy in a clever Apache disguise.

Foster dad says, "The tattoo is the last straw, Wylie."

One more thing I should have hidden.

I say, "Lots of people have them. Indians especially."

Sometimes *The Fosters* need reminding—I am Wylie E. Chatto, descended from an Apache scout who tracked Geronimo down just to prove he could. I'm wearing a T-shirt with pictures of Apaches on the back, Geronimo, and Cochise, and maybe Victorio. It's hard to tell because I can't read the names any more than I can read the tattoo hiding underneath the Indians. According to Foster Dad it says, *WHITE POWER.* The things he hates most are the two swastikas, one on each of my shoulder blades, propping up the hateful words like bookends.

I tell him, "Words don't matter when you can't read." That disappoints *The Fosters,* too. I want to explain how Apache warriors painted white men's power symbols on their bodies when they rode into battle. American flags and crosses, anything the spirits liked.

"It's all about pleasing the spirits." Another disappointment. *The Fosters* don't want to hear about heathen gods—even Usen, who's almost the same as the big white God who lives in the sky.

"Just another name for God is all," I say before I remember we are talking about tattoos.

Usen makes me think about my real mother, who met him when she huffed paint. My real mother would understand about the tattoo, and not being able to read, and even the voice of Geronimo, who always talked to me in dreams, but now talks to me all the time.

"*White man's power runs through copper wires,*" he whispers too softly for *The Fosters* to hear. "*When the wire is cut their clocks all stop. The white man's time is finished.*"

Geronimo has secrets for me, but I can't hear them all. His voice is louder than it used to be but the most important words are still too quiet.

"Geronimo can't read the tattoo either," I tell *The Fosters.*

"I think he should see somebody," Foster Mom tells Foster Dad. She reaches into her plastic alligator skin bag for a cell phone. I wonder if Geronimo knows about that kind of white power.

He says, *The wire spirits still run the show.* He's about to tell me something else when Foster Mom touches her fingers on the cell phone screen. With each touch the room smells more like trouble.

"Rosemary," I tell *The Fosters*. "The smell of complicated things. The smell of trouble brewing on an electric range," I tell them. "The favorite herb of crooked spirits." The more I explain, the less they understand.

"Dr. Goldberg, please." Foster Mom holds the phone next to her ear and looks at the ceiling. Taps her foot in time to the music Dr. Goldberg plays for her while she works out the best way to get rid of me.

Foster Dad looks at his watch—a clear sign it's time to act.

My Apache war cry makes Foster Mom drop the phone. I stomp on it and run out of the house. I'd go faster if I had a horse, but Apaches on foot are fast enough—if they aren't huffing paint.

Geronimo floats beside me so I'll know he's a ghost. His lips move without sound, but Geronimo doesn't have complaints stuck in his throat. He's telling me what I need to know about visions and directions and bravery. I listen carefully, but at first Geronimo's not loud enough and then he isn't talking.

It's hard to know about Indian ways when your teacher is a dead medicine chief. Maybe I should ask somebody else. Another Indian, who's alive and not so full of Apache ways. Geronimo doesn't say no, so I start looking.

—

OKLAHOMA CITY'S FULL OF INDIANS. Lots of Choctaw and Cherokee—mostly civilized, but at least they weren't saved from being Indians by White Fosters. Maybe one of them can tell me what Geronimo can't say louder than a whisper—what every Indian in the world knows except for Wylie E. Chatto.

"Indications are positive," Geronimo talks like the Magic 8-Ball Foster Mom gave me on my tenth birthday. It told the future in printed words I never learned to read.

"What does it say?" I asked *The Fosters* after every Magic 8-Ball question.

"Indications are positive," was what they told me. Sometimes without even looking. Magic 8-Balls can't solve spirit problems. That's what visions do.

Visions need things like fasting and chants and steam and drugs. But Geronimo says huffing paint is the wrong way to get them. He and *The Fosters* agree on that much. Geronimo says Indian spirits are hard to find, not like the white man's spirits that talk to you on the telephone.

"Peyote," he whispers in my ear.

"Where do I find that?" I ask, but my Geronimo service is temporarily interrupted. So now I have something else to ask a real live Indian. The trouble is finding one, because most Oklahoma Indians are so civilized they look like Fosters.

Somebody with dark skin and black hair and eyes filled up with death— that's who I'm looking for, but nobody fits that description all the way.

This one's too frightened. That one's eyes are blue. Some of them push their fingers over cell phone screens instead of looking out for enemies. Some listen to the electric spirits sing through little speakers in their ears.

Strangers don't like it when I study them close up. Most look somewhere else, hoping I'm harmless-crazy instead of dangerous. They're not brave enough to tell me what I want to know.

But there is one across the street. Hard muscles show underneath his T-shirt with the picture of Geronimo on the front. It's a spirit sign, like when I found my good luck key in the front seat of a police car with an open door, a beam of sunlight shining on it through a cloud. Usen's finger pointing out a miracle.

Indications are positive. The man across the street has death behind his eyes. He has a shaved head. He has tattoos, a swastika on his neck and words that might say *WHITE POWER*. I can tell from his broken nose, he's a warrior.

In a handful of heartbeats I'm across the street looking at Geronimo on his shirt, waiting for another sign, because you can never be too careful when it comes to spirits.

Geronimo's lips are moving but picture Indians hardly ever talk out loud. The words on his thin angry lips might be English or Apache, but I'll never figure it out because the owner of the shirt says, "Get lost Tonto."

Now I see he's not all the way Indian. The hair stubble on his head is brown not black, and even though his eyes are full of death, they are halfway between brown and green,

"Hazel," I tell him, as if we've been talking about his eyes all along.

His hands turn into fists and he bobs his head forward. It comes so close to mine I can see the broken veins in his eyes and the pimples on his chin and the hateful way his lips turn up at the corners. He has blue letters on his knuckles, and green numbers on his forearms and black spider webs on his elbows. He pulls up the edge of his Geronimo T-shirt that's not tucked in so I can see the pistol in his belt.

Now I can read the shirt-Geronimo's lips perfectly.

"Take the gun, Wylie. It's a gift from Usen."

There's no beam of light like with the good luck key, but Geronimo never lies, so I snatch the gun while its owner finishes his last cuss-word.

". . .ucker."

I say, "Thank you," before he has a chance to say another one. *The Fosters* taught me all about politeness. Say thank you whenever you take something you shouldn't. Say, "Thank you God," when no one is around to hear—just in case. Send a thank you note even for gifts you don't like. Have Foster Mom write them if you don't know how.

The gun-giving-man doesn't have much death behind his eyes anymore. He backs away really fast, because now he knows I'm not a pretend Indian. He moves fast and jerky like a movie running backward on *The Fosters'* television.

He says, "Holy crapola," when he's too far away for me to read Geronimo's lips anymore. He breaks into a run. Not nearly as brave as I first thought.

I untuck my T-shirt and stick the pistol into my pants. I cup my hands like a megaphone and shout, "Thank you," once again, because now I have a pistol and a lucky key and that is sure to help me learn what every other real Indian in the world already knows even without peyote.

—

"LET ME SEE YOUR HANDS." It's a cop voice behind me, like the ones on *America's Most Shocking* shows Foster Dad likes to watch.

I hold up my hands, criminal style and get ready to say, "Is there a problem officer?" the way *The Fosters* do when they get pulled over for speeding. But this isn't a speeding ticket, because the cop has one hand on the butt of his pistol and he's reaching behind him with the other one.

Handcuffs. I've always wondered what those are like, and now I'll find out, because the cop pushes me toward the car and makes me, "Assume the position," like I've seen on TV hundreds of times. He snaps the cuffs on—way too tight.

The air smells like it did when Foster Mom called Dr. Goldberg.

Rosemary. Trouble on the way, cooked up by white man spirits in their complication kitchen. Geronimo tells me, *"Look out Wylie,"* but I already know indications are way positive this cop wants to arrest his very first Apache.

Pat down time. He spins me around, getting ready to find the pistol in my pants, but I can't let that happen, because it's a gift from Usen and Geronimo.

So while he's looking at the bulge under my shirt, I lurch forward and crack my forehead against his.

I say, "Ouch," before I can stop myself—embarrassing, because Apaches don't say ouch. The cop moans and slumps to his knees, while I take off running with my hands cuffed behind me.

People watch, instead of turning away like they usually do. They see me when I leap into the air and swing my arms under my feet like a jumping rope.

"I have extra-long arms!" I shout, so everybody will know how it's done. I don't say, "Like a monkey," the way Foster Dad described me to a doctor. I don't say, "It's not quite a syndrome, but close," the way the doctor did, or "It's God's will," like Foster Mom. I'm too busy running.

The cop is on his feet, but still not ready to move fast. "Stop!"

I listen for, "In the name of the law," but that never happens.

I run into an alley that turns into another alley that has a gray dumpster where it opens to the next big street.

I climb into the dumpster, lower the lid, and spit my good luck key into my hand. In three heartbeats the cuffs are off—Usen always knows what he is doing. I throw the cuffs away because I don't like them, and I throw the key away because it doesn't taste lucky anymore.

"Apaches know how to run," I tell Geronimo. He knows that already so he doesn't have to speak.

The air inside the dumpster smells like garbage instead of rosemary, but that doesn't mean I'm safe. Red rat-eyes stare at me from half-eaten chickens and cans of pork and beans. Albino rats, bred by white scientists to be satisfied with cages and laboratory food, but still clever enough to escape. Black rat eyes glitter in streaks of sunlight poking through the misfitted dumpster lid. Black and white together—the rats have done what people haven't.

My heart is steady and my breathing is too, so I'm not afraid of rats.

I call them, "Brothers," even though they can't understand me anymore than I understand Geronimo when he whispers in Apache.

"Brother rats." I empty a green plastic bag and pull it over me like an Indian blanket. The brother rats climb over it like I'm not underneath.

When the policeman opens up the dumpster lid, he believes them.

"Rats!" he tells the electric voice that lives in a black box on his shoulder. The voice says my name mixed in with static and numbers. The wire spirits know my name.

"Not your real one," Geronimo tells me. *"Not your war name."*

I don't know my war name either, but I have one. That's why the rats are hiding me. That's why Usen gave me a lucky key and a pistol. That's why I have to learn what every real Indian in the world knows except for Wylie E. Chatto, who was stolen from his mother before anything important happened.

But important things are happening, anyway.

The electric voice sputters and spits as the cop walks away, wondering how a wild Apache with syndrome arms and handcuffs can hide in the middle of Oklahoma City.

"Thank you, brother rats."

The rats twitch their noses at me like a handshake. Usen likes them. Geronimo likes them. Wylie E. Chatto likes them, but cops and Fosters don't. When the wire spirits sleep the rats and the Apaches wake up.

I feel Geronimo's flat angry smile behind me as I climb out of the dumpster. He can hate white people and be happy at the same time.

The Indian knowledge I'm trying to figure out is very close now, the way rats are always close even when you can't see them. Indian knowledge is bigger than the rats—important and invisible, like the moon hiding in the shadow of the earth. Like a mountain top hiding in the clouds.

I hear Mexican words mixed up with English a few steps away—right around the corner. Mexicans are Indians too, conquered by the Spanish, pretending to be white long enough to take their country back. They gave Geronimo his name, so maybe they can tell me what I need to know.

Their ears are turned to the street so they don't notice me until I'm close enough to touch them.

"Yaa ta sai." That's how Geronimo says hello when I can hear him. I smile at these Mexicans before I remember that's a white man thing.

There are three of them. Exact copies of each other with their short hair and goatees. The Mexicans keep their normal length arms crossed and remember about not smiling.

One of them says, "You smell like garbage, *puto*."

"*Puto*. Is that my war name?"

"*Tonto del culo.*"

Now I see it. The leader's eyes are filled to the brim with being mean.

"Stupid *pendejo*."

"*Mayate.*"

They all talk at once, frowning like the Indians on the back of my T-shirt. I turn around so they can see.

"What you want man?" I can't tell who asks me that because I'm giving them plenty of time to look at my Indians.

I want to tell them about the tattoo under my shirt, because these Mexicans have lots of ink on their skin. *The Fosters* call it jailhouse ink, but I've only seen it on the street.

When I turn around again, they are standing like a formation of geese with the meanest one in front. He lifts up his T-shirt and shows me his pistol.

"Already got one." I lift my T-shirt and show him the pistol Usen gave me.

The Mexican takes his pistol out and points it at me, holding it sideways like the black gangsters do on television. The three Mexicans back down the sidewalk spitting Spanish words into the air. When they get to the corner, the one with the gun fires three shots before they take off running. I don't shoot back because I don't know how many bullets I have, and it isn't a good day to kill someone.

Cars skid to a stop behind me. Doors open and slam. People shout things about wild Indians and guns. They all take off running when I turn around to see—except for a big man who steps out of an old pickup truck wearing overalls and an oil field cap with the bill in front.

He walks up to me like there hasn't been a one-sided gunfight in the street and says, "Buddy, you'd better get out of here."

I tell him my name's Wylie E. Chatto and he tells me, "Mine's Governor Annotubby—and not those Annotubbys that run the Chicasaws, neither."

He's the most Indian-looking man I've ever met—not afraid of anything, not even rats or an Apache kid with long arms and a pistol.

"Power failure." He points at the traffic light that's gone dead. Horns are honking at it, like the wire spirits will hear and make things right. Only horns aren't honking behind Governor Annotubby, because everyone has run away from the gunfight but him.

"They'll be after you when the electric comes back on," he says. "And it always does. At least it has so far."

I tell him, "When wire spirits sleep, the rats and Apaches wake up." That is one of the things I'm supposed to figure out, but there is a lot more… "What is it every Indian in the whole world knows except for me?"

"You better take off, Wylie. Somebody's sure to call the cops."

The stoplights are flashing red now, and Governor Annotubby tells me, "They'll start working proper soon."

I can see he's right about that. Before long, people are driving through green lights and stopping for red ones, except for the cars that are stuck behind Governor Annotubby's old pickup truck.

And pretty soon, even those cars manage to get clear, and there is no one on the street but me and Governor. He's still not told me what I need to hear.

There are sirens all over town, cops and ambulances cleaning up after the power failure, and Governor tells me I'm part of what they want to get off the street.

"*The Fosters* are tired of me," I tell him. "Didn't know what it would be like to live with an Apache who can't read or write."

Governor Annotubby doesn't mind my crazy talk. "You'd be a holy man back in the day, but now. . ."

I tell him about my *WHITE POWER* tattoo. I tell him about Geronimo. I tell him about the spirits who live inside electric wires and give white people their power.

"You got to go, Wylie. Before they come for you." Governor Annotubby sounds exactly like Geronimo only louder, and the air fills with a trouble smell that's stronger than the garbage splotches on my T-shirt.

I look past Governor Annotubby and see a policeman with a bruised forehead getting out of a police car, and a man in a khaki uniform getting out of an ambulance, and *The Fosters* watching everything.

The air is so full of rosemary it stings my eyes, and the man in the khaki uniform has a rifle like the ones animal police use to tranquilize tigers.

Am I one of those? Indications are positive.

I can read *The Fosters*' lips perfectly—even better than Geronimo's. They're taking turns telling each other, "We really had no choice."

The man in the khaki uniform says, "Put up your hands," but he's already taking aim.

Even though I do exactly what he says, he pulls the trigger—once, twice. Two darts sting me on the chest like yellow jackets. I pull them out but it's too late. The electric gods sing their victory song.

"The cowboys always win," I tell Governor Annotubby, who looks exactly like Geronimo now.

"Your time will come," he tells me. *"Got to wait until the sacred alarm clock wakes you up."*

The man in the khaki uniform stands beside Geronimo, waiting to catch me when I fall.

"Peyote?" I ask him. Geronimo is winding his sacred alarm clock, one that doesn't need electricity. It's got to be a vision.

"Ketamine," the khaki man tells me. "I guess they're pretty similar."

He catches me as I pitch toward the pavement. Then he lets me down gently, like white people always do.

A DIFFERENT KIND
OF INDIAN

SOME KIDS SELL TACOS AFTER school. I make arrows. Four of them a day, because that's a sacred number. I haft them to shafts of white aspen harvested from the spirit-mountains somewhere in Montana. I fletch the shafts with wing feathers of the red-backed hawk—that's Crazy Horse's spirit bird. Mom sells them for a hundred bucks apiece on the Internet.

The flint is real, but everything else is as phony as my website name. In cyber-space I'm Joseph Little Wolf, a cool old dude whose great-great grandpa was the Cheyenne Chief who kicked Custer's butt.

Joseph Little Wolf doesn't care about things like making friends or why girls don't seem to like him. He's too busy selling Authentic Cheyenne Medicine Arrows so he can pay for Authentic Native American Struggles, like freeing Leonard Peltier and tearing the white presidents off of Mount Rushmore. I don't mind being Joseph Little Wolf. It's better than being Joseph Beaver. That's who I am everywhere but cyber-space.

Mom says taking the white man's money is an act of revolution. She says I'm a cyber-warrior, even if I am a fifteen-year-old Choctaw kid instead of a grown up Northern Cheyenne.

"It's Karma, Joseph." Mom talks about Karma a lot.

Karma is how the Choctaw will get back everything we've lost. Our land. Our history.

"One Authentic Cheyenne Medicine Arrow at a time." Mom says it might take a while.

Mom says the white man's world is falling apart and pretty soon America will belong to us again. She's not talking Ghost Dances or bulletproof shirts like the Indians at Wounded Knee. We're Choctaw, after all, one of the civilized tribes.

"It's the riots," she says. "The power failures, the strikes, the murders."

In the old days the cowboys always won. They had the most guns and the cavalry. They've still got the most guns, and now they have armored cars and tanks and airplanes instead of horses.

"The Indians are winning quietly," Mom says. "It's our way."

"We're used to cars that don't start," she says. "We don't fly in airplanes or ride in tanks." She says Indians can get by without electricity, and gasoline, and all those things that are going to quit working pretty soon. Mom's been talking about Indian ways ever since we moved to Oklahoma City so she could be with her girlfriend Chris.

That's something I've learned to be quiet about. Cowboys hate lesbians even more than Indians.

Mom says, "Indians win plenty, but we don't brag about it, so no one notices."

I tell her, "Quiet's kind of lonely." Sometimes those feelings just slip out.

She says, "It won't be forever. Things will change when the time is right. Karma is another Indian thing, but a different kind of Indian entirely."

—

OLD-TIME CHOCTAW BLENDED INTO GRASS and trees like rabbits and white tailed deer. Three steps into the woods and we were gone. One extra tree in a forest that went on forever.

In the city we blend into crowds. Not the tallest, or the shortest, or the best dressed, or the worst. Someone is always first to be noticed. Someone is always last. Invisible people aren't noticed at all. Eyes skate over them and land on someone prettier or uglier or more unusual. One more Choctaw is never noticed if he stays in the shadows of important people where everyone's attention naturally goes.

An invisible Choctaw can walk through a crowd without anyone noticing. He can watch the prettiest girl in Putnam City Central High School from a few feet away and she won't complain to her boyfriend that, "Some Indian kid is stalking me."

But that's really difficult, because girls are harder to sneak up on than buffalo. Girls are the most observant creatures in the world, except for Mom, who never notices how miserable I've been since we moved here.

The lunchroom is an easy place to go invisible, because everybody there is either looking at their food or talking with friends who have to listen because their mouths are full.

No one in the cafeteria uses an inside voice, and everybody has a lot to say. People cheer when a glass breaks or a tray hits the floor. The place is so noisy I don't have to take careful steps or avoid accidental bumps. Anyone can go invisible in a lunchroom, but it takes a real Indian to infiltrate the athlete's table.

The most important jocks leave the campus for lunch, but the second-string football and basketball players sit together. Each one talks louder and nastier than the next to see if anyone notices. Of course everyone does.

I move among them smoothly and suddenly at the same time. No one knows what to expect, so after a while they give up trying. First one way, then the other, and pretty soon I'm at the table where the jocks are playing who can boast the loudest. No one notices when I sit down. Almost like I've been invited.

If they were catfish, I could pull them out of their hiding places. If they were deer, I could smoke their meat and feed my two mothers for a month. They aren't any of those interesting things. They talk about girls, but the things they say don't help me and I lose my going-invisible-attitude.

The second-string quarterback says, "Get lost Chief Red Cloud."

The other jocks laugh at that, even though Red Cloud was an Oglala Sioux and not the tiniest bit Choctaw. I don't tell them, because I'm busy drifting on the wind again, going invisible so fast they barely see me leave.

—

WHITE PEOPLE HAVE THIS THING about eye contact, and talking all the time. They don't understand how hard it is to stand up under the weight of a steady gaze, or how difficult it is to breathe air that's thick with words. White people think you're lying when you look at your feet. They think you're stupid if you shut up for a minute. It's hard for a Choctaw boy to fit in.

I watch the popular kids and imitate them in front of the full-length mirror in my room. Over and over, until I've almost got it. White means you're the center of attention. Exactly the opposite of being Joseph Little

Wolf. That should be easy for a smart Choctaw boy who's only Joseph Little Wolf when he's making arrows.

The Internet has lots of tips on making friends.

Introduce yourself.

I figure out a little too late, the P.E. shower room is not the place for that one. White boys scream while they are getting wet, like they're emptying out all of the dirty stuff inside. Soap and steam, like a warrior cleansing his spirit before going off to battle. I think maybe I'm beginning to understand, but then the naked dancing starts and the towel popping and genital grabbing and loud talk about blowjobs and anal sex and queers.

Everyone's an expert but me.

It's hard to be an Indian when you're naked and unarmed, a good place to go invisible, but I've made up my mind to change my ways. I try my friendship skills on a black boy first. He's an oppressed minority too, so maybe he'll understand if I don't get it exactly right. He doesn't look at me when I say hello the first time, and I wonder if he has a little Indian blood.

"Hello." This time I say it in my loudest, least invisible voice. I stick my hand out in the white businessman shake position, and then I remember black boys have a special way of doing this.

I can't back out now, because the locker room is suddenly quiet and everybody looks at me and the black boy. My eye contact is perfect—strong, aggressive, a little bit dangerous. My hand is out, the fingers wiggling the way they would if I was sneaking up on a sleeping catfish.

"My name is Joseph Beaver." My voice hardly quavers, but it's the only sound in the room. Dead silence for a dozen heart beats, then everybody starts laughing all at once.

Except for me.

The black boy says, "Pussy name." He doesn't shake my hand. He claps both of his instead and does a little dance while everybody else in the room shouts, "Pussy name! Pussy name!" so loud it makes the lockers rattle.

I don't know what to do, because nobody is getting dressed and there are so many enemy eyes turned toward me that I wonder how long it will be till someone goes looking for a rope.

The mostly naked boys form a circle with me at the center. Their faces look like the faces of the rioters on TV who break store windows and set fires when the electricity goes out. Mom says that's how the white man's world will fall, but right now it looks like it is going to fall on top of a Choctaw boy who is trying to make friends.

Before that happens, the coach pushes through the door. He yells at everybody in general, but the only one he's looking at is me. One more enemy, but not the kind who'll kill me. The Internet doesn't tell you things like this can happen when you introduce yourself.

—

MOM SAYS GIRLFRIENDS AREN'T IMPORTANT, but she moved us to Oklahoma City so she could be with hers—even though Chris is white. Mom says some white people are just fine. Especially lesbians. In the end everything comes down to girls.

Chris says a girlfriend will happen at exactly the right time. "The way it did for your mom and me. That's Karma."

Lesbians must all know about Karma.

"Meanwhile you should get a dog," she says. "A dog will let you be yourself. A dog doesn't care about your lifestyle or how much money you have."

Chris is driving me to school because I slept in late. Indians get up with the sun, so maybe sleeping in late means I am finally fitting in.

Chris says, "A dog doesn't care what kind of car you drive."

I think she is talking about her old Volvo with the rusted fenders and the cracked windshield and the engine that works perfectly except for a little blue smoke.

"I don't have a car," I tell her. "I don't have a driver's license."

"A dog wouldn't care about that either," she says.

We are a block from my school and I can already see some students walking in, smoking cigarettes, flipping cars the bird. The girls all look pretty and the boys all look mean. No dogs anywhere around.

"Let me out here," I say, but Chris is busy sharing her worldly knowledge so she doesn't pay attention. Pretty soon it will be too late. Maybe it's already too late, because it's impossible to go invisible when you are riding in a rusty old Volvo with a lesbian who looks like Chris.

"I can walk from here," I tell her, but she is still going on about how dogs are so much better than girlfriends.

When she pulls into the drive-through to let me off, one of the cigarette-smoking guys flips her off. The pretty girls all laugh. I can hear them through the Volvo's cracked windshield.

Chris slams on the brakes and jumps out of the car. The Volvo's engine doesn't stop right away, and Chris doesn't stop either. She can kick anybody's ass—even the jocks are afraid. The cigarette smokers scatter before her the way the U.S. Cavalry scattered before Joseph Little Wolf's great-great grandpa. She could catch them if she wanted, but she just puts her hands on her hips and spits. She will take no scalps today.

I jump out of the car and run to the front door, like I'm scared of her too. I'm not exactly ashamed of Chris, but I don't want to be seen with her. I don't want the other kids asking questions. I'm a little bit ashamed of the things I don't want. It's hard to go invisible when you feel that way.

—

NO PEOPLE IN THE HALL, as if everyone is hiding from something I don't know about. The lights are dim, the way they get before the power goes out completely. It hasn't done that much in this part of Oklahoma City. Chris says that's because this is the newest part of town with buried power lines and good transformers. I walk back to the front doors to see if she is gone.

Before I get there I hear footsteps move in behind me. Two people, scraping their heels across the floor like they don't care about leaving marks. White kids, pretending to be thugs. Chris says moms never know when their boys act like gangsters. I wish she was here right now, because the thug-steps head my way.

"Hey, Geronimo!" Only one of them speaks. He thinks it is an insult to call me by a dead Apache's name.

I practice my quiet Indian ways while I wait to see if they will take things past the talking stage.

Chris would say, "It's only two of them."

Mom would say, "That's two too many."

I don't say anything, but I turn and give them my best Joseph Little Wolf expression while the lights dim in the hallway and there are no coaches anywhere around.

"Did your girlfriend drive you to school?" The talker makes a nasty looking gesture with both hands that probably has something to do with sex.

They stop six paces back, well beyond the danger zone, but then the lights dim more, except for a pair of halogens canisters above my head. Those keep me illuminated while the hallway fluorescents fade to black. I'm the only show in town. I consider running into the darkness, but then I'd have to look at a coward's face when I practice being popular in front of the mirror.

I raise my hands into what I think must be a pretty good boxing stance, but there's laughter beyond my zone of light and the sound of thug-steps closing in, and I wonder if Mom is right about the white man's world falling apart, because I know she's right about two being two too many.

A light flashes behind me. Once, twice, three times, bright and stroboscopic, like the light shows at rave parties I've only heard about. The two white boys move in jerky motions, but they move toward me. So when the lights start flashing again I hit the closest one in the nose, and swing a wild punch at the other. It lands somewhere soft, but I don't know exactly where until the fluorescent lights come on. He's lying on the floor with both hands on his stomach.

A cheer goes up in the classrooms. It's for the lights coming back on, but it still feels good. The next three flashes don't look so impressive now that the hallway is fully lit.

I turn and see a girl with a camera. She takes a few more pictures of the thugs on the hallway floor, who are looking for their gangster ways on their hands and knees.

"These won't make the school paper," the girl tells me. "But I can give you all the prints as you want. I've been watching you for a while."

I wonder how that's possible. She must know how to go invisible like me. Like a real Indian. The girl isn't pretty right away, but she turns prettier as she talks and she is really pretty when she smiles. Brown hair, brown eyes, a little taller than I am, but she makes up for it by slumping.

Her eyes look at the floor. "Been meaning to talk to you for a while. This seemed like the perfect time."

"Perfect." I extend my hand white businessman style again. This time it works.

"My name's Joseph," I tell her, even though I'm sure she already knows. I don't say my last name because I remember what happened in the locker room.

"Mine's Karma." Her voice cracks a little, but her eyes sparkle in the fluorescent lights when they meet mine.

Karma, what else could it be?

TWENTY PERCENT OFF

WORK'S DONE FOR WYLIE E. CHATTO.

"For today anyways," the boss tells me. " Maybe tomorrow too. Can't shred paper when the electric's off. Go on out and wait for the bus, Chatto. Time is money."

I give my wristwatch a nice long look, because that's what people do when time gets mentioned. I touch it on the side like there's some kind of button that helps me keep track of something, but my watch doesn't have buttons or batteries or confusing hands that point at different numbers every second, every minute, every hour. It's a present from my best and only friend, Hyannisport Larkspur Smith. She says time is useless to an Indian, especially one who looks a little *off.*

I tell the boss, "It's half past early thirty," as I walk through the front door of Discrete Document Destruction, the only place in Oklahoma City that won't hire you if you know how to read.

I say, "Hyannisport Larkspur Smith," out loud to remind myself there's someone waiting for me back at the halfway house. Something to keep in mind while I try to figure out which bus to take at half past early thirty.

Two girls stand on the sidewalk a few feet away trying to make their cell phones work. They're backed up against the wall so I guess they heard me think out loud.

I tell them, "She's my best and only friend." Now they know I had a reason for saying Hyannisport Larkspur Smith. I could tell them things about her—

like how she gave me my Indian-time watch, and braided my hair into a tail, and whispered my war name so no one else could hear it—but I don't. That was two calendars ago. Maybe three.

Hyannisport Larkspur Smith said, "Your war name is Wylie E. Coyote. Don't tell anybody." I make the zipper motion across my lips to remind myself.

The girls get mad at their phones so they won't have to look at me. They use angry-girl-words, halfway between shouts and tears like, "Not even," and, "Whatever."

One of them is blonde with skin that looks like the inside of a peach, and the other has brown hair and a woodpecker nose. Their eyes are outlined in solid black, so it's hard to tell if they are pretty.

Coyote magic could make me go invisible. These girls wouldn't have to think about a big Indian standing so close he could grab them in a minute, but something bad is coming so I keep on looking solid and dangerous.

The air smells like rosemary. The scent is weak so the badness is a might-be-thing and maybe Wylie E. Coyote can turn it into a never is. I flip my braided tail over my right shoulder so I can see it while I work out a plan.

The girls edge away like they're balanced on a narrow ledge. They slide along as slow as a pair of snails moving over brambles. The rosemary smell gets stronger, so I speed things up with a war cry and a wild Indian face.

That starts the white girls moving fast. They run away just as tires start screeching like someone wants to stop real bad but can't. The screech-noise turns into a car crash right into the front of Discrete Document Destruction exactly where the girls would be if not for coyote magic.

They are running faster now, all the way to the corner. The blonde one stops long enough to shout, "Goddamned retard." She makes an upside down fist with her right hand and flips her insult finger straight up.

"I'm not retarded, just a little off," I call after her, and then feel kind of bad because nobody says retarded at the halfway house. It's hard to yell exactly the right thing when the insult finger goes up.

"Excuse me," says a woman's voice inside the wrecked car. She's behind an airbag that's going down a lot slower than it should.

"Can someone help me please?" The words have music in them, like a song that hasn't quite taken hold.

"The door is stuck, and I think my leg is broken." A flirty song. The kind of song that gives me ideas the halfway councilor says are *inappropriate.*

Hyannisport Larkspur Smith calls them dangerous but natural.

When I get around to the driver's side window, I see how pretty this woman is—prettier than the blonde girl and the brown-haired girl put together. This one's hair is too red for a real color, but it looks good all messed up.

"Hyannisport Larkspur Smith's hair looks just like that," I tell her, "Except it's brown." Then I realize that Hyannisport Larkspur Smith's hair is nothing like this woman's—except in those dangerous, natural, inappropriate ideas I have sometimes.

The pretty woman gives me a big salesgirl smile, the kind that means I'm just in time for the best bargain ever. She puts her left hand through the window and tells me, "Delilah Munson is my name. What's yours?"

She wiggles her fingers like she's trying for a magic spell, and it might be working because I take her hand and tell her, "Wylie E Chatto."

I shake her hand way too long, but I can't tell she wants me to quit until she says, "You think a big strong boy like you could get my door open?"

"Sure." I squeeze on the handle until I hear a pop, and give the door a jerk—quick and violent, the way a coyote breaks a rabbit's neck. *Going Batshit* is what I call it, but that might scare the pretty lady so I just tell her, "Easy as pie."

That gets me a bigger salesgirl smile.

"Everything went crazy when the traffic lights quit working." She turns herself on a bucket seat made of so much leather it must have used the outside of a whole cow. Her skirt is red—almost the same color as her hair—and so short I can hear the slippery sound her legs make on the upholstery.

When those legs stick all the way out of the car, they are almost all the way out of the skirt too. She pulls the material back a little more and says, "Look."

I don't have a choice.

The skirt is just a little scrap of cloth, but it folds across her legs like curtains over a crystal clear window that will let the sun shine in if you pull them back a little more. She takes my hand, guides it to the most naked leg. She moves my hand in circles over the spot she thinks is broken. I count the circles quietly, hardly moving my lips at all.

When I've counted four, the pretty woman says, "What do you think?"

Her eyes are as green as the bottom part of the traffic lights that quit working and caused the accident. I remember green means go, but I also remember what Hayannisport Larkspur Smith told me how *inappropriate* ideas are only okay if we keep them to ourselves.

"Is it broken?"

It takes me a few seconds to figure out what she is asking.

"This is the most unbroke leg I ever saw." Not a bruise or even a rough place where the hair isn't shaved away. No stockings either. "I need to go."

The woman and the car and even the broken front of Discrete Document Destruction smells like rosemary so strong coyote magic can't fix it.

"Somebody has to take me to the hospital." She shows me the screen on her cell phone. "No signal at all." She smiles at me the way Hyannisport Larkspur Smith smiles at the halfway councilor who comes around on Saturdays.

"Power's off all over the city." She waves one of her hands the way pretty magician's assistants do on HBO magic shows, and I hear sirens coming from all over town—fire engines, ambulances, police cars all going different places at the same time. I try to open the front door of Discrete Document Destruction, but the boss has it locked up tight, and knocking won't do any good if a car crash didn't make him curious.

"Carry me." She holds her arms straight out with her hands dangling like ripe fruit ready to drop onto the ground where it won't be stealing if I take it.

So I scoop her up. I try not to run my hand under her bare legs but her skirt is too short for that. I put one arm around her waist, so my fingers are nowhere near her breasts, but she wriggles until they are. She reaches over my shoulder and takes hold of my coyote tail—the first woman ever to do that except for Hyannisport Larkspur Smith.

"You don't look like a Wylie to me. I think I'll call you Samson." She sits in my arms like I'm the most comfortable recliner in the whole wide world and waits for me to say something.

"Get it? I'm Delilah and you're Samson."

"Bible," is all I can think to say. It's one of those story's religious white people tell each other, I can't remember it for sure, but I don't think things worked out too well for Samson. "Don't know where the hospital is."

She kicks her legs around like a little girl on a swing, which I don't think she'd do if one was broken. She whispers in my ear, "Don't worry Samson, I'll tell you exactly what to do."

Those words go into to my ear all warm and whispery. It feels like a promise that pretty white women don't usually make to an Indian who's a little off. She gives my coyote tail a kiss and clucks her tongue like I'm a carriage horse.

"Giddyup Samson," she tells me, and that's exactly what I do.

—

"GO THIS WAY, SAMSON. TURN that way. Faster. Slower." When Delilah Munson doesn't tell me what to do, I freeze up like a picture of a statue.

She presses her fake red hair against my shoulder. She touches my face with the tips of her fingers like she's a blind person trying to figure out the floors on an elevator panel. She moves my head around so I'll look at exactly the right place.

"Look Samson. There's our reflection in a store window." Delilah Munson kicks her legs so I can see exactly what she's wearing under that short skirt. I try to look away but can't get my head to turn. My eyes won't stay closed and neither will my brain.

"Look at us, Samson. Don't we make a cute couple?"

Our shadows fall inside a Bass Pro Shop window that has a special percentage sale on rifles. The numbers are big, which means the prices are small—at least according to the emminent Hyannisport Larkspur Smith.

"Twenty percent off," I say, because some of those numbers are twenties.

Delilah smiles like twenty is the smartest thing she's ever heard. She kicks her legs like a little girl again, and one of her shoes falls onto the sidewalk.

"Oh my!" Her voice is excited but it's not surprised. She points a finger at the shoe so I bend over and pick it up.

"Put it on me, Samson. Put it on my poor broken leg." She talks the way you talk to a dog when you want to make him whine. She wiggles her toes one at a time. So graceful I can't take my eyes away.

"Over there, Samson." She traces the shape of my lower lip with a fingertip, licks it, and points at a concrete bench. It's cold and hard, so she shivers a little when I set her down, and even though it's probably the concrete, I kind of think she's shivering for me.

Delilah puts her bare foot in my hand and I slide the shoe on. It's red, like her dress and her hair and the feeling building up behind my eyes.

"Breathe, Samson." Delilah knows I'm holding my breath even though I don't.

After a couple of deep breaths I feel normal again except for being watched by those traffic-light-green eyes and being touched by fingertips that I'll bet have never touched an Indian before.

Delilah slides one of her hands between the buttons on my shirt. It's delicate but hot.

"Your heart is beating really fast, Samson."

Her words travel through her fingers and tell my heart to gallop like an Apache horse running from the U.S. Army.

"Carry me, Samson." She keeps her fingers over my heart while her voice tells my legs where to go and her messy red hair makes me think of Hyannisport Larkspur Smith when she comes out of her private sessions with our Saturday councilor.

Delilah's green eyes cross a little when they look at me, like there's too much to see in close, but she doesn't want to move away. Those eyes are a lot more complicated than I thought they were—prettier too, like green leaves hanging over clear water after a heavy rain.

I hardly notice the rosemary smell until I hear someone say, "Watch out, you clumsy bastard."

We're on a footbridge over the Oklahoma River, and I'm about to run into a big, fat white man in a cowboy hat.

"Retard." He rolls his shoulders like the fat is muscle, like he beats up Indians every day.

I don't say, "I'm not retarded, just a little off," because I've already made that mistake one time today.

"My, you're a big one." Delilah keeps her magic fingers over my heart while she turns her green eyes toward the fat cowboy.

"Isn't he a big one, Samson?" She takes her hand out of my shirt and picks up my coyote tail. She kisses the tip of the braid then blows the kiss right at him.

His brain is so cluttered up with feeling fat and strong he can't decide whether Delilah is insulting him or flirting. She clears that up by making her hand into a finger pistol and letting the thumb hammer fall.

"Bang. Why don't you kill him, Samson?"

I put Delilah on the concrete railing. It's exactly the right height to let her cross her legs in a way that leaves me wondering what they look like at the very top. The fat cowboy is looking at them too, so hard he's almost forgotten about the crazy Indian he's just insulted.

Until Delilah points that finger pistol at him again and says, "Get him, Samson," without a trace of flirt.

"Get him." Her green eyes are hard as broken glass and her voice sounds like a command to a killer dog and her finger stays pointed at the fat man.

That *Batshit* feeling comes on really fast, and I take a couple of steps toward the fat cowboy, trying to figure out which part of him I'm going to break first. I swing my coyote tail over my shoulder so he can see it when I come for him. I turn my hands into fists that are big and hard enough to break a fat man's head.

"Oh shit." The fat man falls on his butt and scoots along backward like a crab with broken legs. He rolls onto his feet and waddles down the bridge so fast he makes the whole thing shake.

"Twenty percent off," I shout at his back, so he'll know he's been scared away by a wild Indian who knows his numbers.

"Samson." Delilah pulls me to her with a curled finger and a smile. She pats the concrete railing, so I'll know what she wants me to do.

"Two men fighting over little old me." She kisses me on the cheek and takes hold of my coyote tail.

"You'll do anything I say, won't you Samson?"

Anything's a lot. More than five, or ten, or even twenty percent, so I have to think about that for a while. I look at my Indian-time watch like people do when they don't know what to do. That reminds me of Hyannisport Larkspur Smith, which reminds me of my war name that nobody knows but her.

"Maybe not," I tell Delilah Munson. "Maybe not anything."

She pokes out her lower lip, like I just told her something really sad, like maybe we're not a cute couple anymore.

"You know what happened in the Bible?" She takes my coyote tail in one hand and sniffs at it, like she's wondering where the rosemary smell is coming from. "You know what happened when Sampson disappointed Delilah." She makes a pair of finger scissors and pretends she's cutting off my tail.

I remember how those fingers work. How they change things in a minute—the way you think, the way you act, how fast your heart beats, how much you breathe.

Batshit is what happens next. I jump up. Delilah screams. She tumbles off the bridge right into the Oklahoma River. The dirty water washes her prettiness away.

"Goddamn it, Samson. I can't swim." But the Oklahoma River isn't very deep and she's standing on the bottom. Her hands are on her hips and the makeup on her face that I didn't see before is running down her neck.

"You're leg's not broke," I tell her. "You can walk to the hospital." I run away before she turns her magic on again. A coyote is no good without a tail.

LOVE AT
THE LAST MINUTE

MY MOTHER'S NAME IS HYANNISPORT Larkspur Smith. She wrote it in oversize shaky letters at the bottom of the lavender-scented note she left for Dad, telling him she wouldn't be around anymore. A big nervous signature, the way John Hancock would have signed the Declaration of Independence if they had amphetamines back then.

Dear Bob,
You know I can't stay here anymore.

Love,
Hyannisport Larkspur Smith

P.S. Take care of Karma.

That's me, Karma Chameleon Smith, a P.S. on a *Dear Bob* letter. Dad says the name came from a song Mom listened to when she was stoned. Well he doesn't exactly say it. Dad doesn't talk much, but he plays Mom's old Culture Club CD while he fans himself with the note and looks at our one and only family picture. I figured the stoned part on my own.

I ask him, "Did she love me?"

He points to the word love on the dear Bob letter, but she didn't mention me until after that.

I ask him, "Is she still around?"

He blinks once, which means yes in Dad language. You have to get really good at reading people when you have a dad who barely talks.

"Do you know where she is?"

He looks at the ceiling for a second, then at his feet, then back at the sepia tone picture of the dysfunctional family of three. A father with a five-year-old girl sitting on his lap and a crazy mother standing behind us with her arms crossed. He's wearing a suit. I'm wearing a dress. Mom's in a pair of jeans with holes in the knees and an Oklahoma State University t-shirt that says, *GO COWPOKES* in big letters.

I can tell a lot more from that picture. A friend of Dad's is the photographer. Mom doesn't like him. She loves Dad a little, but hasn't made her mind up about me. I see things in the way people stand, how they hold their hands, where they put their eyes. Dad says I always could.

Well, he doesn't exactly say it.

I ask, "Think she'll ever come back?"

He says, "No," the ordinary verbal way.

"I'm nothing like her, you know."

One blink.

"I want to hear you say, I'm nothing like her."

"Nothing."

"Thanks, Dad."

"Call me Bob." He gets up slowly and stretches as if all this conversation is wearing him down. It's his way of telling me the parent-child relationship has run its course. Time for us to be friends.

"Yo." Dad clinches his right hand into a fist and holds it out for me to bump. Some days he's a regular chatterbox.

—

MY ALMOST-BOYFRIEND JOSEPH HAS two mothers and no father. I have one father and no mother. It's a perfect match, except for the fact that he's Native American and I'm not.

When he introduces himself he says, "I'm Joseph Beaver. I'm Choctaw."

He doesn't say, "Kiss me. I'm Choctaw," but almost. Oklahoma Indians are proud. Oklahoma white people are guilty. Another perfect match.

Joseph and I are only children, but he might have lots of half-brothers and -sisters because his dad was a sperm donor at a Tulsa fertility clinic. His Dad's name is Anonymous, which is even weirder than Hyannisport Larkspur Smith.

Chris is Joseph's Dad/Mom. She has hard muscles and soft eyes. She'd throw herself in front of a bear for Joseph, but not in front of Mona. That's his Mom/Mom. Joseph has Mona's chromosomes, and all he's got from Chris is her bear-fighting love.

Mona isn't sure her boy should have a girlfriend yet, especially a white one. When Joseph introduces us she starts right in on safe sex. According to her there's no such thing, and the path to getting STDs starts off with a kiss.

She says, "Boys just naturally carry STDs around, once they finish with collecting rocks and baseball cards." She puts an arm around Joseph's shoulders to show she loves him anyway.

"Besides diseases, there are babies." Mona gives Joseph a squint-eyed look. "Be careful, Karma." She kisses Joseph on the cheek, and he flinches. Who can blame him?

Chris says, "Don't mind Mona." She shakes my hand—starts off in the ordinary way but turns it into one of those elaborate rap-singer-shakes-with-fancy-finger grips. She tries to end it with an overhand two-person clap, but by then I'm totally lost.

After we listen to the sound of one hand clapping for an embarrassing two seconds, Chris says, "Tell me, Karma, have you got any Indian blood?"

That's the real reason for Mona's safe sex lecture. I know because Joseph's already told me about his Mom/Mom's "Indian thing." She'd think sex was a lot safer if I was Native American. Mona is a quarter Choctaw. That means Joseph can document an eighth. That would be watered down to a sixteenth if he and I had children. Evaporating identity.

"The tribe is so diluted already," Mona says, as if that's totally reasonable. Her all-white girlfriend tries to change the subject, but Mona's already talking about revolution and anarchy and Indians taking America back. She runs her hands through her long black hair and runs her voice up and down the scale. Her eyes get anime-big and beautiful. Her skin tone deepens from slightly tan to spray on bronze. Mona is a wild Indian who might not make a lot of sense but you listen to her anyway because she's beautiful.

My almost-boyfriend's mom is prettier than me.

Mona says, "The white man's world is coming to an end."

I'm not supposed to be offended because I'm a white girl, after all.

"Systems are failing," Mona says. "The electricity, the food supply, medical care, the military."

Just as she tells me this, the lights dim, and her computer backup batteries sound a warning that would make a dog howl, if Mona and Chris had a dog.

"You see." She puts her hands on her hips. She gestures to the lights, gestures to the howling backup batteries.

"Technology is their Achilles heel." She shrugs and holds it until I give her my best photo-ready smile.

"Golly," I say, because that's a word for all occasions if you're under twenty. I want to change the subject, but no subject-changing words come to mind.

"Technology will sink the white man." Mona's eyes get a little wider. Her skin blanches into one of those ugly designer colors that everybody's supposed to like but no one does. She's just remembered I am white and she's told me the Indian Revolution Plan.

"Please don't tell anyone."

I say, "Mum's the word."

Joseph smiles at my cross-cultural pun. He says, "Got to go, Mum," then Mona and Chris get the joke.

They wave as we leave the house. Their waving hands go stationary but stay suspended like Mona and Chris are swearing an oath.

Joseph and I wait till we are a block away before we laugh, because we don't want his two moms to think I'm a bad influence.

—

A POLICE CAR STOPS BESIDE us before we walk another block. The passenger cop gives us a hard look. There aren't as many cop cars as there used to be because Oklahoma City is broke. The mayor says we're in a temporary slump. Mona Beaver says it's permanent. My dad doesn't say anything as usual.

"Hey, you kids!" The passenger-cop is trying to think of a reason to make our lives miserable. The expression on his face tells me he has children. The way he puts both arms out the window and turns his hands into fists tells me they don't get along. His anger drowns out everything else.

The driver-cop looks at his watch. He wants to be someplace else—any place but in this gas guzzling police car beside his kid-hating partner.

"You!" the kid-hater stares at Joseph. "I'm talking to you, Sitting Bull." He looks back at his partner, who looks a lot more like Sitting Bull than Joseph.

The driver-cop says, "Cool it William."

My almost-boyfriend doesn't say anything, but that's not unusual. He almost never talks. Like my Dad—it occurs to me—but I don't want to think about that.

Before I can say, "Is there a problem officer?" the radio inside the police car makes a noise like wood scraping across concrete. A robot-girl-voice recites numbers and words, and the driver-cop turns on the police car's flashing lights.

He says, "Got to go, William. That's a 10-24." He gives his partner time to tell us, "This is your lucky day, assholes," before he accelerates so fast he leaves rubber patches in the road. Too fast when gasoline is in such short supply unless it's something like a 10-24.

"What's a 10-24?" Joseph asks.

"Magic numbers that make cops disappear." Talking about magic is the one sure way to get a one-eighth Choctaw boy to smile.

Now that there aren't so many cops, you'd think they'd all be busy enforcing all the laws, but that's not how it works. When there's more crime than ever and not enough police, the cops mostly give up.

Joseph and I aren't going anywhere special so we don't hurry. We walk without talking, but that's OK because the world is talking to me all the time. I point to a stray dog and tell Joseph how its owners moved away and didn't take it with them.

"Pit bull mix," I say. "Non-violent for the time being, you can tell by the way it holds its head."

The dog crosses the street as we get closer because it doesn't trust people anymore. It sniffs the air in case someone's left a bowl of dog food out.

"Maybe I should take it home," Joseph says. "Chris says I should get a dog."

I say, "It's a girl dog. You can tell she's spayed because there aren't any boy dogs around. She knows every square inch of the neighborhood because her people used to let her out to do her business."

"Dog business." Joseph laughs, the way boys always do at bathroom humor. He looks at me and says, "Dog business," again, because I'm not smiling and he thinks I didn't get it.

"When that dog stopped being a cute puppy her owners didn't want her." Maybe I'm talking about my mother now, but still, I've got it right.

"You can tell that just by looking?" Joseph starts to take my hand, but he remembers Mona's warnings about safe sex.

"Dogs are easy reads. People are even easier." I point to a group of three boys standing in front of the 7-Eleven across the street.

"The short one is the leader."

The tallest boy is standing close to him listening to every word he says. He crowds so close the short one takes a step back. He puts a hand on the tall one's chest so he won't follow. The tall one smiles and leans into the touch.

"See the boy standing farthest away?" He might be Hispanic, or Indian. "That one's thinking about what his mother told him earlier today."

"Don't hang around with white hoodlums," is what she said. That boy looks my way when I tell Joseph this.

I ask Joseph. "Got your phone?" You can never tell if those things are going to work anymore, so I don't carry one.

"Call 9-1-1," I tell him. Those boys are going to rob the store.

By the time he fishes the phone out of his pocket and punches in the numbers, the short boy has a pistol in his hand. He and the tall one go inside, but the maybe-Hispanic boy doesn't.

Maybe they'll get a hundred dollars. Maybe they'll get a case of Oklahoma 3.2% beer. Maybe they'll kill the Iranian clerk who came to this country to get away from boys with guns.

The same two cops who bothered us before are the ones who come to save the day. They slide into the parking lot, draw their guns, and charge into the store. We can't tell what is happening inside until there's a gunshot. Then another. Like thunder and lightning behind the windows.

The might-be-Hispanic boy walks across the street and joins us.

The two cops and the Iranian clerk walk out together and stand by the police car. An EMSA siren wails in the distance, getting here fast because traffic is light since gasoline got hard to find.

One of the cops shouts at us. "You kids move along."

Since he's in a killing mood we do.

Joseph doesn't usually talk, but he pats the might-be-Hispanic boy on the back and tells him, "Must be your lucky day." Then we go to my house, because that had been the plan all along—even when there were just two of us.

—

IT TURNS OUT THE MIGHT-BE-HISPANIC boy isn't after all. His name is Rajneesh Patel. Indian was my second choice, but not that kind of Indian.

"People call me Raj," he tells us. "Nobody likes to say Rajneesh."

"Pleased to meet you Raj." I introduce myself while we're shaking hands. "My name is Karma."

Raj thinks I'm making fun of him, but Joseph comes to the rescue.

"Really, dude. That really is her name." Raj smiles because nobody ever called him dude before.

I can see this guy wants someone to like him so I tell him, "My mom was kind of crazy, and my dad was way too agreeable, otherwise my name would be something normal like Heather, or Amy."

Bingo! Raj is smiling. He and I have something in common—we both have mysterious and exotic mothers. Doesn't everybody?

Joseph says, "I'm Choctaw," so he won't be left out while everybody else is bonding. "I have two Moms."

Now Raj is grinning like the DMV is open for business again and he's passed his driver's test the very first time. He's met two people who will never think he's weird for not wanting to hold up a 7-Eleven.

As long as we are on the subject of Moms I tell him how mine abandoned me when I was five years old and my Dad won't tell me where she went, and I'd really like to find her.

"Just to be sure I'm nothing like her." We walk along in silence while I try to figure out if that's the real reason. "And to ask her if she loves me."

That makes Joseph uneasy, but Raj asks, "Do you love her?"

"Golly!" I throw out my all-purpose response again. No regular American boy would ask me that, but it sounds completely reasonable coming from Raj.

"That might be another reason you need to find her," Raj says.

"And to ask her why she left," Joseph says. "I'd really want to know that."

I want to know it, too, but my Dad won't talk about her and nobody else knows anything. Mom doesn't have family except for us. No old friends who come around. She doesn't send birthday cards or Christmas presents.

Raj is really excited to hear about my missing mother, and I can tell by perky way he walks he thinks he can find her.

"People don't just disappear." Raj waves his arms around like he's selling used cars on TV, probably because he thinks that's what regular Americans do when they want to look sincere. "We need to look for clues."

It's not like there is Mom-stuff lying around the house. There's nothing in the closets or in the garage, or anywhere else. Nothing except the dear Bob note and the sepia tone picture Dad looks at while he listens to Culture Club's greatest hits.

"How about the attic?" Raj asks. "People hide the best clues in the attic."

The three of us walk down the street side by side, so close our elbows touch, me on the inside, Joseph on the outside and Raj in the middle. It seems like the most natural thing in the world when Raj puts an arm around each of us, like we've been friends for years instead of minutes.

I ask, "You really think we'll find something?"

He says, "Knowledge overcomes ignorance as sunlight overcomes darkness." Inscrutable.

—

THE TELEVISION NEWS IS SO bad nobody follows it anymore, so nobody knows when power-downs are going to happen. By the time Raj, Joseph, and I get inside my house, the lights are starting to dim.

"It's OK. We have lots of flashlights." Dad works for Allied Radio Shack, guarding the warehouse where they keep all the supplies people never buy anymore. That includes batteries, so we have plenty sitting around.

He says, "It's not exactly stealing when they stop paying you."

Of course he might not work for Allied Radio Shack any more. Maybe he's been fired so he's just going to the warehouse to hang out and take batteries. I guess he'll keep on doing that until he gets a termination letter, and that won't happen because the mail stopped coming weeks ago.

The way we get up into the attic is through a door that pulls down from the ceiling in Dad's closet. Raj knows exactly where it is.

Joseph asks "How?" Which makes Raj and me laugh because he sounds like a television Indian from the old time cowboy movies.

"Most attic entries are exactly like this," I explain, but what I'm really thinking is, "Raj is a mystic from the east."

Dad's closet contains exactly four suits, two pair of Florsheim wing tips, a dozen shirts, six pair of dress slacks, and no jeans or T-shirts. I think that means he's depressed. Joseph thinks it means he wants to be a lawyer.

Raj says, "No man is truly free who owns more than he can carry." When he pulls down the ceiling doorway, we can see the light is still burning in the attic. It's one of those old fashioned incandescent bulbs nobody can buy any more, glowing a dull brown, because there is barely any electricity in the wires.

The attic is much hotter than the house. Dustier too, and full of spider webs that look like cotton candy in the flashlight beams.

Raj holds out his free hand like he's pushing an invisible barrier, the way panhandler mimes used to do at art festivals. He pretends his hand is a mystical antenna searching out mysterious broadcasts from inside the dusty crates.

"Here." He points to an old chest that looks like it belongs at the bottom of the ocean. There's a keyhole on a large metal latch but Raj says it won't be locked because everybody loses keys to things like that before they store them in the attic.

He runs his fingers over the metal latch, like a magician at a children's birthday party, and it pops open.

Joseph gasps. "Dude, you're a regular wizard."

I say, "Golly," again, because I sort of believe in magic too. I know that feeling will pass in a while, and I also know I need to stop saying golly if I want to sound mature and responsible.

Joseph shines his flashlight into the trunk. Raj makes passes over it because he's really getting into the mystical East Indian thing. He tries to say some Hindu words, but they come out sounding like an old time evangelist speaking in tongues.

"You were born in America weren't you?" He looks really embarrassed when I ask him that.

Raj says, "Look at this picture, will you?"

He's holding up a photograph of my mother breastfeeding me right after I was born. She looks glad to see me, but she looks worried too.

I pick up my certificate of live birth, held here for safe keeping in case I ever want to be President of the United States. It says I weighed six pounds and four ounces, and my mother's name is Hyannisport Larkspur Smith, and my father is Unknown. Anonymous, just like Joseph's dad.

Why hadn't I been able to see that in the old sepia tone dysfunctional family picture? I see it now in my memory. How Dad loves me in spite of everything. How he watches his reflection in my eyes, and listens for his name in my voice, and doesn't say anything, because he might let something slip and he's promised not to.

Raj picks up a plastic brown bottle of pills. It says aripiprazole 5mg on the label. It tells my mother to take six tablets daily in divided doses. For schizophrenia. That's something else I didn't know.

Raj has found other things—a picture of Mom looking at the camera with crazy eyes, a diary unlocked and ready to reveal everything.

The diary pages are filled with tiny words almost too small to read, and when I start reading them I wish I hadn't. Page after page, all about me. Drawings of me with blood running from my eyes and word balloons filled with threats written in a mysterious language only schizophrenics understand.

The sound of the front door opening drifts up the stairs. "Dad's home."

I start heading for the attic door, but Joseph makes a grunting sound and holds both hands over his head like a robbery victim. That's how he tells me, "Finish what you're doing. I'll keep him busy." Joseph's been waiting for the opportunity to do something special for me since we met, and here it is.

I stay in the attic because it's my mother who wants to kill me. Raj stays because he's the mystical East Indian who figured out where the clues were hidden, and Joseph engages Dad in conversation because that's the only way I'll have enough time to figure things out. The problem is, neither Joseph nor Dad have much to say, so we won't have very long.

"Look." Raj holds up a folder with my mother's name printed on it. Underneath her name is *CONFIDENTIAL* in big red letters. Inside the folder are a series of one-page letters from the Oklahoma Department of Health and Human Services, and another from Flanders Mental Hospital detailing Hayannisport Larkspur Smith's progress.

"This one's the most important." Raj shows me a formal looking paper. Like a college application, only this is an application for voluntary admission to Flanders Mental Hospital.

Mom's picture is on the upper left hand side of the first page. Her whole history is in her eyes—the daughter she loves and hates at the same time, medications that stop the voices but make her want to die, psychiatrists who finally say there is no hope.

The final sheet of paper in the file is her release, and her admission to a halfway house in N.E. Oklahoma City. There is an address, and a phone number, and a recommendation that she have no contact with her family.

Me and Dad.

"I know what I have to do," I tell Raj. I fold the paper up and put it into my back pocket. By the time we are back in Dad's closet every light bulb we can see is shining bright again. I take that as a sign. Why not?

Raj and I walk out of Dad's bedroom and interrupt him and Joseph. They are in the middle of a wordless conversation about the decline and fall of everything.

When I walk into the living room with Raj, Dad's expression changes. I can see the thoughts forming in his mind, molding his posture into a slump, shaping the muscles of his face into concern.

He's wondering if it's time we had that father/daughter talk about things like pregnancy and morality and STDs. I wonder how he'll manage without words.

—

THERE AREN'T TAXIS ANYMORE, OR buses. I don't have a driver's license or a car, and gasoline's too hard to get even if I did.

"Bicycles still work," Joseph says. He and Raj rode theirs over to my house, so it's too late for me to object. Joseph brought his bow and arrows for protection.

Raj says the bow is compound, "Like a sentence with lots of ands and buts." He's fascinated by the pulleys and metal cables. "Designed by a mad scientist somewhere in China." Raj points to an engraving on the black matte finish. "Mandarin characters."

I can tell he has a lot more to say, but all this talk about mechanical engineering and China embarrasses Joseph. He pulls an arrow from his quiver and twirls it like drummer in a rock and roll band.

"Cheyenne Medicine Arrow," he tells us. "Full of spirit power. I make them. Mom used to sell them on her website."

Internet business is slow since Paypal went out of business and electricity is undependable, but the arrows are still arrows. Joseph looks crazy dangerous with a quiver on his back, and everybody will be able to see it when we ride our bikes to the northeast side of town. Mostly black people live there and I'm a little scared of them, even though I know I shouldn't be.

"I don't think white people are welcome there," I say. "Unless they live in halfway houses."

Raj and Joseph roll their eyes. It's easy for them to judge. Their ancestors didn't invent the N-word.

"So are we going or not?" Raj gets right to the point. Before I can answer he says, "There is no greater enemy than pride." He tells us it's a translation from Sanskrit so we won't bother trying to figure out what it means.

"Dad has an old cowboy pistol in his bedroom," I tell Joseph. "Maybe we should take it."

"People who carry guns are looking for a fight," Joseph says.

He has a point. Besides, none of us knows anything about guns.

Raj points to the front door and says, "Who stands still in mud sticks in it."

I think he means we need to get going.

———

PEOPLE ALWAYS LEAVE OKLAHOMA WHEN times get hard. Raj says it's because they read *The Grapes of Wrath* in high school. Joseph says it's because everybody here came from someplace else. I say it's because this is the Sooner State, and it's already later than we think.

Anyway, people leave. The empty houses look dark and dangerous, especially the ones outside our neighborhood. Some have broken windows, and yards grown up with weeds tall enough to hide wild animals.

Cars line the curbs where people left them when they ran out of gas. Who knows where they were going or how they planned to get there when their automobiles quit working?

Joseph wants us to call him Joseph Little Wolf while we are on this trip, because that's the name he used when he sold Authentic Indian Artifacts on the Internet. It's easy to go along. We call him Joseph, just like we always did, but we remember his new last name.

He rides no-handed holding his compound bow while Raj and I hang back. I wear a helmet, like I always do when I ride a bike. It's bright red fiberglass, strong enough to stop a hammer blow. Uncomfortable and safe.

Joseph says, "Indian warriors don't wear helmets."

Raj says, "What does courage look like in a man?" which would sound much more convincing if his voice didn't crack.

We plan to go down Northwest Expressway, but there's a group of motorcycles about a mile down the road, so we turn onto a side street. Big mistake.

A large black dog jumps through the broken window of a house and charges. A boxer-mix follows, and then a pit bull and a border collie and several other mid-size dogs that move too fast to identify. All of them have big snarling muzzles and ribs that look ready to poke through their skin. They sprint toward us, but stop at curb, still not sure where we fit into the food chain. The leader of the pack comes out last.

"Damn," Joseph says. "A coyote."

Joseph and his mom know lots of Indian stories about coyotes, and all of them come to the same conclusion. They are more than extra smart dogs. Coyotes have spirit-power, like black cats and eagles. Hard to kill, not afraid of people, and if their magic fails them they can bite.

Joseph takes an arrow from his quiver and puts it into Indian Warrior position. He'll threaten but he won't shoot until the dogs come into the street.

"Go on," he tells us. "I'll catch up."

Right now he's Joseph Little Wolf without a doubt. The coyote pulls back a step or two when he sees the flint arrowhead, but the dogs don't know enough to be afraid.

Raj and I ride our bikes back onto the highway, but we don't go far. I take my helmet off and toss it in the road, because I don't want to die with a piece of colored plastic on my head. And it looks like I might die pretty soon.

I say, "Golly," one more time, because now I probably won't be ever be mature and responsible and I like the way the word feels on my tongue.

I ask Raj, "What should we do when the dogs attack?"

He can't think of anything brave or useful.

I jump off my bike and pick up a half-brick that's lying beside the highway, and Raj tries the doors on some of the abandoned cars, but they're all locked.

"The inner soul is not sullied by the miseries of the world," he says as he finds a rusty tailpipe that will never scare a dog away. I guess that's his version of, "Golly."

The black dog charges into the street, and Joseph fires an arrow into his throat. When the dog skids onto the pavement, the coyote yips and all the other dogs go right for Raj and me.

Joseph kills another one, but the rest don't slow down. It's Raj and me they're after.

I'd kind of like it if those bikers drove up now, and Raj must be thinking the same thing, because we are holding onto our pathetic weapons looking down the road where the motorcycles used to be.

I listen to the coyote yipping orders to his band of killer dogs. I listen to the sound of growling and claws on the pavement. But I'm afraid to look and see what death looks like when it's running me down on an empty road.

I draw my half-brick back, determined to hear one yip of pain before the dogs tear me apart. Raj holds his tailpipe like a baseball bat, but I'm going to throw like a girl and he's going to strike out. We both know how this thing will end. Joseph kills another dog, but the coyote stays safely out of range.

Raj and I turn our attention to the animals charging us. They used to be man's best friend but don't remember anything about that now.

I throw my brick. Raj throws his tailpipe—I guess he might as well—and we wait in the middle of the street not facing death bravely, but at least we're facing it. I'm breathing so fast the edges of the world turn black, like I'm looking into a tunnel at the end of time. So I don't see the big white Ford pickup truck until it crashes through the pack of dogs.

A sign on the side of the truck says—*Cheyenne Drilling Supplies. Natural Gas Powered Vehicle. Tsis Tsis Tas.*

The driver is an Indian man wearing a cowboy hat. He might be forty, or fifty, or sixty, or a hundred years old. It really doesn't matter, because there have always been Indians like him in this part of the world, riding up in pickup trucks at exactly the right time.

He shouts at us through the open window on the driver's side. "Don't waste time. Jump in."

Joseph jumps in first. He pulls another arrow from his quiver and points it at the surviving dogs. They've lost interest, and the coyote is gone.

After a block or two, the driver pulls over.

He leans out the driver's window and asks us where we're headed.

Joseph says, "I'm Joseph Little Wolf. We're on a mother quest."

I show him the paper with my mother's address.

"I'll take you there." Our Indian savior doesn't think we're crazy.

"I saw what you did," he says to all of us, but mostly Joseph. "Very brave."

Joseph hands him an Authentic Cheyenne Medicine Arrow, with a flint knapped point. The driver knows the arrow is a real power object, even if it was made by a one-eighth Choctaw boy to scam white collectors.

"Maybe we should ask if Karma can ride inside the cab?" Raj says

Joseph tells him, "It's better if we don't separate."

So we ride down the deserted highway in the back of that natural gas powered truck and hardly think about our bikes.

—

THE NORTHEAST SIDE OF OKLAHOMA CITY was the poorest part of town. Now it's exactly like everywhere else. Empty cars line the streets. Yards are grown up in weeds. Houses all have broken windows. Money doesn't matter when the world falls apart. At least that's how it looks from the back of a natural gas powered pickup truck.

Joseph says our driver is Cheyenne. "It's printed on the side of the truck."

I tell him *Cheyenne Drilling Supplies* is just a name. "Like Cheyenne, Wyoming, or Sioux City, Iowa?" I add a couple of football teams with Indian names and Raj throws in Crazy Horse malt liquor, but we don't convince Joseph.

"I know a real Cheyenne when I see one."

"Tsis Tsis Tas." The driver has both hands on the side of his pickup bed. We were too busy talking to notice when the truck stopped.

"Arrow Boy got it right." He tips his cowboy hat and tells us *Tsis Tsis Tas* is what his branch of the Cheyenne call themselves. The T and S words sort of mean, "The Human Beings," but not exactly. "Name's Charley Sweet Medicine. Pleased to meet you."

He points to a brick bungalow. Its windows are intact. A sign on the door says *Licensed Mental Health Facility*. There's a wooden front porch with a brown floor and a white banister and lawn chairs occupied by crazy looking white people—one man, one woman, and two who might be either one.

Charley Sweet Medicine says, "This is the address on your paper." He climbs the steps and introduces himself, not scared at all. He shakes hands and listens to the crazy looking people tell complicated stories all at once.

I walk as far as the first step and wait for a break in the conversation. Charley Sweet Medicine creates one by crossing his arms and looking right at me. The crazy people stop talking and notice the three kids standing in the yard.

The crazy woman jumps out of her chair and runs down the steps, exactly the way the dogs came at us on the highway. I step backward until I run into Joseph. It's the first time we've really touched, so I stop dead still.

"Karma?" the crazy woman knows my name. There's only one way that could happen. She doesn't look like the sepia tone mother in Dad's family picture. She doesn't even look like the photograph in the upper right hand corner of the Flanders Admission form we found in the attic. But this woman is my mother, Hyannisport Larkspur Smith.

I remember things about her—the way her eyes never settle in one place, the way she holds her hands together as if she's about to pray. I remember why my mother would rather live in a Licensed Mental Health Facility than with her husband and daughter.

She wants to kill me—not always, but often enough—especially when she hasn't had her medication, and she looks like she hasn't had it for several weeks. She ran away to save my life, but now she knows it wasn't far enough. My mother takes a couple of runner's paces toward me, but her legs cramp. She stumbles but doesn't fall. Her lips struggle to find words, but her mind is going too fast for her body.

She wants to say—"I tried to save your life, but that's impossible now."

I see those words as clearly as if they are written in blood. The crazies on the porch see them too. Hyannisport Larkspur Smith has told them all about me. And what she's told them scares them to the bone.

A crazy man lunges out of his chair. His thin blond hair stands up like he's full of electricity. Charley Sweet Medicine steps away.

Charley says, "Let's talk a bit."

Raj says, "Shoot him, Joseph."

I hear a Cheyenne Medicine Arrow fitting into its place in Joseph's compound bow.

"Sic Semper Tyrannis." The crazy man pulls a little pistol from his right front pocket and points it right at Joseph. John Wilkes Booth said that after he shot Abraham Lincoln. I don't know when I learned this or why I remember it. I know it means someone is going to die, because I had to find out if my mother loved me—and I still don't know.

I step in front of Joseph, so the crazy man can't shoot him.

I say, "Please," because sometimes that works when nothing else will.

The pretend John Wilkes Booth cocks back the hammer on his little antique pistol. A flintlock or a cap lock. I don't know the difference, only I know it is a very old gun and it might not work when he pulls the trigger.

He takes another step toward me, so I can look right into the barrel. It's black in there, like a peephole through a door with no light on the other side.

My mother screams. No words, but her whole life is in that scream, from motherhood to madness.

She steps between me and the gunman as the hammer falls.

A spark. A puff of smoke.

Hyannisport Larkspur Smith falls to the ground.

She looks at me and says, "I love you."

Now I know for sure.

"Catch her," says Charley Sweet Medicine.

I want to tell him it's too late, but then I feel Joseph's arms around me, and I realize I'm falling, exactly like my mother after all.

"She's hit in the chest," Joseph says as the pain closes on my lungs so I can barely squeeze in enough air to stay alive.

"Load her in the truck," Charley Sweet Medicine says. "Keep pressure on the wound."

Joseph tells me I saved his life. Absorbed all the killing power of the gunman's bullet after it passed through my mother. I'm a hero just for standing there.

"You're going to make it," Joseph says.

"Right." Raj is trying hard to think of an East Indian proverb but he can't.

They both are lying.

"I love you," Joseph says, just like my mother did.

And I know that's not a lie.

I want to answer back but I don't have enough air. A smile is the best I can do.

THE GROCERY
GAME

BOB TOLD ME TO CALL him Robert while he closed the deal on the condo. It made him sound more important. It made me sound more educated.

"Say yes when I give you the cue, Cindy. Otherwise let me do the talking." He fanned himself with a copy of the lease agreement, but all that did was move hot air around.

"Global warming." Bob didn't believe in things like greenhouse gasses and carbon footprints except as an excuse for the sweat circles under his arms. He looked at the clock over the property manager's desk, but it had stopped at ten fifteen this morning along with everything else that ran on electricity. He fidgeted in his chair and complained about the lack of air conditioning.

"Incomprehensible," is how Bob described the manager's desire to include me in the meeting. He was the one with a college degree and a guaranteed job as high school history teacher.

"It's probably the riots," I told him. Those had pretty much stopped since the National Guard came to town, but still... "I'm sure the manager wants to check out her new tenants personally."

"Stephanie," Bob reminded me. "Her name is Stephanie. She isn't like the girls back home."

He'd introduce me. I'd say hello and he'd take everything from there. But when Stephanie walked through the door, Bob forgot all the plans he'd made. A pleated mini skirt will do that to a man.

She really wasn't like the girls back home. She had shoulder length black hair that didn't hide the dozen piercings in each ear, or the tattooed snakes that stuck their heads out of her nearly-see-through blouse and wrapped their forked tongues around her chin. Stephanie wore black lipstick, and mascara underneath her eyes so dark and thick it made her look like death.

I had to admit, she made death look sexy. Bob thought so too. I watched him struggle with his vocabulary for a few seconds, then I introduced myself.

"Hello, I'm Cindy Silver, Bob's significant other."

"Robert!" Bob finally found his voice, but just enough to remind me I'd forgotten to sound educated.

"Cindy Silver." Stephanie put a little whistle in the S-sounds. She walked around the room in a big circle with her eyes on me. Like I was the center of the universe and Robert was a piece of cosmic garbage that happened to float by.

"Bobby, why don't you make some coffee while I get to know your girl?" She chased him to a coffee pot into the corner of the office—don't ask me how—and before Bob knew what was happening, he was looking for someplace to fill it with water.

She said, "I don't usually like girls who are prettier than me." She moved in close and traced the contours of my face with a bright red acrylic fingernail.

She leaned forward and kissed me on the lips just as Bob returned with a carafe full of water.

"Hey there!" He sloshed a little water as he took a step toward Stephanie, then spilled a little more when he took a step away.

"Something troubling you, Bobby?"

He raised the carafe as if he were offering a toast. "No electricity, and. . ." He trailed off, partly because he was about to say something really stupid, and partly because he noticed the little girl sitting on the chair beside the office door he'd just come through.

The child was a miniature version of Stephanie except for the piercings and tattoos. Same shoulder length black hair, same pleated mini skirt, same dark circles under her eyes.

"My daughter, Mary. She's learning to be invisible," Stephanie said. "It's good for little girls to be invisible when their mommas play the grocery game."

"Grocery game?" I waited for an explanation, but all she gave me was a Mona Lisa smile.

Stephanie walked to the chair where Mary had been sitting, but wasn't anymore. She looked at me until I asked, "Where'd she go?" exactly like she wanted.

"Since you asked so nicely. . ." She leaned forward and whispered in my ear, "Bobby is a pig," and then told us it was time to sign the lease.

Bob wanted to know what Stephanie said, and why she had to say it so he couldn't hear. But he couldn't ask while we signed the papers, or while Stephanie walked us to our condo.

"Right across from to mine," she said. "Just think, Cindy and Bobby living next door to Mary and me."

I'd almost forgotten about the little girl.

"Where is she?"

Stephanie opened the door to our unit and handed me the keys without answering. She gave me a little wave, ignoring Bob as though he was as invisible as Mary.

I wanted to explore our new place once our next-door neighbor was gone, but Bob wanted to talk.

"What did she say, Cindy?"

I didn't need a college education to know the truth would never do. "She told me you were hot."

Bob loved to have his hotness confirmed by girls like Stephanie. "Tell me exactly what she said."

"She'll watch you from her window when you move our furniture in." Men always believe lies like that. Bob flexed his biceps and stood like he was posing for a muscle building ad.

—

STEPHANIE SAT ON ONE OF my brand-new kitchen chairs and showed me her tattoos. Pretty weird, but Mary cuddled on my lap and put her head against my chest and that made everything seem natural.

"Every tattoo tells a story." Stephanie pulled the hem of her miniskirt up and scratched at an illustration on her left inner thigh, a rainbow colored arrow pointing north with a message below it in small blue gothic letters—too small and too gothic to read from a respectable distance.

I leaned in close and read it out loud to make it clear I wasn't up to anything personal. "Deposit empties here."

"I keep things humorous below the waist," Stephanie said. "Ask every man I know."

I was sure Stephanie knew a lot of men, but I was only curious about one of them. "So how about Mary's father? Does he like the body ink?" I wasn't just making conversation. Girls like Stephanie usually had guys who were a whole lot worse. Maybe Mary's dad was in prison, or maybe he was dead, or maybe he'd walk into the room any minute wearing a jacket made of human skin, looking for a matching pair of gloves.

"Tell Cindy about Daddy, Mary."

The little girl sat quietly on my lap and watched Stephanie unbutton her blouse, which was sheer enough to blur the graphic details while letting major features shine through.

"Tell her baby. Who's your daddy?"

"Broken condom." Mary struggled with the R in broken, the way a three-year-old is supposed to, but she said *condom* perfectly. Then she gave me a big, wet toddler kiss on the cheek and clapped her hands.

"Mary's dad isn't in the picture." Stephanie pulled her blouse open, poked her chest forward, and said, "Now look closely at my breasts," like a naughty stage hypnotist.

I wanted to say no, but Mary burrowed deeper into my lap and put her arms partway around my waist and hugged me, so I let Stephanie show me the circle of miniature Jack Daniel's bottles tattooed around her left nipple and the string of tiny cowboy pistols orbiting the right.

"Really fine work," I said. That sent Mary into a giggle-fit and made her clap again.

Stephanie pointed to her left breast. "This one's Yin." Then the right. "This one's Yang. I think of them as my twin girls."

According to Stephanie, her girls represented liquor stores being looted by angry mobs. "Liquor stores are the first to go when civilization comes apart. The one down the street gets robbed twice a week." She shimmied her twin girls in Yin and Yang order. "Liquor and guns. Take it as a sign."

She gave me a few seconds to think about how things had gone to hell in the last few years and how they were getting worse instead of better.

Since Stephanie was so talkative, I asked about the tattoo snakes on her neck that looked ready to eat her head.

"You're not ready for the snakes quite yet."

But I was ready for the red, white, and blue dagger running down her spine with its point at her tailbone and its handle between her shoulder blades.

"People always stab you in the back," she told me. "Your enemies stab you first, and your friends stab last, but in the end, stabbed is what you are."

She backed up to me and sat on my knees like a lesbian lap dancer, crowding Mary between us. "The inscription on the blade's kind of small. It says *Et tu Brute!*"

"Stephanie—" Before I could come up with a polite but firm objection, Mary put a hand on each of my cheeks and gave me a smoochy Hollywood kiss.

She said, "I love you Momma Cindy," only she couldn't quite do V's so it came out, "I lub you Momma Cindy." That smattering of baby talk nearly made me cry.

Stephanie looked over her shoulder old-time-stripper-style as she walked back to her chair. She spun, like a ballet dancer, sat down hard enough to shake the room. "Good girl, Mary. You set the hook real good."

Mary giggled and clapped her hands some more. She jumped off my lap, ran behind Stephanie, and peeked at me under a not-so-maternal arm covered in a multicolored Asian vine.

"She likes you Momma Cindy. Ever think of having one of your own?" Calm and natural, as if she was fully clothed.

I told her, "I don't think Bob and I are ready to be parents," trying hard to avoid eye contact with Yin and Yang.

"Bob doesn't really figure into it. Does he?"

"Well, I'm not ready to be a mother yet."

Stephanie sat there in my new kitchen chair naked from the waist up and stared at me without speaking for a full minute. I didn't realize I was holding my breath until it came out all at once.

"Let's see what Mary has to say about that, shall we?" She hugged her daughter's face against the pistol-decorated breast and asked her, "What about it Mary—Momma Cindy and motherhood?"

"I lub you Momma Cindy" she touched her chubby baby fingers to her lips, blew me a kiss, and smiled. "I lub you sooo much."

"Mary does just fine with women," Stephanie said. "She needs more practice with the men before her turn comes around."

Mary waved to me and smiled in spite of everything. Natural and unnatural, crazy and ordinary. "Her turn for what?"

Stephanie licked a fingertip and wiped away a smudge on Mary's forehead. "Her turn to play the grocery game."

ONE HOT DAY IS LIKE another in OKC, especially when soldiers are in the street and gasoline is rationed. When there's not enough electricity to run a fan, much less an air conditioner. They call it a brownout, but burnout is a better word. As soon as Bob walked through the door he started opening windows.

I didn't tell him that was useless because the air outside was hotter than the air inside. He'd come up with a scientific sounding argument and open windows anyway.

"Damn, it's hot," he said, way too loud. That's how Bob talked when he felt guilty. Like when he cheated on me back home with a girl who "didn't mean anything."

So when he walked around living room chairs talking in his I-had-an-affair voice, it didn't take me long to figure out what had happened.

"The power went off while I was teaching about the Magna Carta," he said. "Can you imagine what that's like? In the dark with thirty snickering teenagers talking about history so old it's got a Latin name."

"Like *Et tu Brute?*" I said. "Inscribed in ink on the tattooed knife on Stephanie's back."

"What?" The expression on Bob's face looked like one of the actor mug shots I used to look at on the Internet.

I stepped in front of him and put my hands on my hips while he ran through his list of explanations. Finally he settled on the truth.

"Sometimes things just happen, Cindy. You know, like when you move into a nice place where your girlfriend will be comfortable, and there's somebody next door who won't leave you alone."

"Did Stephanie show you her whisky bottles and pistols?" I knew he'd play close attention to Yin and Yang, because Bob liked breasts a lot, especially those he'd never seen before.

"But nothing happened." Slow, clear, like the president of the United States lying into a microphone about how things would be getting better in no time at all.

"Nothing I expected, anyway." Bob tried to open the windows wider. He opened the front door and closed it again—gently.

"Jesus, Cindy. It was really strange."

I shrugged.

"She's got tattoos everywhere." Bob circled a spot with his index finger, somewhere between his groin and his navel.

"Dates and pictures. Names too. Bob is tattooed right above her. . ."

Bob knew a word or two that would pinpoint the location, but they didn't seem right for the occasion.

"I get it, Bob."

"But the weirdest thing was Stephanie's little girl." Bob's voice slowed down. His volume lowered too, until his words were hardly more than a whisper. "Mary sat on my lap while Stephanie explained how it took a hundred years for Rome to fall but we'd get there in another month." He said Mary was so quiet he thought she'd fallen asleep, and then, "She kissed me on the mouth. Not the way a baby kisses, Cindy. Not that way at all."

He walked around the room again, shutting windows this time. Waiting to hear what I had to say, but Bob was never good at waiting.

"That's when I ran out," he said. "Really, Cindy, what else could I do?"

—

KNIVES ARE REAL CONVERSATION STOPPERS. I'd never thought about that until Stephanie met me at her front door carrying one. Then I couldn't think of anything else, except that maybe now wasn't a good time to talk about what happened with her, and Bob, and Mary.

She saw me staring at the knife and said, "Oh this old thing," like she was showing off a dress she'd picked out for a special occasion. "Her name is Raven Blood."

"The knife," Stephanie told me. "Knives have names, you know, especially knives like this."

She handed it to me hilt first, which made me feel a little better. Then she handed me a sheath.

"Fits around your ankle if you're wearing pants. Above your knee if you're in a dress—at least the kind of dresses you wear." Stephanie did a little spin that made her red pleated mini skirt fan out like the rings of Saturn. "Bought it on Craigslist before the power got so bad. Couldn't be sure the order took, but FedEx delivered it." She told me, "Raven Blood has a titanium alloy blade. The handle is gunmetal and bone. Perfect balance for throwing. Feels powerful doesn't it?"

She walked me to her kitchen and watched while I fastened the knife around my ankle.

"Wear it all the time." She kneeled in front of me and checked to see I'd done it right. "You have to protect yourself, Cindy. Piggy Bob's a coward."

I'd planned to slide into the subject of Stephanie and Bob, like easing into a cold shower, but I felt like taking a more direct approach now that I had a knife strapped to my leg.

"Kind of looks like the one tattooed on my back." Stephanie stayed on her knees. She folded her hands together like a Buddhist monk, asking my pardon for her little scene with Bob, using body language instead of words.

"You showed Bob Yin and Yang." I said it cold and sharp the way I imagined Raven Blood's edge would feel, but it still made Stephanie laugh.

"So how much did Bob the Pig tell you?" Stephanie stood and dusted off her knees.

"He said Mary kissed him—you know. Not like a three-year-old."

"Girl power is the most important thing," Stephanie said, "She'll get it right eventually."

It occurred to me I hadn't seen Mary since Stephanie let me into her apartment. I spent a few minutes searching out places a three-year-old might hide. I made a clicking sound with my tongue that might bring a puppy running but would never work with a little girl.

"She's practicing invisibility again," Stephanie said. "It's the second most important thing."

"You're teaching a three-year-old girl to seduce a grown man?"

"Her technique needs polish. Maybe I'll turn her loose on someone who's less prissy than Bob." Stephanie's smile was hard to read.

"You're joking, right?" But how could someone joke about a thing like that?

"A little girl can't stay invisible forever," Stephanie said.

At exactly that moment, the electricity came on and Mary hopped out of the oven and said, "Hi, Momma Cindy."

—

BOB SCOOTED A KITCHEN CHAIR in front of the living room window so he could watch Stephanie's condo. All the schools were closed until the government got things working again.

He couldn't get there even if the school was open, because a tornado tore up all the houses around the school and the National Guard kept everybody out.

"Another man on a motorcycle." Bob watched Stephanie meet the biker at her front door and accept a paper sack full of groceries.

Mary stood on her tiptoes beside Bob so she could see. "Momma likes potatoes a lot. Corn, too, and beer. Things that keep."

I stood behind Bob, put a hand on his shoulder, gently so he wouldn't jump. He had a union contract, so I guess the school made direct deposits in the bank, but the bank was closed and nobody had much confidence in money. The only thing that still worked in Oklahoma was the weather. Black clouds hung over the city for weeks at a time. Now and then tornado sirens sounded but the shelters weren't open and the televisions were off and the radio batteries were hard to find.

A few drops of rain fell while the biker was inside. Fifteen minutes at the most for a sack of potatoes, corn, and beer.

"Looks like a wall cloud in the south," Bob said. Everything looked like a wall cloud since the schools had closed.

"Any more of that hot Bud?" All he did anymore was sit at the window and complain about the weather, and the warm beer, and the groceries Stephanie shared with us. "Mighty poor pay for child care," Bob said. "Right, Mary?"

The little girl hopped into his lap and kissed him on the lips. He pulled away, but not as quickly as he should have.

—

BOB SAID STEPHANIE WAS THE best show in town now that TV didn't work. "Too bad the X-rated stuff happens behind closed doors." Mary watched with him and kept him posted on the male players in the grocery game.

"That one's Papa Lobo." She hefted herself onto the windowsill and shouted, "Hey, Papa Lobo, did you bring me anything?"

Bob scooted his chair back as the biker strutted over to the window.

"Hi there, baby doll." He fished a Tootsie Roll from a pocket of his greasy denim jacket and handed it to Mary.

She tried to show her prize to Bob, but he'd already backed his chair into the middle of the room. I moved in close, hoping to pull Mary into the safety zone, but I wasn't fast enough.

She reached into the biker's jacket pockets. She found a bag of M&M's, which she kept, and a packet of white powder, which she returned. "I'm not old enough for crank, right Papa Lobo?"

"Right as rain, baby doll." Lobo looked past Mary and searched my body with his eyes. The knife strapped to my ankle felt large and obvious. Maybe a man like Lobo could see it through the jeans.

I hadn't washed properly since the electricity quit three weeks ago. I knew my lack of personal hygiene wouldn't deter Lobo. Bob wouldn't stop him either if it came to that, but a knife can change any man's attitude.

The biker kept his eyes on me but ran his hands over Mary's face. He lifted a lock of her glossy black hair to his lips and kissed it.

"Be back for you later, baby doll. Take you for a ride on my hog after your mom and me are done." Lobo turned his hungry look toward Bob. "If your boyfriend don't object."

Bob's lips moved but no sound came out.

Lobo stood, framed in our living room window, waiting for Bob to summon up a challenge. Dark clouds covered the sky behind him. Lightning flashed. Thunder rolled over the city in perfect harmony with the three bikers who pulled into the parking lot escorting a Winnebago recreational vehicle. The RV driver climbed out and took a seat on Lobo's motorcycle.

"RV with eighty gallons of gas on board," Lobo said. "That's what the little girl cost me." He hardened his look. "Be back before the rain starts falling. Have her ready."

—

SPARSE RAINDROPS THE SIZE OF marbles fell from low hanging clouds accompanied by occasional hailstones. They made a drumming noise on the Winnebago. If the television worked, we'd be getting warnings to go to the shelters, but we didn't need television to tell us something bad was on the way.

The temperature fell twenty degrees while Lobo went into Stephanie's condo, and the southwestern sky turned the color of corroded copper.

The bikers crowded their machines underneath a dying oak tree in the parking lot. There weren't enough leaves to keep them dry once the real storm started, and it would be here soon. Chain lightning made their movements look jerky. The green color in the south deepened into a solid black wall.

Lobo left Stephanie's front door open as he walked onto the parking lot. A second later she followed him, struggling with her miniskirt and blouse, which didn't seem to fit as well as usual.

She grabbed at Lobo's arm and he slapped her across the face hard enough to be heard over the thunder and rising wind. Hard enough to knock her down, but Stephanie didn't fall. She grabbed Lobo's arm again, and this time he didn't hit her.

"A deal's a deal." Lobo looked from Stephanie to the Winnebago, then at Mary, who sat on the windowsill dangling her feet over a dead boxwood hedge.

Before I could stop her, Mary slid out the window and ran to her mother. Violence didn't scare the little girl. A slap, a shout, bruised eyes, and bloody lips were all part of the grocery game.

"Do *something*," I told Bob. "He'll take Mary. You have to do something now."

Bob made a face like maybe he could fix all this if I'd just give him enough time to come up with a plan. He could explain to Lobo about the Constitution, and the Declaration of Independence, and the Magna Carta.

"We'll call the police," he told me, as if the phones would ever work again, as if there were police.

A two-second hailstorm peppered the parking lot with pea-size ice crystals as I walked out the door. The four bikers underneath the tree started their engines but didn't leave the shelter of the half-dead limbs. Tornado sirens wailed as I approached Lobo.

Bob called out, "Don't be crazy, Cindy." Taking Lobo's side, the winning side, because that's what men with college degrees in history do.

"Good advice, Cindy." Lobo scooped up Mary with his left hand, drew a pistol from inside his jacket with the right, and shot Stephanie in the chest.

Mary covered her ears against the noise, but her back was turned away from Stephanie. So the little girl didn't see her mother fall. Lobo did. He watched a pool of blood mix with ice and water, much more interesting than Cindy Silver. Lobo didn't see me lift my ankle. He didn't know about the knife.

Raven Blood.

The dirty jeans slid off the hilt. My hand closed over it as if I'd done this thing a hundred times. In one easy circular motion I drew the weapon and carried through with an overhanded thrust into the biker's neck.

"Surprise!" I said, but Lobo didn't look surprised.

He stared at me through eyes already glazing over, blue eyes that looked as innocent as the child's whose mother he just murdered. He handed Mary to me, as if we'd planned it just that way, and then he slumped to the ground.

"Jesus," Lobo said. The word sounded wet with blood like a confession given with a mouth full of holy wine. I could barely hear him over the storm warning siren.

"Jesus." Lobo's right leg trembled for a moment, and it looked as if he might reach for the knife, but he died before that happened, with a rush of air and a few bloody bubbles from his nose.

I held Mary so she couldn't see Stephanie, but Lobo lay posed before her like a crime scene photograph. "Momma says if you die with Jesus's name on your lips you go straight to heaven."

"Maybe so, baby."

The bikers rolled our way. Rolled into a circle with me and Mary in the center. I looked each of them in the eye as they drove by, because there was nowhere to run, nothing for me to do if they decided to leave another body on the parking lot.

The siren faded. The bikers broke out of the circle like a lesson in centrifugal force and drove off the lot. Maybe because a storm was on the way. Maybe because even men like these couldn't kill a woman holding a small child.

"Cindy?" Finally Bob came out of the condo. "That was really crazy, Cindy." He nudged Lobo with his boot. He pointed to Stephanie. "Is she. . .?"

"Shut up Bob."

He looked ready to object, ready to be brave now that there was no one to confront.

"Get in the RV *now*, Bob," I told him, "If those bikers come back, I don't want to be here."

Bob looked around the parking lot the way a stray cat looks at the place it used to live before its people didn't want it anymore.

"We're leaving," I said. "The city's no place to be."

"My job," Bob said. "I have—you know—responsibilities."

"School's out, Bob. History's in front of us now." I handed Mary to him and climbed into the RV. "I'm driving. I think I'll be driving from now on."

WAKE UP
CALL

DELIVERIES DON'T COME REGULAR TO the halfway house since the electricity started going brown. Then it went all the way black so there's no TV, or ice to put in tap water to wash down our capsules of RG1068, and after a couple of no-electric days there are no RG1068 capsules to wash down while we sit in dim rooms and listen to emergency sirens.

The councilor asks me, "How are you feeling, Wylie?" Bobby Tuesday is his name. He touches the tip of his extra sharp Mongol #2 pencil lead onto the surface of a yellow pad that used to have the power to take away my freedom, but doesn't anymore.

I won't speak until he calls me by my full name. Proof positive he can't boss an Apache warrior around.

At first Bobby Tuesday doesn't know why I'm not answering. He looks at his watch—reminding me this is his hour—then all of a sudden he gets it.

"How are you feeling Wylie E. Chatto?" Bobby keeps his voice flat so his anger doesn't show until he gets to my last name, but Chatto comes out way too fast.

I tell him, "Fine, thank you." Polite and careful, because things could still change if the electricity comes back. "Better every day." I give Bobby my biggest Apache smile.

What would he do if I told him the voices are back? What would he do if I told him how the scent of rosemary fills the air again when bad things are on the way? What if I told him Chief Dan George's ghost is standing right behind him? Chief Dan wants Bobby to leave so he can tell me all I need to know about girls but he won't talk until we are alone.

I look at my watch so the councilor will know his time has all run out. Hours mean nothing to an Apache warrior, so the watch has no hands. Bobby is too busy looking at his powerless yellow pad to notice.

"Bobby Tuesday is a funny name," I tell the counselor—to show him I still know about laughing. "So is Wylie E. . . ." I almost say, *"Coyote,"* but at the last minute I remember there are things you never tell a counselor. Like where you hide your knife, and what Chief Dan George tells you, and the war name your best friend gave you before someone shot her in the chest.

So instead of saying, *"Coyote,"* I make a zipper sign across my lips. I give the drop-in counselor a wink so he'll have something else to think about. That's how psychology works.

"I guess you'll be okay." Bobby doesn't mean it, but there is nothing he can do. He can't up my dosage of RG1068. He can't even call the police when I shove him aside and walk out of the halfway house, because telephones don't work anymore. He can't wrestle me to the ground because I'm too big and too strong and just crazy enough.

He can't stop me because I'm an Apache warrior coming back from a long visit with RG1068.

But I stop in the front yard anyway. I spread my arms the way Chief Dan George did in Little Big Man. I tell Bobby, "The Sacred Alarm Clock is ticking. Apache warriors are waking up."

The Sacred Alarm Clock doesn't really tick, but I don't tell him that. When you keep white people guessing, they usually guess exactly wrong.

"Wylie. . ." Sometimes the Sacred Alarm Clock sounds like a counselor running out of words.

———

OKLAHOMA CITY STREETS ARE FULL of people wearing paper scrubs and masks, like the hazmat workers who came to the halfway house to clean up my best friend's blood. The police have masks, too, but they keep their regular cop uniforms so citizens don't worry about their guns. New Flu makes them dress this way.

New Flu wants to kiss you on the lips and ride on your blue jeans and fly into your face with a sneeze. The first person with it had a number name—*Patient Zero*. He had a virus in his brain.

"Temporal lobe," according to Counselor Bobby Tuesday. "The virus starts out like all the other germs and then it travels to the brain where it makes you crazy in a special way, like Joan of Arc, or Jim Jones."

People wear masks and throw-away clothes and sometimes rubber gloves so the virus can't tell them what's on God's mind. Halfway house residents know all about being crazy so the New Flu doesn't scare us.

I hear ghost footsteps behind me on my right and left—movie star Indians and dead warriors follow me in two noisy invisible lines like geese migrating back to the way it was in fourteen hundred ninety-one.

Tonto, Cochise, Will Sampson, Black Elk, Rudy Youngblood, Red Bonnet. The ghosts string out behind me like the wake of an Apache powerboat that washes white Oklahomans into the street. Being an Apache is good. Being a crazy Apache is even better when the Sacred Alarm Clock wakes everybody up and for a few minutes they can't remember where they are.

The police sit on their horses waiting for a reason to draw their guns. Gasoline is only for emergencies now. Mules pull trolleys of shoppers from store to store where they spend money before it loses all its magic. The air is filled with the sharp, clean scent of horseshit and trouble.

Rosemary is what trouble smells like when exhaust fumes blow away. Like the strings of herbs that cooks wrap around pork tenderloin. The smell of trouble makes me hungry.

Apache warriors used to eat U.S. Army mules and wild buffalo and Pueblo corn. We had everything we needed on the plunder trail, but that's in Arizona and this is Oklahoma City—the place Indians came to rest between the wars.

On the corner is a 7-Eleven. It's a number name, like *Patient Zero*, but they write part of it in letters so it's hard for me to read. Letters move around like Hopi dancers calling on the rain, but numbers are as still and quiet as deer hunters in a blind. Like 4.85 and 99/100. The price of regular gasoline the 7-Eleven used to sell when there was enough to go around.

Tonto's ghost tells me, *"Apaches never had a use for gasoline."* He doesn't call me Kimosabe—that's for masked white men. He calls me Coyote. All the Indian ghosts call me Coyote. Spirits know your war name.

Tonto leads me into the convenience store, which really isn't convenient without gasoline. He points to racks of corn chips and jerky.

"Some jerky is buffalo." Tonto makes me guess which ones.

The man behind the counter is a Persian. I used to buy things from him with incidental money from the counselors, but Apaches live off the land when their RG1068 wears off. The clerk doesn't know that yet. He gives me a big white Persian grin that isn't hidden under a mask. His name is Mohared, but nobody will try that, so everybody calls him Mo.

"How are you, Wylie E.?"

I don't make him say my full name because he isn't trying to be the boss, but I zip my lip so my war name won't come out by accident.

Mo thinks I am worried about New Flu. He zips his lip, too, but unzips it again right away. "Just got some Doritos in. Maybe the last ones in the world."

Those are made of corn, so I grab a giant pack and tear it open. Corn and salt and other things disguise the scent of corn chip machines.

"Rosemary," I tell Mo, because his store is suddenly so full of the trouble smell that even ranch seasonings can't hide it.

"Hands in the air!" A man in a blue paper scrub suit with a pink doctor's mask and a white cowboy hat points a pistol half way between Mo and me. This isn't the kind of pistols cowboys used to take our land away, but it still smells like rosemary.

I crunch a Dorito, so I'll die with a good taste in my mouth.

"I said get 'em up." He makes a bobbing movement with the gun as if there's some kind of connection to our hands. Mo raises his as high as his shoulders but I don't raise mine at all.

"The boy is mentally challenged," Mo says. "Don't shoot him, please."

Sometimes the Sacred Alarm Clock sounds like a Persian clerk begging for your life.

Tonto stands in front of Mo, because the clerk is as brave as an Apache warrior. "A ghost won't stop a robber's bullet, Coyote," he tells me. "You'll have to think of something."

Ghosts aren't much good at all. I'm feeling kind of guilty about not having any money to pay Mo for the corn chips.

Tonto says, "Living off the land isn't the same as stealing," so I don't have to feel bad about taking things like Doritos and jerky.

I say, "As long as I'm not taking money," so Tonto will know I get it.

He says, "A handful of corn turns defeat into victory."

He talks like that when I'm supposed to figure something out. Something complicated, like how to stop a robbery when all I've got is a large bag of Ranch Flavored Doritos. I haven't got a clue, but I reach inside the bag and take out the biggest handful I can hold and offer it to the robber, like he might trade it for his gun.

"Drop it, retard!"

That word makes me crunch the Doritos into a little pile of seasoned dust while the robber watches. It looks like a little golden pyramid when I open up my hand.

"Drop it!"

The man with the gun is trying hard to be boss, but I won't let that happen now that my RG1068 is gone. I draw a double lungful of rosemary-filled air and blow Dorito dust into the robber's face.

His eyes open wide with surprise and then close quickly when the pain comes. He fires a wild shot over my head and another wild shot into the jerky rack. He opens his eyes into a squint that looks like a pair of dog anuses over his mask, and I know his next shot will kill me, so I punch him in the surgical mask with my Dorito fist.

I shout, "Bam!" like in the word balloons in superhero comic books my best friend used to read me.

The robber's white hat falls onto the floor. His gun falls to the floor. He goes down on his knees crying ranch flavored tears and shouting, "Jesus!" like the televangelists used to do.

The mask soaks up so much blood it looks like the flags truck drivers used to put on loads that stuck out too far.

"Jesus, Jesus, Jesus!" When three Jesuses don't help him, the robber tries to pick up his pistol.

I put the heel of my boot on his hand until he changes his mind. I step back and kick him in the chin before he finds a robber-prayer that works. I pick up his pistol and stick it in my pants. The barrel is hot but not too hot for an Apache warrior.

Horse hoofs make a western movie sound on the 7-Eleven parking lot. A policeman dismounts like he's got all the time in the world.

He asks, "Somebody call the police?" as he walks through the door and nudges the robber with his foot. Cops used to come after a telephone call, but now they only come after gunshots—when the worst has already happened so there isn't any hurry.

He puts a hand on his pistol grip and looks at me, but Mo tells him I just saved the day.

"Wylie stopped a robbery," Mo says. "He came in for corn chips."

I show him the Doritos bag in case he has any doubts.

The cop looks at the corn chips but he sees the pistol in my pants. He thinks about a gunfight, but there's a robber on the floor, and a white cowboy hat that is exactly his size.

The cop fastens his handcuffs on the robber before he puts the hat on his head. "I'll need help to get him on my horse." He looks a little like the Lone Ranger, even if the mask is wrong.

Tonto laughs when I call the policeman Kimosabe.

"You can have the Doritos for free," Mo says. Persians clerks never give anything away unless you save their lives. "Soft drinks too."

But there's no refrigeration, and even an Apache can't drink hot Dr Pepper.

"Anything you want," Mo tells me. "Any time from seven a.m. to elven p.m. On the house."

Tonto tells me on the house is not the Apache way. *"Has to be taken, Coyote. Otherwise it's charity."*

Charity. I push the cop aside. I grab three bags of Doritos and a bag of jerky with a bullet hole in it. I run out the door, as if I'm stealing. It is hard to live off the land with Persian clerks like Mo.

When I run my ghosts can't follow. The policeman could follow if he wanted to, but he has other things on his mind. Sometimes the Sacred Alarm Clock sounds like a cop not coming after you.

—

THERE'S A SMOKE CLOUD COMING OUT of one of the buildings in the center of town. It's the biggest and the tallest and the most useless building of all. No one can get to the top without electricity, so people on the street just watch it burn.

A siren howls like the biggest coyote in the world, and a red fire truck races by me as if this is an emergency. When the firemen reach the building, they jump out of the truck and pretend they have a plan. Nobody cares about the building, so the men unbutton their firemen coats and drink warm bottles of beer while they lay their hoses on the street.

"In case it gets out of hand," the boss fireman says loud so everyone will know he still has a job. The men look hot in their firefighter hats and suits. They have special masks like scuba divers wear so they can breathe under water, but the firemen don't put these on because even they can't stand that much heat.

The boss fireman is Indian. Choctaw, I think. They are usually friendly so I stand beside him and pretend to read signs in the smoke.

"I met a Choctaw once," I tell him.

"No civilians allowed in this area," he says. "Get back beyond the line."

The line is invisible, like the medicine lines around states and reservations and Chickasaw casinos. It's one of those dream things everybody thinks is real until the Sacred Alarm Clock wakes them up.

When I say, "You don't have to pretend anymore," he finally looks at me. He counts my bags of corn chips. He looks at the bullet hole through my jerky bag. There's a cartoon Indian on the front of the bag, but I'm still not sure I picked the right one.

I ask him, "Is this buffalo jerky?" He sees the gun in the front of my pants. "The gun barrel is pretty cool now. Want to touch it?"

The firefighters aren't interested in the fire anymore. They watch me wave my pistol in the air.

"It's taken, not charity, like the chips." I try to hand my pistol to the Choctaw fire-boss, but now he wants to stand on the opposite side of the truck—beyond the medicine line where civilians are supposed to go. I drop my chips and jerky, because it's really hard to hold onto so many things at once, and when I try to catch them, the pistol fires.

A hot brass cartridge flies inside my shirt collar and burns me on the tattoo between my shoulder blades that I got by mistake a very long time ago. It feels good to watch the firemen run away—like Custer running from the Lakota at the Little Big Horn. I don't mind the burn so much.

"It's time to go," I shout at the firemen's backs. It's always time to go when a shot's been fired, but I check my handless watch and pretend I'm keeping track.

———

AROUND THE BLOCK WHERE NO guns have been fired, a half-dozen men stand in a circle with a girl in the center. It's a big circle, because she hasn't got a mask.

The men look sideways at the girl, pretending they barely notice her. Like she's a ghost they shouldn't watch too closely, but they have to look at least a little because she is so pretty. Not pretty in the church way, not pretty in a clean dress with ribbons in her hair way. This girl is pretty like the girls who dance around brass poles while men stuff paper money in their panties.

Her shirt is so tight the buttons pop open to show she's not wearing anything underneath. Her dress is almost short enough to let you see where her legs meet at the very top. The men step away when she approaches them, just like they step away from Tonto and Geronimo and Chief Dan George, but I'm pretty sure she's not a spirit. I'm having feelings about this girl. *"Inappropriate feelings,"* according to Bobby Tuesday, and you don't get *inappropriate feelings* about ghosts—except maybe for ghost of Natalie Wood taking off her clothes in *Gypsy.*

The closer I get, the more *inappropriate* I feel. Her lips are pouted out like she's sucking on a lemon drop that's turned her spit too sour to swallow. Her bright red fingernails are too long to be real. Her eyes are so blue it's a sure bet she doesn't have one drop of Indian blood. They don't quite move together, so it looks like she's watching something nobody else can see—New Flu eyes.

The New Flu girl has a bundle in one arm, and a book in one hand, and she's moving around the circle like a Victoria's Secret model who isn't tall enough but more than makes up for it by looking crazy.

This girl's had lots of practice being crazy. I can tell by the way she listens to voices nobody else can hear, and the way she walks, like her RG1068 has worn off and she wants to make up for lost time before Bobby Tuesday writes her name on his yellow counselor pad.

Our eyes meet like lovers' used to in the old time black-and-white movies. The bubble of men pops and splatters them in all directions. Two crazy people are way too many when the cops ride horses and the Sacred Alarm Clock is about to ring.

I move toward the girl slow and steady, like a warrior on a vision quest. Her blue eyes track together long enough to find my brown ones and they hold on long enough for me to say, "My name's Wylie E. . . ."

"Coyote." She finishes my name like nobody could except for one of my ghosts. "I'm Hannah."

Her gums show a little when she smiles, but that doesn't make me feel any less inappropriate. She hands me her book and plucks at the wrapping on the bundle as if she's removing petals from a bouquet of roses.

"This here's Darryl. He was immaculately conceived in the Travel Lodge Motel yesterday. Found him on the nightstand beside a twenty-dollar bill."

Darryl looks like a Cabbage Patch Doll—but he's probably a Chinese knockoff because his eyes don't close when Hannah tips him back and forth.

Hannah runs her tongue over her lips and smiles again. "That book you're holding is the Bible. It came from the motel, too. It's not stealing when you take a Bible."

"How'd you know my war name?" Tonto and Geronimo finally catch up, but they aren't any help. They step away from Hannah like the circle of men I found her in.

"Signs and wonders," Hannah says. It's hard to tell who she's talking to because her eyes are moving in different directions again. "Everything is foretold in the book of Road Runner." She points her lemon drop lips at the Bible I'm still holding, but the only thing I can read are numbers.

"John, three-sixteen," I tell her without looking. Televangelists say that all the time, so it must be important.

Geronimo crosses his arms and shakes his head. Chief Dan George locks his lips with an imaginary key. It's time to practice my Indian ways, but white girls like Hannah want the air to be filled with words, so I tell her, "Usen is the Apache name for God."

I've never been this close to such a pretty girl before.

A girl who'll look me in the eyes.

A girl who'll let me hold her Bible.

A girl who knows my war name.

"Wylie E. Coyote." It sounds important when Hannah says it. She laughs, like I make her so happy she can't help herself.

Hannah says, "Usen is God's lookalike cousin." She gives Darryl a kiss.

I kiss him in the same place, so it's almost as if our lips are touching.

"Look!" Hannah tips Darryl back and forth and his eyes open and close just like they are supposed to. "It's a miracle."

Now Hannah kisses me for real. For the first time in my life, my lips are touching a real live girl who is not my Foster Mother. Her tongue sneaks into my mouth before I know what's happening and I'm feeling more inappropriate than ever.

"So that's what happens in a kiss." I'm talking to Chief Dan George but Hannah thinks I'm talking to her.

She puts an arm around my waist and guides me down the street like I'm an Indian pony and she's the best rider ever. A little nudge turns me. A cluck of her tongue speeds me up or slows me down. I know exactly what she wants and doing it makes me as happy as the first time I saw Geronimo's ghost.

"There's something we have to do." Hannah's hand has found my pistol. Her fingers explore the barrel. I hold my breath while she pokes a bright red acrylic nail in the place where the bullets come out.

"Okay," pops out of me like a belch that's a complete surprise. I'd do the zipper trick with my mouth, but one hand is wrapped around Hannah's waist and other hand is holding her Bible.

"St. Gregory's isn't very far." Hannah points the pistol the direction she wants to go. I walk beside her pretending I have a choice.

Horse hoofs fall in behind us. I want to turn around, but I already know what's there.

"A cop," I tell Hannah. "Maybe the one from the 7-Eleven." A picture of a policeman grows in my mind like it's sprouted from magic seeds. Pretty soon the policeman is all I can see. He's on a brown horse with a golden mane. He's wearing a white hat. He's thinking about the gun he saw in my pants earlier today—the one Hannah is holding now. He's thinking he might have to shoot us later on.

The policeman's image fills my mind so much there's no room for anything else but Hannah and the scent of rosemary. The trouble smell is so strong it makes my eyes water.

Hannah quotes Bible verses full of thees and thous and double numbers, the way the white preachers talk. The horse sounds fall back a little to keep away from the New Flu viruses riding out on Hannah's religious words.

For a second I understand perfectly that sanity and terror are exactly the same thing, and I haven't felt so sane since I was twelve years old and knew my foster parents didn't want an Indian son who couldn't read.

"Miss." Exactly like the cop's voice in the 7-Eleven, only this time there's no Persian clerk to calm him down.

Hannah says, "We're here, Wylie, St. Gregory's." She ignores the cop who's beside us now, with me between him and Hannah, because he knows which one of us is most dangerous.

He tips his white cowboy hat back on his head and pulls his doctor's mask down so I can see the John Wayne smile on his lips.

Hannah keeps her eyes on St. Gregory's steeple, which points toward the sky like a rocket ship getting ready to take off. She points the pistol at the sky, harmless for a little while but ready for action in a second.

"Miss." The cop has his hand on his pistol. He's blurry through the rosemary haze that makes it hard to breathe, but I can see the arteries in his forehead filling up below the brim of his white confiscated cowboy hat. Getting ready to kill somebody, like he always knew he might, wondering how his horse will react to gunshots.

The cop eases his pistol out of his holster like a five-year-old boy sneaking a cookie. I'd reach for my pistol but Hannah is already holding it and the only thing I have is the Bible from the Travel Lodge Motel.

Hannah steps away from me. She sets Baby Darryl on the pavement and holds my pistol in a double-handed grip. She points the pistol at St. Gregory's steeple, but that doesn't make the cop feel better. He has his weapon out, trying to take aim and control his nervous horse at the same time.

A Bible will stop a bullet. Everybody knows that—even a hardback Gideon Bible stolen from a Travel Lodge. But Usen doesn't want Apaches to use holy words as a shield. For us they are a weapon.

I hurl the Bible like a Frisbee at the policeman's face. I send an Apache war whoop along to curry Usen's favor. But the book twists in the rosemary scented air and opens before it finds its target. It flutters in the horse's face.

Good enough. The horse's front legs are off the street, fighting with the word of God. The cop slides out of the saddle and bounces on the pavement, just as Hannah fires a shot.

I snatch up the policeman's pistol, just in case the fall hasn't knocked thoughts of killing Indians out of him.

Hannah fires again, and again, adjusting her stance with each shot. Altering her weight with little movements of her tongue against her upper lip.

Gunpowder smell fills the air now. No more rosemary. The policeman is content to lie beside the open Bible while the horse dances to the sound of Hannah's bullets.

She goes down on one knee and mumbles a prayer, naming St. Gregory and God and his lookalike cousin, Usen, and then pulls the trigger one last time.

The bell in St. Gregory's steeple rings, louder than it ever rang before.

"The Sacred Alarm Clock," I tell the cop in case he hasn't figured it out yet. "Now everyone can hear it."

Hannah blows the smoke away from the pistol barrel. She places it beside Baby Darryl on the pavement in front of St. Gregory's. She walks over to the Bible beside the policeman.

"It's open to the *Book of Jamaicans,*" she tells me. "St. Gregg's nuns will see to Darryl. That's what it says."

I climb on the policeman's horse and extend a hand to Hannah. They both know about Apache warriors. Everybody does, now that the Sacred Alarm Clock has rung.

MANNING
UP

BEFORE THE TROUBLE STARTED THERE were lots of different bars in Oklahoma City—Indian bars, gay bars, hillbilly bars. Not anymore. Since the power grid went down, and the New Flu came to town, everybody gets drunk together. Lesbians like me stand next to rednecks in dark rooms lit by kerosene lamps and tell the barkeep, "Do it again." Not exactly social drinking.

The good old boys trade jokes about bull dykes and farmer's daughters. They bump into me and say, "Excuse me buddy."

When I come out of the restroom somebody shouts, "Hey mister, you went in the wrong one." Everybody laughs except for me and my girlfriend Mona.

"Don't let it bother you," she says. "Don't start trouble Chris."

But trouble is headed my way and there is nothing I can do about it. The loudest redneck in the bar walks over and spits tobacco juice on the floor. He slides his big drunk cowboy eyes up and down Mona's body and tells her, "You're the prettiest Injun girl I ever seen."

When Mona doesn't answer he spits on the floor again, closer to my boots this time.

Mona says, "Ignore him, Chris. He'll go away."

I look at the tobacco juice on the floor and count to twenty. He's still there when I look up, staring holes through Mona's Wrangler Jeans—an ass man unless I miss my guess.

All night long he's blamed his troubles on the niggers and the Injuns and the homo-lesbo abominations. Quoting the Bible over boilermakers, making it sound like a dirty book. Now he's ready to overlook Mona's race and sexual orientation, share his precious bodily fluids with her. Men like that never go away when you ignore them.

The cowboy puts a grease-stained hand over his crotch, gives himself a squeeze, and says, "Why not try a real man, sweetie."

"Well, welcome to the monkey house." I step between him and Mona. We don't quite manage to lock eyes, because his don't track together and I can't figure out which one he's using at the moment.

Sometime between the tobacco juice and the crotch squeeze the bar has gotten quiet. Back in the Wild West days a piano man would start playing and the bartender would shout, "Drinks on the house," but that doesn't happen.

The cowboy digs at his nose with his crotch-hand then points a finger right at me, like he's got something important to say but it hasn't come to him yet.

"'Bomination."

His finger shakes a little, but it could be an effect of the lantern light.

"A-bomination." He says it with a long *A* so it sounds explosive and radio-active. His breath blows over me with the next to last syllable. It smells like the kitchen in a German restaurant. I'm probably never going to feel good about cooked cabbage again.

"Let's go, Chris." Mona pulls at my shirt. She's an abomination too, but she's so good-looking cowboys like this one never notice.

"Pussy," the cowboy tries to stand a little straighter. Tries to suck in his belly back across the western belt that probably has his name tooled into the back.

"Pussy," is the nicest word he has for me. Much nicer than "A-bomina-tion," or "Bull dyke," or a string of others I've heard before.

The cowboy's vocabulary is pretty good as long as he's talking about perverse sexual acts or describing his penis. He knows the exact length of it—like every other man on the planet earth—and according to him it's exactly what Mona needs to bring her back over from the dark side.

What would he say if he knew my girlfriend is a virgin? A virgin who's had a baby, something like Jesus's mother, only Mona went to a sperm bank in Tulsa.

Without asking me.

When I wasn't looking.

I wonder if that would make her an a-bomination in the cowboy's eyes after he stopped thinking about how she'd look naked.

I'd bet anything his imagination's not that good. Nothing about him is good enough for a girl like Mona. I'm not good enough either, but she loves me just the same.

Homemade beer and thoughts of Mona soften me up for a second, and I'm ready to walk out of the bar, but I don't want to turn my back on the cowboy. I don't want to walk out backwards, because that would build him up for the next time he gets drunk and starts thinking about how he backed a dyke out of a saloon.

"Look partner, I don't want no trouble." I use the double negative so we'll have some common ground. I try my best to look ignorant and bigoted, like I hate everybody he hates except for people like me, so maybe he can overlook it for the time being. "Let me buy you a drink. While the money's still good."

That comment brings a smile—evidence of his tobacco habit and poor dental hygiene.

"E-conomy sucks," he says. It's the biggest word he knows except for A-bomination. He names all the minorities that messed things up for people like him, and doesn't mention lesbians once. He extends a hand. This time it's not pointing an accusing finger, but I don't really want to shake it, because I've seen where it's been.

Mona nudges me.

"Man up," she whispers in my ear, close enough so the cowboy can't hear. Close enough so the warm air reminds me how much I want to go home with her without cuts and bruises and regrets.

I resist the urge to do one of those complicated handshakes with fist bumps, hand signals, and high fives. I press my palm against the cowboy's, and wince when he closes his fingers in a grip that's been strengthened by years of masturbation.

I figure it's Mona's whisper that did it. I had the cowboy won over until then, until he decided the pretty lesbian was whispering something bad about him in the bull dyke's ear. Probably something about his penis—what else could girls like us have to talk about?

The bones in my right hand grind against each other like the gears in a society that's run out of transmission fluid. The pressure in the room changes like it does before a tornado. All the insults I've heard since junior high school pump up my arms and shoulders like a bodybuilder's muscles—only these muscles aren't just for show. They're lesbian, cowboy-butt-whuppin' muscles wired into a brain that's turned all the way up to kill.

The cowboy says something about AIDS and herpes and some other venereal diseases he's certain lesbians invented. He doubles down on his power squeeze and talks about the New Flu that started out in Tulsa.

He says, "Tulsa's a homo-town."

He says, "Jesus loves cowboys, but he can't stand queers."

He says, "Queers ruined the whole damned world."

People gather around us now, gays and lesbians, rednecks, unemployed blue-collar people who came here to get too drunk to worry. They can't watch football on TV anymore, but they can watch a boxing match between a low estrogen woman and an obnoxious redneck.

Maybe the cowboy would quit trying to break my hand if he didn't have an audience. But he has an audience, and he has ahold of a bull dyke's hand, who's stronger than he thought she was. His free hand goes behind him, where he'll have a knife or a gun, or some little something that's just right for detonating an A-bomination.

So I catch him in the nose with a solid left hook.

The cowboy doesn't know how to fight, but he doesn't understand that yet, so I give him a couple of quick, almost feminine jabs in the solar plexus—just enough to let him consider the possibilities.

Mona doesn't like for me to fight, but even she can see I'm going easy. I take a step back, give him the chance to walk away, but now the cowboy has decided somebody has to die. He finds a crappy little revolver in the back of his pants. A .22-caliber Saturday Night Special good for killing copperheads and lesbians.

He points the weapon at me and recites a list of pretty good reasons for pulling the trigger.

He says, "Get the picture, sweetie?"

Blood and snot from the cowboy's nose give him sort of a New Jersey accent and he takes the time to wipe it on his sleeve.

"Get the picture, sweetie?" More East Texas in the accent now. Suitable words to say before a shooting. He closes his left eye, as if he has to take careful aim from five feet away. He puts the tip of his tongue between his teeth, but pulls it back when he tastes blood.

"Mister." Mona walks beside me with her hands on her hips, the way she talks to her boy, Joseph, when he annoys her. "Think about what you're doing." She takes a graceful step and kicks the cowboy in the balls.

Mona used to be a forward on her high school soccer team. One kick is plenty for the cowboy. Some girls would have kicked him again, just because he deserved it. Not Mona. She's Choctaw, one of the civilized tribes.

"Let's go, Chris." She takes my arm like she's the homecoming queen and I'm her escort to the throne.

The cowboy doesn't say anything while we head for the door. He just massages his testicles and watches us get smaller.

—

"I COULD HAVE HANDLED IT," I tell Mona.

It's really dark and there aren't any streetlights. We have a flashlight, but batteries are hard to get, so we won't turn it on unless we really need to.

"That cowboy wasn't going to shoot." It hadn't felt that way back in the bar, but now I remember how he hadn't cocked the hammer back. Cowboys always do that, tease every bit of drama out of a murder before they actually pull the trigger. It makes the story sound better when they tell it to their buddies who haven't killed anybody yet.

Mona kisses me on the cheek. We can do things like that now that the electricity is gone. Two romantic lesbians trading kisses in the dark, the way they used to do a thousand years ago before the world got illuminated.

"You don't know anything about men," Mona tells me. "Even though you sort of look like one."

She's right, of course. Girls like Mona know everything there is to know about men, but girls like me only know about the ones who hate us.

I ask her why she kicked him and she tells me, "To preserve his dignity."

According to Mona a man without dignity is as dangerous as an injured wolf—sure to bite somebody.

"What's that got to do with kicking a cowboy in the balls?"

"It's more dignified to be kicked in the balls by a pretty woman than to be beaten up by a dyke."

I guess Mona's right. I don't know anything about men.

Even without cars, or humming electrical wires, or police sirens, the night is full of noise—insects, catfights, feral dogs trading songs with coyotes. You don't hear people noises often, but when you do, hiding is the best option.

It's easy. Slip into the darkest place you can find and quit moving. Sane people always take cover, so crazy ones are all you see. There are lots of crazies in the street since the New Flu came to town. Religious crazy. Jonestown Crazy. Jehovah's Witnesses with machine guns crazy.

Some scientists say it's a retrovirus that drills into the religious centers of your brain. Somewhere in the temporal lobe. Others say New Flu is just a lame excuse for going batshit. It's one of those questions people make up their minds about and then don't worry about the facts, like global warming, or whether life begins at conception, or if Coca Cola in bottles tastes different than Coca-Cola in cans.

It really doesn't matter when you are out at night and hear people sounds. You slide behind the closest abandoned car and wait until the danger passes. That's another reason not to use a flashlight, even if you have batteries. You can see fairly well for twenty feet, but crazies can see you from miles away. They know exactly where you are long enough to plan an ambush or just shoot you and be done with it.

So, Mona and I stand as still as lawn statuary and wait until the owners of the footsteps walk by us in the middle of the street. Twenty people at least, some of them men, some of them women, none of them gay or lesbian or Native American as far as I can tell. The scientists don't say why New Flu doesn't infect Indians or homosexuals. Mona says it's because we're already crazy in another way.

The New Flu people are going somewhere they all know about, so they don't have to talk. The last time something like this happened, Christians hung witches in Salem and burned Jews in Spain.

Everybody gets together and starts killing everybody else, until almost nobody's left—in this case nobody but homosexuals and Native Americans.

The New Flu people have noisy feet. They aren't afraid of anybody because everybody is afraid of them. When they are about a block away they start singing all at once. The song they sing is "Amazing Grace."

"Pretty good," I tell Mona. "Perfectly in tune. Perfectly synchronized. A capella." That's everything I know about music.

Mona doesn't want to talk about "Amazing Grace." She says, "We've got to get out of town, Chris. I have to think about Joseph."

When Mona starts thinking about her son, she stops thinking about everything else. I'm sort of Joseph's mother too, except in the biological sense. Biology means all final decisions about Joseph belong to Mona.

"What about his school?" I ask.

"Closed."

"What about his girlfriend?"

"Karma's in the hospital."

"Yeah." I'm wondering if that might give us a little more time in OKC, just in case everything works out in the end.

"Joseph might want to wait until she gets out." I know that's not going to work for Mona. Karma has already been in the hospital for a month. Shot by one of the growing population of crazies.

Mona wants to go to the Choctaw part of the state, where people aren't as likely to kill us. But she forgets I'm not Choctaw. She forgets I'm a really obvious lesbian and Choctaw aren't too keen on people like me.

"They'll get used to you. I did."

—

LONG WALKS IN THE DARK used to be romantic, but now they give Mona and me time to talk. It's dangerous when lovers talk. The conversation bobs and weaves like Muhammad Ali used to do when he floated like a butter-fly. At first the argument looks like a conversation, but then Mona gets down to business. She talks about the time I left her, right after Joseph was born.

"That was thirteen years ago," I say.

She doesn't like my tone. "It seems like yesterday."

So I explain how all couples go through rough patches, and she tells me how abandoning your wife and child is more than a rough patch.

"We weren't exactly married," I tell her. "And Joseph's father is some anonymous sperm donor, and you didn't even tell me you were pregnant until it was too late to back out."

Oops.

When Mona starts crying logic gets put out for big trash day.

"Please don't," I say a little too loud. "Please don't." Softer this time, but she couldn't pull those tears back now, even if she wanted too. Big saltwater drops spill over her Native American cheekbones, perfectly visible in the dark-ness. Tears work on dykes about as well as they work on men.

Mona's tears burn my heart like sulfuric acid. The only thing I can do is walk away before I say something else that she'll remind me about for the rest of my life. So I walk her into our rental house and make sure she's safe and then I leave.

Joseph asks me, "Where are you going?" He has eyes exactly like Mona's so I can't ignore him. Joseph is only fourteen years old and doesn't understand how easily beautiful lipstick lesbians like Mona can out-argue muscular butch girls who box with rednecks in taverns.

I'd do anything for Joseph except fight with Mona in front of him, so I say, "Got to take a walk," calm and rational, like anger is an emotional cramp I can cure with exercise. "Be back later," I tell Joseph, loud enough so Mona can hear it from our bedroom where she's waiting for me to come to my senses.

Joseph hugs me—he's the only boy who ever did that—and I feel a bubble pop inside my chest. He's the reason I'll always come back, no matter how angry I am with Mona. I'll always be there for Joseph, except for the next few hours.

Angry walking was easy before civilization collapsed. You don't appreciate things like police cruisers and security cameras until law and order is so much rubble in the street.

One day obnoxious construction workers shout insults at you, and the next it's Visigoths throwing spears. I move through the darkness like a rabbit in a world full of carnivores, fueled with secretions from supersized adrenal glands that make me faster and more afraid than everything that wants to eat me.

Feeling fear more than anger is what civilization's all about, so after fifteen minutes I'm pretty civilized. I'm about a mile from home, and ready to go back and whine about leaving Oklahoma City and living with a bunch of Choctaw who never liked me all that much. I have it all worked out. Exactly what I'll say so Mona will feel guilty enough to owe me something for the sacrifice.

And she thinks I don't know anything about men.

It's important to go back a different way, because someone might be watching. Someone with a knife, or a pistol, and a license to kill issued by the New Flu God.

I hear the motorcycle before I see it, puttering along the moonless night under stars that hadn't been visible in Oklahoma City since World War II. The biker has long hair, no shirt, and posture like a wild cat that's just about to spring. He drives down the middle of the street with a siphon hose draped around his neck, looking for abandoned cars that nobody's set on fire. His headlight is turned off, but his eyes glow—or seem to—as he turns his face my way.

I remember all the things I left back home—Mona, Joseph, and the

.38-caliber Smith & Wesson revolver I used to carry when I was an EMT—just in case. There are no sidewalks in this part of town, so I move out of the street, into somebody's yard full of weeds. They are tall enough to hide behind if I get onto my hands and knees, but all I manage is a stoop. I hold still as a tree, in case he hasn't seen me yet, but of course he has.

I take off running through the weeds as he revs up the bike and heads my way, faster than a man should ride through a weed-infested yard.

Broken bones heal. Chicks dig scars. Glory is forever. He doesn't care if he dies tonight because pretty soon there won't be enough gasoline for motorcycles and who wants to live after that?

I climb over a rotten stockade fence, thinking that's the end of it, but the biker crashes through. So I climb over another one, into an alley where trash hasn't been collected since city government collapsed.

When he crashes through that fence, I lift a trashcan filled with the leftovers of society and use it like a battering ram against his chest. The bike speeds past me, but the biker doesn't. He lands on is back with a sound like a wet drum.

My EMT training kicks in, and I take a step his way, but apparently he's breathing and has a pulse, because he also has a gun.

It's one of the boxy-looking Glocks that holds a lot of bullets and doesn't have a safety. I'm too close for him to miss, so I kick the gun out of his hand just as he pulls the trigger.

The three-foot flame lights up the alley, like a fireworks show on the Fourth of July, and by the time I can see again he is on his feet.

Limping, so he can't chase me, but he's limping toward his motorcycle. I think I should surprise him with a little one-on-one combat, but I don't know what else he's carrying. Guys like him always have backup weapons.

"Later dude," I tell him, as I run down the alley.

"Asshole," he shouts at my back.

It occurs to me he still doesn't know he's been knocked on his butt by a girl. I think maybe I should tell him, but by the time I make up my mind, he is on his bike again.

Maybe he'll give up if killing me is complicated. I duck behind an abandoned car, and he roars by me, not at all worried about using up the last gasoline in the world. He makes a skid-circle in the street, artistic as a stuntman in a motorcycle movie.

I head through another overgrown yard, jumping over a Big Wheel and a sandbox and a dead German shepherd. I jump a three-foot chain link fence, and almost stumble into a swampy swimming pool before I regain my balance. There's a gate into the neighbor's yard standing wide open, so I run through and close it behind me.

Through an abandoned house.

Cross the street.

Jump another fence, then another.

This goes on so long, I think the biker must have given up, but when I stop to catch my breath, I hear his engine idling as if it's sniffing the air, trying to catch my scent.

The house I'm in has no broken windows or locked doors. It's pristine except for spider webs and dust. Every dish in the kitchen has been washed and put away. Every knife and fork in its proper place, even the high-dollar cooking knives on their magnetic rack, so shiny I can see them in the dark.

I take the longest, strongest, sharpest butcher knife and carry it into the backyard where maybe I'll be able to use it and maybe not.

It is a big backyard but with almost no grass. Everything is pressed concrete and dried up water features, well maintained except for the cable I trip over as I head for the back gate. Coaxial cable—all the news and movies in the world used to come into the house over this little wire, and now it's fallen from wherever it's supposed to be onto the cement deck that keeps weeds and disorder at bay.

Rabbits have ideas when they run from foxes. How high to jump, where to turn, when to hide. When they run out of ideas, they die. Butch girls like me have thoughts that won't fit into rabbit brains. I cut a ten-foot section of coaxial cable. I open the back gate and tie it across, wondering if a war movie is trapped inside, or maybe a slasher film, or a pornographic movie about girls kissing girls.

I go to the front gate. I open it and wait for the motorcycle sound to come my way.

If the biker hasn't given up.

If he hasn't found someone else to torment.

If he hasn't lost my trail.

It doesn't take a minute until his engine roars to life. The bare chested biker of the apocalypse rides down the road too fast for the almost total darkness of electricity-free Oklahoma City. So fast I don't have time to shut the front gate before I run. So fast I have barely enough time to duck out the back gate under the cable that he won't see from a speeding motorcycle in the dark—not even with his glowing eyes.

It catches him on the throat and throws him backward like a slingshot. His motorcycle crashes through the fence across the alley and keeps on going.

The biker isn't going anywhere. He lies on the pressed concrete deck thrashing his arms and legs like he's trying to make a snow angel.

His eyes still glow. They fill with hate when they find me. That's the last thing on the biker's mind when life slips out of his grip with a nasty gurgling sound, like water going down a drain that's plugged with hair.

I could try to save him, but I don't.

I look at the place on my wrist where I used to wear a watch when punctuality mattered. "My, look at the time."

I don't know if he heard my smart aleck remark, but I hope so.

—

THE SUN PEAKS OVER THE horizon, filling the eastern sky with the color red. Darkness is scary but light is scarier. People can see you in the daytime, watch you walk down the street, wait for you at a blind corner, and make you wish you had a gun. I take a twisted pathway home in case I'm followed.

Mona and Joseph will be up already, wondering where I am, because people go out and don't come back all the time.

They can't call the police, because the phones don't work, and the cops are all gone anyway. They can't post signs or ask around, because then everybody would know I'm not watching out for them anymore. So they'll wash down their worries with powdered orange juice and fill their bellies with pancakes made from scratch.

We still have gas and water, so we are warm and clean and eat cooked food. That's how much is left of the civilized world.

By the time I reach the front door of our house, I have my story edited and ready for the morning edition. Beginning with, "This is why I'm late, you guys." Ending with, "I'm just glad to be alive."

I'll delete the part about watching the biker die, because I want Mona and Joseph to be glad to see me.

The front door is unlocked—a bad sign.

No sounds inside—another bad sign.

No breathing noises or air moving around bodies as they change position. No bare feet slapping the linoleum. No clinking sound of dishes being washed and put away.

No breakfast smells. No people smells. No people.

"Mona!" I call out. "Joseph!" I know the place is empty without looking, but I look anyway. I call Joseph's name again and add, "Alli alli oxen free," just in case it's a hide-and-seek game I don't know about.

"Please!" That's a one-word prayer, because the house is so quiet and the only thing I know that could make it that way is death. "Don't let them be dead," I whisper, barely loud enough for God to hear. I think about rephrasing that statement, make it more humble and less demanding, but if there is a God, he'll understand, and if there isn't, it doesn't matter anyway.

I take a quick tour of the house, not looking at anything too closely in case there's blood.

No bodies in the living room—so far so good.

I keep on walking and praying through the bedrooms, and the kitchen. No bodies, no blood, no signs of violence. Panic pulls back so I can look for something besides dead people, and I see the note stuck to the refrigerator door under a magnet advertising *Jean's Plumbing*. The fridge is a bulletin board now that the electricity is gone. Not cold inside, but there's a cold hard fact stuck to the door.

"We're gone!" the note says, as if I hadn't figured that out. *"We can't stay in OKC any longer. Follow us to Choctaw country when you're ready to man up."* It's signed, *"Love Mona and Joseph,"* with a series of little x's and a smiley face.

It's written on the back of a flier from St. Anthony's hospital. That's where Joseph's girlfriend is getting over being shot. Joseph won't leave town without saying goodbye to her. So that's where I'll go first, to a hospital with a Saint's name.

I take a few minutes to eat breakfast, because now that I'm not so worried I'm ravenous. Kashi Go Lean and powdered milk is quick and easy—fiber rich crunchy particles that look like statues of alien bacteria. I read a promise on the box—regular bowel movements and a slim waist. Those things still come in handy.

I take a few more minutes to pack everything I know Mona and Joseph will forget. By the time I'm ready to go the sun is high, but I have my pistol in its cowboy holster, and my cooking gear, and my EMT equipment, and my Swiss Army knife with the fancy blades and the ivorine toothpick and the tweezers. Everything a girl needs to man up.

—

CHOCTAW BOYS LIKE JOSEPH HAVE uncles, who can teach them all kinds of Indian things. Joseph has boy cousins too, and a grandfather who is old but still manly, but I'm the closest thing to a father he's ever had. Women don't make good dads, even if they have broad shoulders and tough attitudes. We can't teach boys anything at all about football, or dirty jokes, or how to pee standing up.

I'm thinking about all that while I'm walking to St. Anthony's Hospital, hoping I'll see Mona and Joseph along the way. I'm cutting across parking lots and climbing fences and taking side streets, so there's not much chance of that, but when the world comes to an end people start thinking about things like destiny.

The street I'm on stops in a cul-de-sac that runs up against a drainage ditch. There's too much water in it to cross, and the water's full of all kinds of things, like shopping carts and broken down exercise equipment. Something makes a big splash that sends ripples across the duckweed. A flock of birds flies all at once, filling the air with a waterfall sound, and by the time I figure out what just scared the hell out of me, my six-shooter is in my hand.

"Quick draw McGraw," says a voice behind me.

It doesn't sound like a threatening voice, so I put my pistol back in its holster and turn slowly toward the words. The voice is androgynous, sort of like mine, and I don't know exactly what to expect.

"Got any spare change, buddy?" The speaker is an old man with a scraggly beard and an even scragglier dog.

Spare change isn't good for much these days, but that's the way the old man says hello. He has a friendly smile with all of his front teeth, and a suit of clothes that tells me he's been living out of rag bins for a long time. Nothing matches, not even his shoes. Everything about him is ragged except for the walking stick he's holding in his right hand. The stick is perfectly straight and lacquered so its wood grain stands out like the lines on a child's finger painting. Probably not much good for walking, but I guess we all love something that has no practical value—a ring, a watch, a polished stick, a pretty Choctaw girl.

"Sorry, Miss." He realizes I'm a woman now, and blushes underneath the sun damage and the grime. "I don't see too good from far away."

He gives me time to take offense, and when I don't, he smiles again. He tells me something lives in the drainage ditch.

"Kills whatever it gets a hold of. Killed a deer th' other day." He sidles up beside me and points at a partially submerged carcass. "Jake squalled like a puppy when it happened.

Jake might be part pit bull and part Chihuahua, or he might be some kind of mutation that comes out at the end of the world, but he has a sensitive face.

According to the old man, Jake has a sense of smell that rivals any bloodhound. "He's a real good dog. Best friend I ever had. Now he's th' only one."

Jake lays back his ears, tucks his tail between his legs, and wags it at the same time. He lifts his left paw, like he wants to shake hands, but pulls it back when I stoop over.

"People call me Andy." The old man extends his hand, and doesn't pull it back. He has a gentle, firm grip, exactly the way I always imagined Will Rogers would shake hands. He knows how hard to squeeze and when to let go, and he doesn't wipe his hand on his pants leg when everything is done.

"My name's Chris." I give Andy the most pleasant smile I have, but it probably comes off like the one on my driver's license.

I try to pet Jake, but the dog backs several feet away. He licks at his front paw, tests it to see if it will hold his weight, picks it up again.

"I met Jake under the Tenth Street overpass right after the electricity went off," Andy said. "Maybe a car hit him, back when there was cars. Maybe one of them wild dogs bit him, or maybe a tick bite got infected."

Jake shakes his head back and forth after each of Andy's possibilities.

"Maybe I can help," I say mostly to the dog. "I'm a trained paramedic."

Jake hobbles over to me as cautious as a five-year-old on his first trip to the dentist. He flops on the pavement right in front of me with his injured paw extended. He turns his eyes toward Andy and whines softly.

"Jake's a real good judge of character." The old man sits cross-legged beside Jake and strokes his head. "It's the scent of reliability. He smells it on you strong."

Dogs and people aren't so different. Lidocaine works on both of them, and the anatomy is practically identical—at least in the forearm. That's where Jake's problem is.

"Abscess in the muscle," I say in case anybody's interested. "There's a piece of birdshot lodged against the radius, distal to the point where a tendon attaches." I can't remember the name of the muscle, or the tendon, and the bone might actually be the ulna, but I like to say the Latin names, even if they're wrong.

The incision is so small it doesn't even need a suture. It doesn't bleed much, and that's a relief, because I'm not really sure how to control bleeding in a dog. I wrap the wound with a strip of gauze, because I need practice doing field dressings, and Jake is such a good patient.

I pet him and tell him what a good dog he is and he gives me a look of one-hundred percent pure love. I've never gotten that look from anybody ever—not from Mona, not even from Joseph when he was a baby.

I bend over so Jake can lick my face. He doesn't want to stop, and I don't want him to, even though I know all the other places he's been licking regularly since he was born.

"Chris." Andy's standing beside us, half-whispering my name, but I'm the busy recipient of unconditional love, so I don't pay attention.

Then I hear the sound of claws scratching on concrete—not running, but coming our way pretty fast. Jake stops licking me and I look up in time to see a ninety pound Rottweiler mix trotting toward us with his head down and his tail up and most of his teeth showing.

Jake struggles to roll onto his feet and I reach for my gun, but it's clear neither of us will have time. Maybe he'll go for Jake, I think without meaning to, and hope the dog can't smell my thoughts.

"Oh shit." I say the words softly and solemnly, as if they are a prayer. As if they are my epitaph. I try to think of something more profound, while my hand slips off the grip of my pistol like it was a bar of soap in a shower room filled with naked men who are all looking my way.

The dog is twenty feet away when Andy makes a sound, like a sneeze inside a vacuum cleaner hose.

I've pulled my gun almost all the way out of my holster. I fumble the hammer back and raise the pistol into firing position just as the Rottweiler rolls head-over-heels and lands on his feet like a Rumanian gymnast dog doing a floor exercise.

He starts at us again, slower this time, listing to the side.

I hear the sneezing sound again, and he stops dead, like the statue of a monster dog. He topples over with a thump and moves his lips and legs as if he's chasing rabbits in a dream.

The Rottweiler takes a breath that's much deeper than necessary for a dog that's lying on its side. He exhales with a rattle that reminds me of a dying biker on a pressed concrete deck.

Jake trots over to monster and sniffs the air for signs of his escaping soul. He looks at me as if to say, "It's gone."

"Blowgun." Andy holds his polished walking stick so I can see it's hollow. "Deadly weapon, concealed in plain sight."

He tells me something about darts made of honey locust thorns soaked in natural poisons. "Sometimes they don't kill so quick. This time we were lucky."

I barely hear what Andy says because I'm inspecting the monster. Flies gather on his eyes. I brush them away and pull the lids closed, even though I know it's a meaningless gesture.

"Maybe we should say some words," Andy says. "You know, a prayer or something."

"I'm glad it was him instead of one of us." I fold my hands together the way I've seen Shaolin monks do in kung fu movies. I'm especially glad it wasn't me, but I keep that to myself.

—

NOW THAT JAKE'S LIMP IS fixed, I can't walk fast enough to leave him behind. Andy says he has to stay with me until his debt's repaid.

"No slackers in the animal kingdom." He tells me the short version of Androcles and the lion complete with voices.

I'm not sure if Jake is my dog now, or just on loan until his medical bill is paid. Andy says Jake will make the final decision. Meanwhile we'll stick together. The old man doesn't seem to walk with any plan, but after a couple of hours we are standing in front of St. Anthony's Hospital, where Joseph's girlfriend is still getting over her gunshot wound.

"If she ain't dead," Andy says. "This part of town's full of New Flu crazies, praising God and killing people."

"Maybe they're all gone," I say. "We haven't seen anybody all day."

"They don't come out except when you don't expect them," Andy tells me. "That's another one of them laws of nature."

According to Andy, the New Flu crazies pattern their behavior after horror movies they saw before the fall. "Once movies and television was gone, people played them stories in their minds. Twenty-four hour slasher films seven days a week."

"What about people who watched Lifetime Television?"

"The slashers kill you with knives," Andy tells me. "The lovers kill you with romance. Either way, you're killed."

—

WOMEN DRESSED IN MULTICOLORED SCRUBS watch me from behind the glass front of the St. Anthony's reception area. It's locked and nobody makes a move to let me in.

"Stand back," I tell Andy. "Take Jake with you." I've decided that a homeless man and a stray dog are scaring the nurses more than a bull dyke with a gun strapped around her middle. It seems to be working.

A nurse opens the door, but she won't let me in. She's wearing a pistol around her middle too and a pair of bandoleers across her chest and a big crucifix around her neck. She holds a translucent white polyethylene squeeze bottle so I can see it, then squirts a tiny stream onto my shoulder.

"Holy Water," she tells me. "We can't be too careful anymore."

I can't come inside unless I'm a friend or family member of a patient.

"I'm looking for some people who might have visited a patient earlier today."

The nurse looks at me for a long time before she speaks, trying to be just careful enough.

"Indians." She spits the word out like it's infested with maggots. "They're here now, visiting the little gunshot girl."

"Karma." She winces when I say the little gunshot girl's name. She crosses herself, takes a sip of holy water from her squeeze bottle. She offers it to me, but I tell her, "Couldn't hold another drop."

She closes the glass door, locks it, shows me the key.

"You can wait outside," the nurse shouts loud enough so I can hear her through the glass. "With all the others."

I turn around slowly, and there they are—three New Flu crazies. When I least expect it, just like Andy said.

All three of them are men. It's easy to tell, because they are naked, except for cowboy gun belts like mine. All three have erections. I've heard men always get those when they are about to kill somebody—also when they die.

The leader has the largest penis—no surprise. He also has his pistol drawn. Both are pointed right at me.

"You a woman or a man?" His pistol and his penis bob synchronously. Marking the last few seconds of my life in the nastiest way possible.

My answer is interrupted by a vacuum cleaner sneeze. Then another. The leader looks at the darts sprouting from his belly. He turns and fires a wild shot at Andy, who draws another breath deep enough to launch a third dart.

The other two men have drawn their pistols now. One aims at Andy, and the other aims at me, while their leader falls onto his back and twitches like a dying Rottweiler.

Jake charges into the scene, giving the surviving crazies another target to consider. Long enough for me to draw my pistol and put two bullets into one man's chest, just as he squeezes off a shot at Jake.

Jake!" I'm at the dog's side, trying to hold back the blood that's coming out of his side in a torrent of foam.

I hear another blowgun discharge and another pistol shot, and the nurses in the lobby run out shouting, "Patients! Patients!"

They wrap the wounded and the dying in paper sheets, flop them onto gurneys, and wheel them inside—even Jake.

Andy's the last to go. The nurses want to take his blowgun, but he grips it tight. *Death grip,* I think, because his shirt is saturated in bright red blood.

He waves at me as they take him through the glass doors to God knows where for God knows what.

I sit down on the concrete where a gunfight just happened and wait for Mona and Joseph to come out. The flies are fighting with the ants for blood and tissue. There isn't nearly as much as it seemed a few seconds ago.

Mona doesn't notice the puddles when she and Joseph come through the hospital doors. She's not surprised to see me, but Joseph is.

He hugs me the way he did when I went for an anger-walk last night.

"Think you're ready to man up?" Mona asks.

"Yes," I tell her around Joseph's hug. "I know exactly how to do it now."

Joseph steps back and sniffs the air. His nose is not as good as Jake's, but close.

"What is that, Chris? What's that I smell?"

It could be blood, or gun smoke, but I don't tell him that.

"It's the scent of reliability," I say. "We'd better leave before the New Flu crazies find us."

THE MOST MYSTERIOUS
WAY POSSIBLE

THE NURSE'S HAIR NEEDS A GOOD shampoo. She's pretty in a worn out, haggard sort of way in her green scrubs with the nametag that says, "Tammy," and her white Keds that are starting to turn yellow. She's worried about her daughter, who is home right now with her alcoholic husband, who used to be a painter back when people cared enough to paint their houses. Maybe she's told me all these things, but I really can't remember. I can't remember anything, not even my own name until the nurse hands me a teddy bear and says, " Karma, I want you to cough as hard as you can. Let those lungs know you're the boss."

I want to ask questions, but it hurts to talk. It hurts to breathe. It really hurts to cough, but Tammy pushes the teddy bear into my arms and makes me do it anyway.

"Got to get into a survival frame of mind." Tammy's eyes tell me she knows all about survival. It involves a lot of pain.

She makes me cough until I'm crying and reaching for the button that might release a drip or two of narcotic into my IV line if I haven't already exceeded my limit.

I probably have reached that limit, because I can't remember how bad the pain can get, or why I'm here.

Tammy says, "You have your whole life ahead of you, but first you have to get through this little rough patch." She pushes Teddy into my arms again and makes me cough until the pain totally rules.

Until I remember who I am.

"Karma Chameleon Smith," I tell her. "I've been shot."

"You sure have sweetie." She leans over the stainless steel rail of my bed and brushes a lock of hair out of my face. Her blue, non-latex glove comes away greasy. How embarrassing.

She reminds me I'm in St. Anthony's Hospital, where the worst trouble in the world has already started. I've been shot on the bad side of Oklahoma City.

"Lots of gunshot wounds these days," She points to another bed only a few feet away from mine. There's a girl in that bed too, but she isn't coughing. There's a plastic tube in her mouth, hooked up to a machine that makes compressed air noises and beeps.

"You're roommate's headed south," Tammy says. "Critical care is full, and our generator's barely able to run all the respirators."

She gives me a playful punch on the arm. "You'll survive, Karma." Another buddy punch to make up for all the coughing, and to prove she really likes me. "How did a pretty girl like you get such a funny name?"

"My mother picked it out."

Those words make Tammy's smile roll over. "Sorry. Sorry for your loss."

The pain-killer must be all used up, because my chest feels like a brick fell on it. I remember how I stepped in front of the bullet meant for my almost boyfriend, and Mom stepped in front of me. Didn't save me exactly, but she slowed the bullet down. It doesn't feel real enough to cry, but I must be doing that anyway, because Tammy's dabbing at my cheeks with a corner of the sheet.

"We're out of tissues," she tells me. "The hospital quit payin' us, but we keep coming in. Helps pass the time while the world falls apart."

The breathing machine keeping my roommate alive makes a monotone C sharp. Tammy walks around my bed and flips switches until it stops.

"This one's gone," She turns off the machines that kept the girl alive too long. She pinches IV lines and disconnects needles. "Guess you've got a private room now." Tammy covers the nameless girl's face with a sheet. "Anything more I can do for you?"

Since I'm the only living patient in the room I answer. "Hand me that teddy bear again and help me to the bathroom." There are some things a girl has to do for herself, even when the world is coming to an end.

—

News all comes from rumors now that television and radio are gone. People used to worry about electricity and the strength of the dollar, but now it's the New Flu.

"First outbreak started in Tulsa." Tammy smiles like that's some kind of Oklahoma accomplishment. We had Will Rogers, and Neil Armstrong, and the first domestic terrorist bombing, and the first F10 tornado.

Now we have New Flu.

She adjusts my IV, which is dripping mostly saline and some kind of anti-retrovirus drug into my veins. The saline keeps me hydrated and the antiviral keeps me safe from AIDS, because I've received five units of blood, and nobody can be sure of the blood supply any more.

"Now we're out of blood," Tammy says. "But that's OK, because the ambulances quit running, so people mostly die when something happens."

She says it's best not to think about those things. "Especially with the New Flu coming." She sounds happy about the brand-new disease that might send hundreds of patients to the hospital. "If they can find a way to get here. And really sick people always do."

The New Flu starts with nausea but turns into schizophrenia.

"Nothing like it ever was." Tammy crosses herself Catholic style. People do that all the time here. It used to be a Catholic Hospital, so I suppose it's natural."Religious riots and mass suicides. It's like the whole world's turned into Jonestown."

I don't know what Jonestown is, so Tammy tells me all about the Reverend Jim Jones, the guns, the cyanide laced Kool-Aid. It started in California and spread to Guyana, where everybody killed everybody else.

"But New Flu started in Tulsa." Tammy doesn't know where Guyana is, but Tulsa's only ninety miles away. "So pretty soon there'll be cases in Oklahoma City."

She crosses herself again and walks over to the only window in my now private room and stares at the sun until her eyes fill up with tears. She wipes her scrubs sleeve across her face and tells me how the antiviral drugs in my IV will protect me from the flu.

That's the good side of getting shot.

"The Lord works in mysterious ways." Tammy looks at me for almost a minute without saying anything. She shifts her head from side to side so she can see me better through her tears.

"Right." I cross myself, the way I've seen her do, so she'll know I think the Lord is mysterious, too. I wonder if we'll be having Kool-Aid for lunch.

—

TAMMY WALKS INTO MY ROOM holding a shampoo bottle full of water. She dabs a little on a cotton ball and draws a cross on the window in my room.

"Holy water," Tammy says. "I'm a Baptist, but I have a lot of respect for holy water. It's been around for centuries. If it didn't work people would have given up on it years ago." She puts a little on her fingertip and traces her lips. "So every word will be a prayer. If I was a vampire, this wouldn't be possible."

I nod my head instead of speaking. I don't have holy water on my lips.

She draws a holy water cross on my forehead. It smells like shampoo. I can't stop myself from saying, "Cleanliness in next to godliness," but I cross myself after I do, so she'll know I'm not making fun of Jesus.

"You have visitors," she tells me that like it's bad news. "They have to wait outside until I sanctify the room."

Tammy's getting pretty weird, but she still knows how to be a nurse, and I'm still hooked up to IVs full of real medicine to protect me from real germs, which are a lot more dangerous than vampires. I don't have to cough anymore, but she lets me keep the teddy bear.

"Won't be a minute," Tammy says to someone in the hall. She sprinkles the soapy holy water in the doorway. "Be careful," she tells the hallway people. "The floor is very slippery." Then she turns to me and whispers, "You be careful too, Karma. They're Indians." She hands me the bottle of holy water, in case they attack.

—

MY ALMOST-BOYFRIEND JOSEPH COMES through the door first. He doesn't slip and fall, but he sniffs the air like a suspicious dog on his way to the veterinarian's office. His mother, Mona, follows him in. She looks suspicious too, like she always does.

"This place is really strange," Joseph says.

"It doesn't look too bad if you just got shot," I tell him. "After that, everything's an improvement."

He takes my hand for a second, but lets go when he sees Mona watching.

"It's okay," Mona says. "You can hold hands with a girl who saved you from a bullet." She smiles at me like it no longer makes a difference that I have no Choctaw blood.

It's always been important to Mona that her one-eighth Choctaw boy doesn't hook up with a no-eighths Choctaw girl like me, so letting us hold hands is a breakthrough.

"Mom's got an idea." Joseph rolls his eyes, but he keeps his voice under control, so only he and I will know he thinks the whole thing's crazy.

Mona is full of crazy ideas, like the white man's world coming to an end, and Indians taking over. Only now that idea doesn't seem so crazy after all.

"Indians are immune to the New Flu," Joseph says.

That's one of the rumors Nurse Tammy told me. "No Indians in the riots or the mass suicides, or any of the new religious movements springing up around the country." Tammy figures Indians are in league with the devil because of all their whooping and dancing.

I wonder if Tammy's listening from the hallway, and that must be pretty obvious, because Mona leans out the door and looks both ways.

"All clear."

"Mom wants you to be her sister in blood." When Joseph tells me this, I reach for the bottle of holy water.

Joseph shows me a knife with a transparent green glass blade and bone handle. "Cheyenne War Society knife. Made it myself. The obsidian is really Coke bottle glass, and the grip is cow bone, but other than that, it's totally authentic."

Mona says. "A two-hundred-dollar value when the Internet was working."

She takes the knife from Joseph and draws a red line across the thickest part of her palm, just below the thumb. Before I can call for help she takes my hand and cuts me in exactly the same place. She presses her cut against mine and mumbles something under her breath. It might be Choctaw words, but it probably isn't, because according to Joseph, the only Choctaw Mona knows is how to say goodbye.

When it's Joseph's turn, he saws the glass blade back and forth across his palm instead of making a clean cut. Mona holds his hand and mine together like she's pronouncing us husband and wife.

Only she says, "Now you are brother and sister in blood."

I pull my hand away, even though it's probably too late. Joseph's sister is the last thing I want to be.

"What's that mean?"

Joseph doesn't look like he knows for sure, but he tells me, "You're a Choctaw now. Rolls don't matter anymore."

Mona cleans the knife off on my bed sheet and wraps it in a red bandanna.

"Keep it safe," she tells me. "An Indian is nothing without a knife." She sets the bundle on my bed beside the bottle of holy water.

"I'll leave you two alone for a few minutes, then Joseph and I have to go." She walks out the door. I can see her shadow on the wall, cast by the hospital lights using the last of the generator electricity.

Joseph leans forward and kisses me on the cheek. Then I kiss him on the forehead. Then he kisses me on the mouth. Then I kiss him on the mouth and include some tongue.

Just when things are getting really interesting, he tells me he and his mom are leaving town.

"The family has a cabin in the Ouachita Forest," he says. "We're heading there today." He tells me I can join them when I'm well, and that shouldn't be too long, because I kiss like I'm in perfect health.

The Ouachita Forest is two hundred miles away. Nobody has gasoline, and there are no buses anymore. "How will you get there?"

"Indians know how to walk," Joseph says. "Especially Choctaw, because we all walked to Oklahoma almost two hundred years ago."

He tells me I can find him again, because we're brother and sister in blood. He kisses me again to show we're not brother and sister in any other way. Joseph is my for-real-boyfriend now, even if it won't last very long.

"It's time, Joseph," Mona says from the hallway. Her shadow turns ninety degrees. She's speaking toward the door without looking inside, because there are things a boy doesn't want his mother to see.

He kisses me one more time and walks to the door. He waves to me and I see the cut on his hand that will pull us together again someday. My name's Karma after all. That must mean something.

I hide the Cheyenne War Society knife under my pillow before Tammy comes back into the room. I take a big swig of holy water so she'll know I haven't made a pact with the devil. It tastes like Jesus is washing my mouth out with soap.

BACK IN THE OLD DAYS, hospitals used to kick you out before you had a chance to get well. Now they want to keep you forever.

Tammy says, "It's dangerous outside," and I know it is, because I see the smoke in the air from all the fires in Oklahoma City, and I hear coyotes singing to each other in the night.

"They've come into town to dance with the devil," Tammy says. None of the nurses go home anymore. They just sleep in empty hospital beds and pray. The generators have used up all the fuel, so the hallways are dark and the only light at night comes from homemade alcohol lanterns that look like Molotov cocktails.

"The Indians call coyotes tricksters," I tell Tammy. "They have lots of stories about them."

The only coyote stories Tammy knows about are Road Runner cartoons. She doesn't want to talk about Indian stories. She doesn't want to talk about me leaving the hospital either. I'm unhooked from the IVs and it hardly hurts to breathe, but whenever I mention going home, Tammy says, "Not yet."

I spend most of my time thinking about Joseph and Mona, even though my dad is probably wondering what happened to me. Tammy says he isn't waiting for me back home, because the National Guard evacuated everyone.

"And then the soldiers left," Tammy says. "No one knows where they went." It's her theory they are fighting a war with Texas.

The nurses all wear pistols strapped on over their scrubs now. Tammy has an old time six-shooter and two bandoleer bullet belts across her chest like Pancho Villa. She looted it from the Bass Pro Shop a few days ago. She says it wasn't stealing, because the owners were so far away and danger is so close.

"God will understand," she says, crossing herself the way she does now after almost every sentence.

Sometimes God tells her what to do like he's talking on a supernatural citizens band radio. According to Tammy, he speaks with a southern accent and knows every 10-code that ever was invented.

"I ask if I should keep you here, and God says 10-4." Tammy says that means yes. "So this is your 10-20 for the time being." Her eyes don't track the way they used to, and I don't think God's voice is the only one she hears.

It's time for me to go.

—

A GIRL IN A HOSPITAL GOWN doesn't look like she's going anywhere, especially if she's carrying a teddy bear. I practice walking the halls at night, when nobody thinks I'd go outside. I have a homemade alcohol lamp and my teddy bear, and a pair of clinic shoes that Tammy gave me because of all the germs on hospital floors.

"They told me I should walk," I say to anyone who asks what I'm up to, and this sounds pretty reasonable, because they always want you to walk in hospitals. Nobody tells me to go back into my room, because I am just following orders, and I'm carrying a stuffed animal instead of a gun.

After a few days, I can go pretty much anywhere I want to in the hospital, and nobody looks surprised. I spend a lot of time in the lobby where relatives used to wait for patients to check in and out. There are glass walls instead of windows, so I can see how dark it is outside.

The cafeteria is a popular place at night, because there is still one generator going that keeps the freezers working. There is soda pop, and Jell-O, and ice cream, and popsicles, and lots of other food that doesn't need electricity.

St. Anthony's has plenty of food in storage, like someone planned for the end of the world a long time ago. No one cares if I eat all the dried meat and dehydrated fruit, and candy bars I want, and they don't notice I'm replacing the stuffing in my teddy bear with turkey jerky, dehydrated apricots, and granola.

Teddy's pretty fat, so he holds a lot of food, and still has room for my authentic Cheyenne War Society knife and my bottle of soapy holy water. Every night I stroll through the lobby looking to see if the moon will give me enough light to run for it.

I've never paid much attention to the lunar phases and the full moon comes a lot slower than I think, but finally it happens.

Tammy walks up behind me while I'm trying to figure out exactly how much light there is.

She says, "The Lord works in mysterious ways."

"He really does."

I mean every word of that, because there's a pack of coyotes outside the hospital lobby and they're yipping at the moon in the most mysterious way possible.

"Do coyotes bite?" I ask her, because I'd like to hear some reassuring news even from somebody wearing a six-shooter and two crossed bandoleers. Now

Tammy wears a big crucifix around her neck on a gold chain from the hospital gift shop. I think the crucifix used to be on the wall in the chapel, but now the whole hospital has become a sort of chapel and Tammy has become sort of a Frito Bandito Priest.

"They mostly bite Road Runners," she says.

"Good to know." I run for the lobby door holding Teddy close to me. I expect Tammy to chase me, but she doesn't. That's because the door is bolted, and she has the key.

Tammy stands there stroking her giant chapel crucifix while I slam my shoulder into the glass and have about as much effect as a bug slamming against a car windshield.

There's a set of wooden chairs around a miniature table where the children of patients used to stack blocks and play board games with missing pieces. I pick up one of those chairs without dropping Teddy. It's made of really solid wood, like oak or maple, and I throw it at the one of the glass walls before Tammy can say, "Jesus Christ!"

The chair bounces off the glass and almost hits me. I'm planning to try it again and again, but Tammy draws her six-shooter and pulls the hammer back.

She's aiming at me with her tongue sticking out the corner of her mouth, and I have no doubt she's going to shoot.

"Tammy!" My shout doesn't distract her at all, and she's closed one eye so she can line the sights up with my body. I suddenly remember what bullets feel like, and I really don't want to feel them again, so I turn sideways and hold Teddy up for protection, the way my mother protected me when I got shot the first time.

The slit in Teddy's back gaps open and a couple of Snickers bars and jerky sticks fall out. My authentic Cheyenne War Society knife is getting ready to drop to the floor. That knife is important to me, since it was made by my boyfriend and brother in blood, Joseph, so I catch it instead of taking cover.

Tammy looks surprised to see the knife, and even more determined to shoot me, because now it might be self-defense. I clutch Teddy to my chest and hold the knife over my head in a Statue of Liberty pose and close my eyes as she pulls the trigger.

Lots of noise, like when I was shot before, but this time there isn't any pain or people gathering around me telling me I'm going to make it. There's just the sound of breaking glass, and coyotes yipping and an alarm bell ringing.

Bright light floods the lobby. Some kind of battery powered security system, I guess, but with all the noise and all the light and Tammy being such a bad shot, I figure now would be a really good time to leave.

Everything slows down when emergency alarm systems go off, and I stand there way too long, still holding my Cheyenne War Society knife over my head like a torch, getting ready to run, but not quite able to make my body move. Coyotes run through the broken glass wall, and when I finally turn enough to see them I move my knife in front of one of the security spotlights and fill the room with bright rainbow colored splotches.

When I twist the blade the colored flashes dance around the lobby like a planetarium light show, and before long, the room is filled with armed nurses and coyotes.

All of them are pretty amazed, especially Tammy. She falls onto her knees and puts her hands together like she's holding an invisible book. Her mouth moves too fast for sound to keep up, and the other nurses see what she is doing and follow suit.

I run for the broken glass wall, because I know the alarm battery will run down soon and the nurses might realize I'm not some kind of Coyote Goddess, but even I have to wonder, because the animals follow me for twenty yards or so, yipping all the way.

They form a circle with me in the center, and the full moon's light shows me that every coyote eye is turned toward Teddy.

"Turkey jerky for everyone." I toss Teddy to the pack and take off running into the empty city, still holding the knife Joseph made for me. The scar on the palm of my hand right below my thumb throbs and pulls me southeast.

FOLLOWING
FOOTPRINTS

MARY SITS ON A PINK sandstone boulder, watching Momma Cindy and Daddy Bob argue with the radio. Momma waves to her. Daddy tries to smile but only one side of his mouth goes up.

Mary says, "I'm getting wet."

It isn't rain exactly. The air is like the vaporizer her mother used to use when Mary's throat got sore.

Daddy Bob points the radio in different directions, listening for words mixed with the hissing sounds.

"Maybe the radio is gone for good," he says. "No more broadcasts ever."

Momma Cindy doesn't think so. "Black Mesa State Park is so far away," she says, "From the news, I mean.

Mary knows about far away. Momma Cindy, Daddy Bob, and Mary live in the RV so they'll be far away when everything turns bad.

"Look, sweetie." Daddy Bob points to a string of puddles. "Dinosaur tracks. Black Mesa's famous for them."

Mary can make the puddles look like footprints if she holds her head just right. A big dinosaur and a little one walked here a long time ago. Before television. Before cars. Before people.

"Sixty million years ago," Daddy Bob says.

The water in the footprints is clear, but he tells her, "Don't drink it. Not potable." Grown-ups have a lot of words Mary doesn't understand. She doesn't understand what the two dinosaurs did here either.

"Where do the footprints go?" she asks.

Daddy says it doesn't matter, because everything that lived back then is dead now anyway. "Extinct." Another grown-up word.

Mary pushes a finger into a dinosaur track. Mud squishes at the bottom, and the water doesn't look clear any more.

"Not potable." She pretends to lick the muddy water from her finger, slowly, so Momma Cindy will have plenty of time to stop her. But Momma's busy listening to popping sounds, like the firecrackers Daddy set off last fourth of July.

"It's coming from the parking lot," she says. "Back where the RV is parked."

Daddy picks Mary up and sits her on his shoulder. "Maybe we should follow these footprints a little farther." He talks to Mary in his story-telling voice. "No telling where those dinosaurs will lead us."

MESSAGES

IT'S NOT STEALING IF YOU take things out of the Goodwill box behind St. Gregory's in the middle of the night.

It's especially not stealing when civilization is so far gone even anarchy sounds good, and you've just escaped from a hospital where the nurses turned into religious Nazis. I pinch the back of my hospital gown so my butt doesn't stick out when I reach into the bin. Those slutty-sick-girl costumes are terrible for self-esteem.

I find a pair of pretty good jeans, and a pair of sneakers that are almost the right size, and a T-shirt with a Jack Daniel's bottle on the front and *Party Till You Stink* written in neon-orange letters on the back.

No socks—who needs them?

No bra—I wish I needed that a little more.

No panties—too bad about the panties.

Too bad about a lot of things. Too bad my mom is dead. Too bad I have a silly name—Karma. What were my parents thinking?

Too bad the world fell apart before I turned sixteen. Before I ever used a tampon or put a condom on anything besides a banana. Before I was grounded even once for staying out too late with my boyfriend, Joseph.

No radio. No TV. No Internet. No trash pick-up on Monday. No electricity. Everything I thought would last forever has gone to *Where the Woodbine Twineth*.

Funny how I remember things from TV programs I never saw and books I never read. I'd like to ask somebody about that, but everybody I've seen lately is way too scary. Armed and dangerous, waiting for monsters who've been hiding under their beds for a thousand years.

A pack of coyotes somewhere close yips at the moon. Another pack yips back. Coyotes used to be afraid of people, but now it's the other way around. Claws click on the pavement of the alley that leads to the Goodwill box. No more time to search for panties.

"Git!" I snap my previously owned T-shirt at the closest coyote. She backs up but doesn't run away. Neither do the others that are waiting to see what the boss coyote does. They look like dogs, but they've never been man's best friend—or even his next best friend. They've waited patiently for things to fall apart so they could take their rightful place on the food chain. Not at the top, but close.

I threaten them with the almost authentic Cheyenne War Ceremony Knife, given to me by my very authentic boyfriend, Joseph, who made it out of pressure-flaked green Coke bottle glass and butcher's bones.

Joseph whispered, "I love you Karma," when he handed me the knife. Well, he would have whispered that if his mother hadn't been outside my hospital room, listening to every word.

So he said, "I love you Karma," with his eyes, before his mother told him it was time to go to the part of Oklahoma that is officially Indian Territory again.

"It's time," she said. "Before Oklahoma City falls apart completely. Karma can find us when she's finished getting well."

Somewhere near Durant if the pack of coyotes lets me live.

Lights shine behind the stained glass windows of St. Gregory's. The whole place is lit up with votive candles. Each one is a prayer for the dead, so it's bright inside church.

"Back up!" I slash my homemade Indian knife at the lead coyote and she backs up a little more. I point the green glass blade toward them and walk sideways toward the front door of St. Gregory's, which I know will be open, because that's how churches leave their doors.

"You'd better run," I tell the chief coyote. "That church will be full of people and they'll be on my side."

I start thinking about what I'll do if the church is full of people, because people got religious-crazy when the electricity went off. They blame it on the New Flu virus that drills into your brain and makes you listen when God sends you on a killing spree, but that might just be an excuse.

I swing the front door open and look inside. Nobody. Just hundreds of votive candles burning like an old time witch convicted by a jury of her peers.

The coyotes are still behind me, eyes glowing green in the candlelight, watching to see what happens next.

I go inside, shut the door, and sit in one of the middle pews. I'm afraid to say a prayer because that might be the first sign of New Flu. But I think one anyway, quick and concise, like religious shorthand.

Give me everything I want and help me find Joseph. The last words in my prayer are, *show me a sign* because it sounds religious. My lips move a little so God has a better chance of noticing—if there is a God.

Instead of thinking, amen, I whisper, "Anybody here?" People have been asking that question in churches since the very first one.

No answer. That means I might be safe for a while.

There's a crucifix. There's a birdbath-looking thing full of holy water. There's a poor-box and a pulpit and a little room against the wall where people used to confess their sins.

The confessional has an electric light that used to come on when it was in use—like a refrigerator, or a recording booth. I've never seen the inside of one so I open the door—to make sure no one will be watching me when I put on my pretty good jeans and my close enough sneakers and my Jack Daniel's T-shirt with the neon-orange words on the back.

As soon as I open the door I wish I hadn't, because there is someone inside. Someone with a pistol in his hand and a hole in his temple and a note pinned to his clerical jacket.

The priest smells like peeled potatoes. One eye is open and the other is closed, like he's winking.

The votive candlelight reflects in the open eye—a wild green color, like coyote eyes. I can see my silhouette in the reflection. Black on green, like a special effects monster in a cheap movie on Syfy.

What kind of monsters will people imagine now that television is gone?

The note on the priest's jacket written in red magic marker says—*Family is when you know everything bad about somebody, but you love them anyway.*

Was that something the New Flu put into his head or something he just had to write in bright red ink and pin to his jacket before he told God, "Sorry," and shot himself?

I shut the door because the peeled potato smell makes me sick. I can't see my reflection in the priest's non-winking eye anymore, but it's hard to stop thinking about it.

So I think about the hole in his temple.

And the note he left for me to read.

And my father, who I haven't seen since I went into the hospital.

—

I WAKE UP ON THE St. Gregory's pew with a stiff neck, a sore bottom, and a stream of drool drying on my cheek.

The first thing I think is, *I forgot to brush my teeth.*

The second thing I think is, *I'm really hungry.* My stomach growls like one of the wild animals that roam the streets of Oklahoma City when the sun goes down. Every McDonald's in the world is closed. And every Taco Bell. And every Long John Silver's. I'll eat anything as long as it's not potatoes.

The priest smell has crawled out under the confessional door and filled up the whole church. Some of the votive candles still burn but most are puddles of hardened paraffin. The church is full of stained glass colors, sunlight broken into its spectrum like a seventh grade science project.

Nightshift monsters are off duty, ghosts, and goblins, and things you hear moving but never see. It's a long walk to my house on the Northwest side of Oklahoma City, where my father might be waiting—safe from looters and rioters and the Oklahoma National Guard because he's so quiet and careful that he's almost invisible. I think he loves me, but he almost never said those words. No one did—not even me.

The only things I have are the underwear-free clothes given to me by St. Gregory's generous Christians, and my Cheyenne War Ceremony Knife with the glass blade.

The knife is a pretty weapon. There's a not-so-pretty weapon in the dead priest's hand, one with a proven history. I've already confessed my sins and I don't want to open that door again, but I do, because, where else will I find a pistol now that all the stores are closed?

The peeled potato smell has picked up a garbage dumpster tone that makes my eyes water. Both the priest's eyes are open now. Blue bottle flies are busy there, and in his nostrils too, doing insect things I don't want to think about.

I try to take the pistol, but the dead priest doesn't want to give it up.

"I read your note. What else do you want?" I pry his index finger out of the trigger guard and say the magic word my father taught me, "Please."

That convinces him. The gun slips from his hand without shooting me. It's a silver pistol with a pearl handle, like cowboys used to carry.

"What's a priest doing with a six-shooter?" I ask.

A beetle crawls out of his mouth, like an unholy answer to my question, and that sends me running for the church door.

I'm a hundred feet down the street with my gun and my knife, looking way too dangerous to mess with, when I remember I didn't shut the church's door. I start to go back, but I see something grey and furry run inside. It might be a coyote, but I think it is a dog, because there's only one, and its tail is wagging.

Don't mind me. I'm just a friendly dog looking for a dead priest to eat.

"From dust to dog food," I tell nobody.

Now I understand why buildings have doors.

—

IT'S A LONG, HUNGRY WALK to Northwest Oklahoma City. I slip the knife through a belt loop, but I hold the gun, ready to shoot anything I see.

There are fires all around the city and no one is trying to put them out. There are wrecked cars, and now and then a body.

Dog packs roam the city—looking dangerous and friendly at the same time, but they know what pistols look like and they stay back. No need to kill a real, live girl quite yet. That's still too far for a domestic animal to go when there are plenty of dead people to eat. The dogs look at me as if to say—"See you later, Karma." I wonder how long it will take for the all masters of the world to turn into kibble.

I think maybe I should protect these dead people, but there are so many of them and I only have five bullets in my six-shooter, because the priest already used one of them.

How hard is it to shoot a pistol? It looks easy on TV. Everything looks easy, like driving a car, or making love, or keeping civilization from going down the drain.

I go into a 7-Eleven, because I'm starving. There are Hostess CupCakes inside—the chocolate ones with the white icing scriggle across the top. I eat four of them and wash everything down with a warm Diet Coke. A girl has to watch out for her figure.

I stuff my pockets full of beef jerky and Slim Jims, because you never know when you'll be starving again. I make sure the door is closed when I leave, and it's a good thing, because the feral dogs try to get in before I've gone half a block. They look at me like they might hold a grudge.

"I have five bullets left!" I cock back the hammer on my priest-killing pistol. "Go ahead. Make my day." Everything useful I know comes from television and movies. Where will I learn about the world now that they are gone? Books, read by candlelight, like Abraham Lincoln? That's one more thing I learned from television.

The hammer on my pistol has a fang shaped firing pin. I know that's what it's called even though I've never seen one until now. It looks sharp and dangerous, and I don't know how to get the hammer to go back down without pulling the trigger, and I don't want to do that because I don't want to waste a bullet, and I don't want to hear the noise of a gunshot, and I don't know what it will feel like when something explodes in my hand.

I make sure my finger is not on the trigger. I walk a little faster, because the six-shooter is really heavy and I'm afraid to put it in my waistband with the hammer back. The Hostess CupCakes filled my blood with sugar and made me hungry again too quickly, so I open a couple of Slim Jims and eat them before the grease makes me too nauseated to swallow.

My hands smell like pepperoni, and my previously owned T-shirt smells like fear, and the feral dogs like those smells better than anything else in the world. Their claws scratch the pavement behind me—no stealth at all. More than five of them, I think. More than the number of bullets in my deadly pistol with its fang firing pin. I wonder if the dogs know that.

Every now and then I pick up a rock with my pistol-free hand and throw it at the closest animal.

They stay out of range, about fifty feet, because I throw pretty good for a girl.

—

TWO HOURS, FOUR HOSTESS CUPCAKES, five Slim Jims, and two Diet Cokes is how far I have walked when I come to my house. It's dark inside, like all the others, but it's not as scary. The door is locked, but there is a key hidden in a gray Keystone that looks completely unnatural in the dried up juniper beside the front door. Two dog packs are following me, poorly organized. One pack might be a little larger than the other but it's hard to tell because some of the dogs switch from one side to the other.

By the time I get the door open, the two biggest dogs are fighting. The others growl and bark at each other, waiting to see who will win. I shout at them to stop, but they ignore me. I'm not the leader of the pack, so I go inside.

Without calling out, I know the house is empty, but I call out anyway, "Dad, it's me. It's Karma."

The house smells stale, but not like something dead, so I walk from room to room, looking at what is left of my life. In the kitchen there's a bulletin board. Dad made it out of wine corks stuck into a frame with Elmer's glue.

"Artsy-craftsy," he called it. "And cheap."

Dad drank a lot of wine, usually when I wasn't looking. One cork for seven glasses. One cork every four days. Quicker if the days were difficult. How much wine did he drink when his daughter went into the hospital, and he couldn't visit because only soldiers were allowed to drive?

I open the refrigerator, but I close it quickly because it smells like the confessional at St. Gregory's.

There's peanut butter in the pantry, and crackers, and Kashi Go Lean snack bars, from when Dad was on a diet. All good food, and the water is still running, so I can drink my fill, and take a shower. I can put on clean clothes that actually belong to me, and cotton panties with a real elastic band.

Dad's room looks just the way it always did, neat and orderly for the end of civilization. The only thing out of place is a pocket watch on a piece of blue note paper in the middle of his bed. His writing—easy for me to tell, because it's neat and perfectly oriented on the page, each letter exactly the same size as if it came from a longhand font on a word processor.

Dear Karma—

This watch is all wound up, but doesn't work anymore. Like the world, I guess. I think that means you should take all the time you need to figure out what comes next. Nobody's keeping track any more.

Remember, friends are precious. Take them where you find them and find them where you can. Don't be choosy. Look for the signs.

Love,
Dad

Neatly written, but hard to understand. The watch has stopped at five o'clock. Dad used to say, "It's always five o'clock somewhere," before he drank a glass of wine.

The watch feels lonely in my pocket. And cold, even though it's late summer and the air conditioning's been off for months.

I pack my Slim Jims, and my peanut butter and crackers, and a thermos full of tap water into the L. L. Bean backpack I bought when I thought I might go camping. Now it looks like I might be doing a lot of that while I go looking for Joseph.

Four pairs of jeans, four shirts, six pair of socks, and eight pair of lovely underwear nestle around the food. A bar of soap, a bottle of aspirin, and Dad's old Swiss Army knife with the ivory toothpick and the useful blades all go into special compartments. The only things I don't pack are my fully cocked six-shooter, and my authentic Cheyenne War Ceremony Knife.

I don't look out the window before I open the door and step outside, because this is home and I never did those things when civilization was still around.

But now I should.

The dogfight in my front yard is finished now, and the new improved pack looks ready for action. The new dog-chief has a bloody ear, and blood on his muzzle, and maybe he's eaten the loser, because that one's nowhere to be seen.

The pack leader might be part chow, because he's big with fur-like armor and a growl like a garbage disposal. He's tired of taking crap from humans who've chained him in the backyard and fed him scraps for years.

I point my pistol at him and shout, "Git!" in my best deranged hillbilly accent, but this dog has heard it all before, and he's not impressed.

The other dogs aren't sure what comes next. They wag their tails and look at me like I might be about to throw them a treat, but what I do is hold my pistol in two hands the way cops used to do on TV shows, and I put my feet into a wide target-shooting stance, and give the dogs a count of three to clear out.

When they don't clear out, I give them another count of three. I'm getting ready to count one last time, just in case they are a little slow with math, when the dog-chief charges me.

I pull the trigger and the hammer falls.

Click. The dog-chief stops for a moment, but now he knows for sure, something he's suspected since I walked out my front door and closed it behind me without checking first.

I'm defenseless.

I prove that by pulling the trigger again and again, listening to the hammer fall onto empty cylinders a lot more than six times. Why didn't I think of this before? Suicide only takes one bullet.

The dog-chief charges me again, and this time no amount of clicking is going to slow him down. It's too late to go back into the house. It's too late to draw my authentic Cheyenne War Ceremony Knife, so when the dog-chief jumps at me with his mouth open, ready to shred me like last week's homework, I swing my nearly useless cowboy pistol at his face.

There's lots of yipping and yelping after that, and I see blood on the shiny silver barrel and cylinder of the pistol, and broken dogteeth on the sidewalk, and a hopeless look in the eyes of the dog who wanted to chew me to death but can't chew anything now.

This time when I yell, "Git!" the big pack scatters into smaller packs with leaders who remember that people are the boss.

"Git!" I yell again, and put the pistol into my waistband in case I need to beat another dog with it later.

—

I'M CHEWING ON A SLIM JIM, taking big steps along the street, hardly thinking of how far I've got to go, or all the ugly things I'll pass on the way. Not thinking at all of how I might never find Joseph or bullets for my six-shooter, or how all the Hostess CupCakes in the world—except maybe for Twinkies—will go stale in a couple of weeks.

Not thinking about much at all, because I'm acquiring a taste for Slim Jims and surviving a dog attack feels really cool after the fear wears off. Until you hear something behind you that you'd forgotten about.

Claws on pavement.

I pull the pistol out of my waistband and get ready to fend off another dog attack, but nothing's there.

I cock the hammer back, even though I don't have bullets and shout, "I'm not afraid to use this." What do feral dogs know about six-shooters anyway?

I see a movement in my peripheral vision, and suddenly there's a coyote where nothing was before, sitting on her haunches not afraid, but not aggressive, either.

I suppose the coyote was always there, blending into the background the way wild animals do, waiting for my eyes to pick her out.

No wagging tail. No subservient look.

There's a sound behind me like a breath being let out in a rush, and when I turn around, there are three more coyotes, watching, waiting.

I tear my Slim Jim into four roughly equal parts and toss them to each of the coyotes. Perfect tosses. Perfect catches. Each piece is swallowed in a gulp.

They saw me defeat the chief of the feral dog pack. Now I'm giving them food. It's a coyote ceremony older than America.

I'm the Alpha Female. The new leader of the pack. They follow me down the street into the dangerous heart of Oklahoma City. Friends are precious now. Like Dad said, I can't be choosy.

—

MY COYOTES LIKE SLIM JIMS, but they like jerky better. They snatch pieces of cured meat out of the air with zero energy. No jumps, no lurches, almost no chewing at all. They're always standing in the right places with their mouths open.

"It's probably not good for you." They listen but they don't stop eating, and I don't stop throwing. It's all part of the canine bonding process.

"Here it comes." A two inch section of Slim Jim follows a parabolic arc like the ones we studied in geometry and intersects a coyote mouth. They've never been to school, but they understand the math perfectly.

"Trajectory," I tell them. "Ballistic vectors," as if these are words they need to know. I fake-toss a time or two, but coyotes can't be fooled. They have no expectations of free meat sailing through the air.

The coyotes space themselves out around me so they can disappear in case of danger. Like I'm their pet human, good for laughs but not so good they'll die for me.

"Sorry for all the things my people did to yours," I tell them. "You know, the traps, the poison bait, the bounties."

I can't be sure they understand, so I say, *"Habla Espaniol?"*

The one in front of me looks back. Just my luck. I'm hooked up with a pack of Chicana coyotes.

Just to be sure I say, *"Viva Zapata,"* and they all look at me.

A quick glance but there's no doubt.

Each coyote has a different face, a different posture, a different way of walking, a different attitude—individuals, like dogs and cats and people. I name them after the four directions, because of the way they space themselves around me, like I'm the center of a compass and they are the four compass points. Joseph would like the direction names. It's one of those Indian things.

North is the biggest and the smartest. She walks in front of me, as if she knows exactly where I'm going. East is to my right, West is to my left, and South walks behind me. As far as I can tell they never change. Coyotes don't look friendly like dogs. Their ears stand up and their tails are high, as if to say, "We've gotten along without you very well for thousands of coyote generations. We'll be fine when you're not here anymore."

They don't mind if I talk about Joseph.

"You can't repeat this to anyone." I toss a little jerky to each of them, starting with North and ending with West. They wait their turns, as patient as house cats. My secrets are safe with them.

"Joseph looks sort of like a movie star." North looks at me over her shoulder. One of her ears twitches as if she can't believe what I'm saying.

"Not in A-list movies, but Disney pictures about lost animals and kids who save the world." North accepts this after another piece of jerky.

I tell the coyotes how I'll probably let Joseph make love to me.

"If he really wants to," and I know he really wants to, but so far he hasn't asked. "I won't let him do it right away." I tell the coyotes about the bases. "First base is just a kiss." That still works even after the sexual revolution came and went. "Maybe the other bases have changed, but I don't have to worry about that now that civilization's gone."

North looks back at me as if to say, *"You call that civilization?"*

The coyotes space themselves around me like a magic circle, as if I were St. Francis of Assisi, or Beastmaster, or some X-man superhero with telepathic power over animals. It feels pretty good, but when I start to tell the coyotes my new theory, I can't find them anymore.

Gone, just like civilization.

I don't have a clue, and all of a sudden, I feel vulnerable. I reach for my empty six-shooter, even though the Cheyenne War Ceremony Knife is probably a better weapon, and I point it at the shadows of empty buildings and abandoned cars, where ghosts might be hiding now that my magic coyote circle is gone.

To my left, the door of a Love's gas station stands partway open, like the spring on the automatic door closing mechanism is stuck. The door is mostly glass, but it's dark in there, full of mysterious superstitious things that I never believed in until this moment.

I cross myself the way the dead priest in St. Gregory's probably did before he put the pistol to his head and pulled the trigger—playing a fixed game of Russian Roulette. I point the weapon at the partially open door and wish the priest had taken the time to fill the empty cylinders with bullets.

A threat sticks in my throat. Saliva trickles past my larynx and makes me want to cough almost as much as I want to hide.

Human, or animal. Which is worse?

I panic quietly and point my useless pistol and wait because I don't know how to turn invisible. My arms cramp and a trickle of sweat runs between my shoulder blades, and the Slim Jims in my stomach are filing a writ of habeas corpus—God how I miss watching *Court TV* with my father.

A big raccoon—at least forty pounds—crowds halfway through the door before she sees me. Her eyes lock on mine, but she doesn't pull back inside. I put the empty pistol into my belt, and step backwards, holding up both hands as if surrendering.

She runs forward a few feet and stops. Bobs back and forth on her feet like an autistic child. Four baby raccoons follow her outside. This might be happening all over Oklahoma City, only I'm not there to see. All it takes is a few broken doors, and convenience stores that were once owned by Iranian and Vietnamese immigrants now belong to Mother Nature.

"Cute," I tell the mother raccoon. "You have cute babies."

She isn't persuaded I'm harmless yet, so she keeps her eyes on me as she leads her family away, as close to an opposite direction as she can go without re-entering the building.

"Bye-bye." I smile and wave the way I would to human babies, making all kinds of new friends in the animal kingdom.

Then my coyote girlfriends are there. Suddenly visible again, surrounding the raccoon family, who all look at me as if I have betrayed them.

"Stop!"

North is the first to attack. Then the other coyote sisters, breaking necks and tossing bodies into the air, pawing them for signs of life. North picks up a baby in her mouth. She brings it to me, drops it at my feet.

"Damn. I'm not part of this." But I guess I am. I'm the raccoon distraction, the harmless threat that misled a mother and her children until it was too late.

The coyotes like fresh raccoon almost as much as Slim Jims and jerky. It's disgusting, but I know this is the part of nature that Disney documentaries never showed us. I have a lot to learn, but I already know this much—family is when you know everything bad about somebody but you love them anyway.

"Good old North."

The coyotes all look at me in turn.

Their English is better than I thought.

——

I WANT TO FOLLOW INTERSTATE 40, because it's easier to walk on pavement than dirt, and I have a long way to go. My magic circle of coyotes has other ideas. They nudge me to the shoulder and into the woods. They'll let me walk close to the road, but not on it.

"What's the point, guys?" There's no reasoning with wild animals. They nudge me farther into the trees and underbrush where I have to watch out for thorns and poison ivy. I drift back toward the road whenever I can, so my pack and I reach a sort of equilibrium—I like that word. It reminds me of chemistry and democracy and it makes me feel like I know more about the world than I really do.

"Equilibrium." I repeat the word out loud, as if my coyote girlfriends will get the idea, but they nudge me deeper into the trees, and there are a lot of trees since we left Oklahoma City.

I push toward the highway again, but before I get into the ankle-high buffalo grass beside the pavement, I hear horses. It's like part of the soundtrack to Oklahoma, and for a moment, I want to run up to the road and sing a couple of verses of "The Cowboy and the Farmer Should be Friends."

But then I remember that people have been killing each other ever since the electricity went off. And even if they have a good excuse like the New Flu virus, people are a lot more dangerous than poison ivy and thorns.

"Maybe it'll be Joseph," I whisper to my coyote girlfriends. "Or some of his Choctaw buddies." I hope so, because we are barely out of Oklahoma City, and the sun is already low in the western sky, and I am so tired and hungry all I can think about is peanut butter and sleep.

Two men ride by, both wearing cowboy hats and carrying rifles—the kind with big bullet clips shaped like mechanical bananas.

"Not Joseph," I whisper to the coyotes, but they are nowhere to be seen.

One of the cowboys says, "You hear that?" He adds a string of curses that probably mean his mother didn't love him. He points his rifle in my general direction and fires a three-shot burst.

The horses don't like the noise. The other cowboy doesn't like it either.

"Damn it, Bill, use the single-shot setting." He's afraid of his horse, and his horse is afraid of the gunshots. It makes him forget all his complicated woman-oriented swear words for a few seconds, but they come back to him when the horse settles down. He recites them one at a time in no special order.

"Heard somethin'," says the trigger happy cowboy. "Ain't you heard it too? Sort of a whisper-voice."

He points his ugly rifle right at me. If he shoots again, he'll hit me for sure, but now he has other ideas.

"A girl's voice. I'll bet anything." He tells his nervous partner exactly what he means to do once he finds the girl who belongs to that voice. It doesn't sound like anything I learned in sex education.

"Ain't heard nothing," the nervous cowboy says. "You just need to get laid is all."

I guess when civilization ended, the women all went into hiding. Good thing I found out about this before it was too late—if it's not already too late.

The horny cowboy turns his horse like it has power steering and rides in my direction. The nervous cowboy follows close behind. They both hold their weapons like they've done all this before. They trade racial slurs back and forth in case the girl with the whispery voice is African, or Asian, or Native American.

I can't help feeling glad about being a plain old white girl, and that makes me feel almost more ashamed than I am afraid.

Maybe they won't kill me. Maybe the nasty vocabulary is just a lot of cowboy words, something interesting to say around the campfire now that football is extinct. But the cowboys are pretty specific about what they plan to do and who gets to go first and how deep they'll bury me after I fall apart like a baseball with broken stitching.

"Never hung nobody before," the nervous cowboy says. "Think I can hang her when we're done?"

"We'll see," the horny boss cowboy says, like he's talking to a three-year-old who can be put off by promises that don't guarantee anything.

There are lots of things these men want to do to me, but they haven't found me yet, and maybe they won't if I don't panic and run into the open like a distracted raccoon.

They are trying to flush me out, and my best chance is to stay right where I am, but my legs really want to run, and my eyes really want to cry, and my mouth really wants to scream.

The cowboys separate and ride around me, one on either side. I slump in the underbrush as much as I can without moving, but I must have moved a little, because the horny boss cowboy's horse looks right at me.

He's been brushed and curried and fed and shod because these cowboys love their horses even though they hate women. He's on the cowboy's side of things, but he doesn't give me away—yet.

Please! I beam out telepathic promises to bring him sugar and apples if he will pass me by, if he will quit looking at me and move on. But he blows hot horse breath into my face and bumps me with his soft as silk horse nose.

"Get up bitch," the horny cowboy says.

There's no fever in his eyes so his mean streak isn't something that hatched out of the New Flu virus. He's hated women ever since he came out of one.

"A white bitch," his partner smiles. "It's our lucky day."

I'm up and running, like a fox in front of a pack of bloodthirsty English gentlemen. Not worried about poison ivy and thorns, or even the whooping cowboys holding ugly rifles.

The easiest place to run is on the interstate, but I head deeper into the trees, wondering which one these men will hang me from when they've finished taking revenge on their mothers. Wondering if they'll shoot me just in case I might get away, short circuiting their fun, proceeding directly to the orgasm without passing go.

The killing is the main thing after all. I feel the spot where the bullet will pass through my body, right between my shoulder blades. Hot as burning gunpowder, faster than the speed of nasty words.

I'll never hear the explosion that sends the bullet my way or the last curses the cowboys mutter before they kill me. But I hear a three-shot rifle burst, and I look over my shoulder in time to see my coyote sisters chasing horses down the interstate.

The horny boss cowboy drags himself toward his partner who has three bloody holes in his chest.

"Goddamned coyotes. Goddamned white bitch." He sits beside his friend who might not be dead yet, but probably will be pretty soon, because assault rifles set to fire automatic bursts aren't particular who they kill.

I step back farther into the trees but I don't run away. I can't help watching the horny boss cowboy cry over his friend, who he killed by accident when my coyote sisters spooked their horses.

My face turns into an ice-cold revenge Popsicle when the horny boss cowboy tries to lift his friend and I take stock of the destruction. One dead, one badly injured.

The cowboy can't chase me with a broken leg, and it must be broken because it's twisted at a painful looking angle. These days a broken leg can kill you, if your horses run away and you just shot your partner because of some crazy white bitch with coyote magic.

"Help me," the cowboy calls to me. "I promise I won't kill you." He's found me in the trees. He tosses his rifle out of reach. It fires another burst because he hasn't changed the setting.

I draw my authentic Cheyenne War Ceremony Knife and point it at him, like it's a magic wand that will make him do exactly what I want. "There is one more rifle."

He crawls over to his partner's rifle and throws it near the first. No explosive discharge with that toss. "Now will you help me?"

I smile and back into the trees without answering. Giving him a reason to hate women, at least until he starves to death.

"Please," he calls to me, full of manners now that his weapons are out of reach. "I'll give you anything," followed by a string of promises and threats that cancel each other out.

After a hundred yards I can't hear him but his hatred follows me until I step behind a live oak tree with limbs that sprawl across the forest floor like the tentacles of a giant octopus. My coyote sisters form a circle around me in their usual positions. I want to pet them for saving my life, but things don't work that way.

"Thank you," I say, mostly to them, but also to God, in case he's listening.

Then I get a good look at the tree that's hiding me from the full force of the cowboy's hate. There's a perfect Valentine heart carved into the trunk with two names inside separated by a single word. I trace them with the tip of the Indian knife Joseph made for me—*Joseph loves Karma.*

"Thank you." This time it's all to God, because I know this is one of those signs religious people talk about. A message, like a priest's final words or a note from your father who you'll never see again.

"We're on the right track," I tell my coyote sisters. "We'll find Joseph before you know it."

I check the watch my father left me to see if God has fixed it. Five o'clock, like always. Maybe it will be five o'clock forever.

I move deeper into the woods, protected by my magic coyote circle. North is in the lead.

IN AN
INSTANT

THE CLOCK ON OUR KITCHEN wall stopped months ago along with everything else that works on electricity, but my mother checks it anyway. "Still five o'clock. In India, mothers don't measure time with machines."

She tells me, "All the really important things happen in an instant." She kisses me on the cheek, brushes the spot with her fingertips and says, "You're a man now, Raj."

Just like that.

"Things change when the world falls apart." Her Bengali inflections turn everything she says into Eastern wisdom. "Now looting and shopping are exactly the same thing. You see, Raj? Whether you're in India or Oklahoma City."

"Well. . ." I'd have more to say if my accent came from the other side of the world.

She puts her hands on my shoulders so I'll have to pay attention, so I'll know Bengali-Okie-men have to listen to their mothers. "Hunger makes all the difference, especially if someone's already broken into the grocery store." She hands me a shopping bag made of recycled plastic. "Think of it as an adventure."

My first assignment as a man is stealing dinner from the Buy For Less.

—

THE RIOTERS MADE A MESS of things. Broken glass, pools of dried blood, piles of crumpled clothing that might have bones inside.

I keep my eyes on the back of the store and my mind on canned goods. Chef Boyardee, Vienna Sausages, Starkist Tuna.

I take careful baby steps through the deepest darkest part of Buy For Less, back where the seafood and meat have turned into a maggot factory. No wind inside the store to move the odors around. They settle in layers that burn my eyes and turn my stomach but I'm still hungry enough to eat canned tomatoes and beets and wash them down with grapefruit juice. The looters left plenty of those things when they ran through the store days ago and cleaned out all good stuff—Wolf Brand chili, beer, Diet Coke.

I'm opening a can of sauerkraut with a one of the twenty blades on my Swiss Army knife when bright lights shine on me from two directions.

A voice behind one of the lights says, "Show us your hands, José."

So I drop the knife and the sauerkraut and push my fingers toward the ceiling. Pigeons roosting in the girders shift positions, not sure if I'm reaching for them. They coo to each other—making plans.

The voice calls me a "Goddamned Mexican." I hear a dollop of saliva splatter on the floor. I hear the hammer of a pistol click into the danger zone.

"I'm not Mexican," I say before I can stop myself.

I point to the American Flag pin my mother made me wear to prove I'm patriotic. I draw a finger under the *Kiss me! I'm an Okie!* legend on my T-shirt.

"My name's Rajneesh Patel," I tell the pair of sealed-beam lights. "I'm Bengali, not Hispanic." The word Hispanic comes out like an obscenity—with accents on *hiss* and *panic*. "My friends call me Raj."

The pigeons flutter toward the broken windows at the front of the Buy For Less. They want to get away from the muzzle flashes and the noise that's bound to come when men with guns and flashlights find a brown-skinned boy eating sauerkraut in the back of a grocery store.

I hear a wad of chewing tobacco move from one cheek to the other. A second spittle dollop hits the floor.

"Goddamned illegal aliens." The nicotine-saturated voice is stuck on Mexico, even though there is no such thing as Mexico anymore. No USA, either. No borders or armies. Not since New Flu swept the continents clean of government.

"Take our jobs," one voice says.

"Take our women," the other voice adds.

The lights bob in unison, perfectly synchronized like the cheerleaders at college football games—with their long tan legs and pleated skirts and breasts as firm and sweet as frozen Jell-O.

When you're a fifteen-year-old virgin Bengali-Okie-boy who just became a man, everything keeps coming back to sex. I think about all the girls who never slept with me. Physiology turns fear into an erection, just in case I have a chance to reproduce at the last possible minute. I wonder if the flashlight men will open fire if I adjust my penis into a more comfortable position. It's a very American thing to do—like the New York Yankees and the St. Louis Cardinals. After a microsecond of deliberation I do it, because there isn't anything else for me to do. My bucket list has turned into a thimble.

Light beams move over my body like I'm the main act in the center ring of a Shriner's circus. The conversation behind the sealed beams takes on a different tone, one filled with dirty words that don't have anything to do with illegal aliens.

According to the Flashlight Men, I don't look Mexican anymore. Now I sort of look like a girl—especially my mouth, and my, "Cute little butt."

I guess the Flashlight Men think about girls, too, now that everything has fallen apart. The longer they go without one, the less choosy they are.

"Been a long time," one of them says through a mouthful of tobacco juice.

"A long, long time," the other man agrees. He speculates about the nature of homosexuality. How it's the partner who plays the female role who's the real queer.

"Even if he ain't exactly willing. Especially if you kill him when you're done."

"Amen, brother." There's talk of K-Y jelly on aisle 20-A and condoms in the pharmacy. Footsteps move toward me.

I'm wondering if I can find my Swiss Army knife in the dark, and how much of a fight I can put up before the Flashlight Men do whatever they are going to do, but I'm no longer wondering why girls are so tepid about sex.

I fold my hands into fists and try to look fierce and dangerous, but I know I'm not pulling it off because I hear the men sliding their pistols into holsters and talking about who'll go first.

A third voice says, "Not yet, Bubba."

The Flashlight Men turn their beams onto a tall white man in a black suit like the ones bankers and ministers used to wear. He has a red tie with a gold clasp that sparkles in the flashlight beams like a battery-powered miracle. His hair is coal black with gray at the temples. His eyes are just coal black.

He points a Photoshopped smile at me and holds out a hand with a glittering ruby ring on the little finger. Gangsters wear rings like that. Powerful men who don't wear capes and can't leap tall buildings in a single bound, but do have secret identities. I thought all the gangsters would be gone, now that nothing is left to rob.

The Flashlight Men step back as I approach the shining man, but they keep the lights turned on him. His image burns into my retinas so deeply it will never go away.

My savior's hand is soft and firm, the way the president's probably was before New Flu put an end to government. His eyes are kind, like pictures of Jesus hanging on the walls of Bible stores.

Amen, brother.

"My name is Colonel." He turns and walks toward the front of the grocery store, and I follow him.

"My name's Raj." I walk a little faster toward the broken glass and sunlight, wondering if I'll run away as soon as I'm outside or just try to stand in Colonel's shadow.

The decision is easy, because there are six men standing around the front of the Buy For Less. White men wearing designer jeans and shirts, with gold chains around their necks, rings on most of their fingers, and eyes full of hunger for things they wouldn't find inside a grocery store. Not usually, anyway.

They laugh when Colonel tells them he found me in the ethnic section between the lentils and the curries.

He puts an arm around me. "We're collectors, Raj. I guess you could say you've been collected."

Colonel points toward the passenger seat of a four-wheeler that looks something like a golf cart. He doesn't make threats or promises, but I do exactly what he wants because there are eight scary looking white men in the parking lot and they are also doing exactly what he wants.

"I thought gasoline was all gone." Four-wheelers and three-wheelers are crowded around the front of the grocery store. They all start at once on Colonel's command. Lots of exhaust fumes, lots of noise. He isn't trying to hide from anyone.

He takes a seat beside me, so I'm crowded up against the driver. Waves of lust and hate radiate from the man behind the steering wheel, but Colonel feels as safe and solid as the Statue of Liberty. He smiles when I lean against him. He looks at me the way my mother did before she sent me off to loot a grocery store. I don't know what he wants me to do, but I'm sure he'll think of something.

"I really should go home," I say.

"This is your home now."

"I sort of have responsibilities." I start to tell him about my mother, waiting for me all alone, but I suddenly realize keeping quiet might be the most important responsibly of all.

Then I can't talk anymore because we are riding down Northwest Highway, weaving around abandoned cars, and Colonel's men are shooting pistols at birds and empty houses and stray dogs prowling the streets in packs.

I wonder if my mother will hear the gunshots and figure out I'm not coming back. I hope she remembers this was her idea. I hope she understands her chance to be mother of the year just went out the window. I hope she knows I love her.

Colonel makes an almost imperceptible sign with his right hand, but somehow all the drivers see it. All the noisy vehicles stop. All the engines turn off at once. Like Colonel has a master key inside his brain. He walks to the front door of an abandoned house and opens it with a kick.

His men file inside and after a few minutes they come out carrying bottles of wine.

"It's the blood of Christ," Colonel says.

They bring out a case of Scotch whisky.

"The single malt blood of Christ," Colonel says. "Twenty-five years old."

They bring out a case of Budweiser in twelve-ounce bottles.

"The urine of Christ," Colonel says.

All his men laugh at once. I laugh too, which I guess sort of makes me one of them—if only for a second.

"In the Last Days, religion and crime are almost the same thing," Colonel says. He doesn't have a Bengali accent like my mother, but his words still sound like they come from the other side of the world.

"Raj here is an Indian," Colonel tells his men. "They know all about religion."

I want to tell him I was born in Oklahoma City, so actually I'm American. I almost point to the flag pin on my shirt and the *Kiss Me! I'm an Okie!* legend written on my T-shirt , but I don't because I really want the Colonel to be right.

I want to say, "Amen brother," but, "I guess," is the best I can do.

"What tribe are you?" One of Colonel's men has opened a bottle of single malt Blood of Christ and gives himself a transfusion.

"He's a *Guru* Indian, not a *Whoo-Whoo* Indian." Everybody laughs when Colonel says that and the man takes a deep swallow of Scotch whisky. I can tell he hates me from the way he wipes his mouth on his wrist and spits on the ground.

"Columbus made the same mistake." I smile at him with my perfectly aligned East Indian teeth and beam friendship and understanding through my eyes, but his invisible shield of hate deflects everything.

My new enemy takes a step toward me, but Colonel stops him with a look.

"There's a carton of cigarettes in the kitchen," Colonel tells him. "Go get them, Bubba."

Colonel never went inside the house, so there's no way he could know this. It makes the man nervous, because if the cigarettes aren't there Colonel will be angry. In a minute the angry man comes out smiling, waving the carton of cigarettes in the air.

Colonel extracts a pack of Marlboros and opens it. He removes a cigarette and places it between my lips. He takes a lighter from his pocket and opens it—the distinctive noise of a Zippo. I don't know how I know this but I do.

"We don't have to worry about cancer anymore." Colonel hands me the pack of cigarettes and the lighter. "Keep them."

The smoke tastes like wisdom and bravery. This is what it feels like to be one of Colonel's men.

I tell myself I'll only smoke one cigarette a day, because nobody makes them anymore. When I run out, maybe Colonel will give me another pack, or maybe he'll decide I'm not the Indian boy who knows all about religion after all. I'm the boy with the cute butt his men won't stop looking at—and occasionally touching.

As far as I can tell all Colonel's men are named Bubba except for me.

"They're interchangeable Raj, like Jesus' disciples." He winks at me and touches the tip of my nose with a finger. A spark of static electricity jumps between us. "Bubba, bring Raj that six-shooter."

I can't tell who Colonel is talking to, but the Bubbas know. One of them hands him a pistol in a Western holster. This Bubba might be one of the Flashlight Men, or the one who fetched the carton of cigarettes. They look as indistinguishable as a litter of wolf pups or a troop of clowns.

Colonel straps the pistol around my waist.

"Boys with pistols don't look so sweet." He lets me take a sip of Scotch from his personal bottle. I smile, even though it's like swallowing gasoline.

"The Bubbas like girls better than boys, but they use them up kind of fast." He slips his pinky ring onto my little finger to remind his men whose property I am.

"Raj is off limits," he tells them. "At least for now."

"At least for now?" I don't like the sound of that, but Colonel tells me it's all part of a complex strategy I'll understand later on. He doesn't say I'll like it.

"Best not to think on it too much," he says. "Maybe we'll find a girl along the way. A nice young one, to remind the boys." Colonel runs a hand through my hair and licks his fingertips, like I'm a piece of chocolate cake he's saving for later.

"Remind them of what?" I ask, mainly to get his mind off chocolate.

"That you're not a girl, Raj. Sometimes the Bubbas need reminding."

—

TEN CIGARETTE DAYS SINCE BUY For Less, and I'm still wearing Colonel's pinky ring.

The Bubbas say, "Look, Raj and Colonel are going steady," but not when Colonel can hear them.

I count the bullets in my gun, where all of them can see—enough to kill six Bubbas if they come for me. I've never fired a weapon in my life and I don't practice with this one because Colonel says I shouldn't.

"If the men see what a bad shot you are, the pistol won't discourage them."

So I just count my bullets to remind them how wrong things can go if they think about my butt too much.

Every night, we sleep in the National Guard Armory where the 44th Medical Evacuation Hospital used to train. There's medicine, and M-16 rifles with lots of ammunition. There are Meals, Ready to Eat, and tents and a chain link fence with razor wire coiled on top.

Most important, there is gasoline. Not enough for Jeeps, but plenty for four-wheelers.

Every day, the Bubbas drive through Oklahoma City, wherever Colonel tells them. They stop when Colonel gives the sign, sometimes at houses, sometimes at stores. Sometimes he tells them what to look for, but mostly he just says to go inside.

I ask, "How do you pick the houses?" because what Colonel does seems like magic.

I'm crowded between a Bubba and Colonel in the front seat of a four-wheeler, so I can't pull away when he leans his lips too close to my ear and whispers, "There's always something, Raj."

A drop of saliva pops out of his mouth when he says my name. I want to wipe it off, but he's watching me so I just let it dry.

He raises his right hand and sticks his pinky finger in the air—the one that used to wear my ruby ring—and the Bubbas all pull over and kill their engines. I'm hoping that's all they'll kill today.

Colonel points at a brick house with no broken windows and tells his men, "This one."

There's a scuffle to see which Bubba will go inside. The baldheaded one with the Nazi tattoos wins this time by using a stun gun. He looks at Colonel for approval and then backs through the door.

Inside, a woman screams. She screams the same thing over and over, but nobody outside can understand.

The outside Bubbas smile and trade buddy punches. Then there's a gunshot. Followed by two more. Followed by three more after that.

Six bullets, the same as in in the pistol Colonel gave me. I put my hand on the pistol grip, because the Bubbas are all nodding their heads and smiling like someone just announced the electricity is coming on again. They look at each other, and they look at the front door. At least they aren't looking at me.

I feel ashamed that I'm not worried about the gunshots and the screams, but relieved it wasn't me screaming—at least not yet.

Colonel puts a hand on my shoulder. "It happens like this sometimes."

I want to ask him, "What happens?" but I don't really want to know, so I just sit beside Colonel and hope the screams are enough to remind the Bubbas that I'm not a girl.

Five minutes later the Nazi Bubba comes out carrying a little girl, who's holding a stuffed animal in her arms. He whoops like a violent weather alert. He tosses the little girl into the air so high it looks like she might reach escape velocity but she pauses in mid-flight and falls into his arms again.

Maybe she's four years old or maybe she's five. It's hard to tell, because the terror on her face subtracts at least a year. She opens her mouth into a perfect capital "O". It looks like she's screaming, but if she is it's in a frequency Bengali-Okie boys can't hear.

The Bubbas collect in a broken circle around their Nazi partner. They look at the little girl the way they've looked at me ever since I came out of the Buy For Less.

I feel like a door has opened letting in sunshine and fresh air as the Bubbas turn their attention toward her. Relief crowds out everything else in my mind. I try hard to feel sorry for this little girl, but I can't quite manage.

"It will come," Colonel tells me, understanding what's going on inside my mind the same way he knows what's inside buildings as we drive past on four-wheelers.

He walks over to the Bubba circle and extends his arms. The Nazi doesn't want to give her up, but Colonel moves so close he can't refuse.

"Her name is Mary," he says.

The little girl nods her head like an antique bobble-head doll, and doesn't stop until Colonel tells the Bubbas, "Mary Magdalene."

They know all about Mary Magdalene. The Bubbas step away from Colonel mumbling an unintelligible mix of curse words and biblical wisdom.

Colonel turns to me and says, "Everybody got religion when New Flu spread around the world, even people who shouldn't."

The Bubbas all ask for the girl at once. They say, "Please."

They promise to take turns, like little boys asking their father for a BB gun.

"Not yet," Colonel tells them. "Take care of her Raj." He sits her in my lap. "This is your lucky day."

Now I have a pistol, a half-pack of cigarettes, a Zippo lighter, a ruby ring, and a little girl—all presents from Colonel.

—

ON THE DAY I SMOKE my fifteenth cigarette, one of the Bubbas finds a cache of drugs.

Colonel looks unhappy when he sees what's in the big cardboard box with *"KITCHENWARES"* written on the side in black Sharpie letters.

"This is trouble, Raj," Colonel tells me. "Keep Mary and your pistol close."

The box has bags of marijuana inside, pressed into solid blocks like the freeze dried vacuum-sealed coffee my mother bought when the stores were open. A dozen baggies full of pills are wedged between the blocks.

"Weed is fine," Colonel tells the Bubbas. "Smoke all the weed you want, just don't take the pills."

According to Colonel, the little blue tablets with the word *SKY* pressed into them are ecstasy. They evaporate among the Bubbas more quickly than twenty-five-year-old Scotch. No one knows where they went.

"Beats me, Colonel."

"Ain't seen 'em."

"Not a clue."

The Bubbas all look at their feet and tell the same lie. The drugs have more power over them than Colonel, so he pretends he doesn't care.

I'm holding Mary in my arms, wondering what I'll do if trouble starts.

Colonel runs a hand through Mary's hair. "Pretty little girl."

He takes turns looking at me and Mary like he's making a decision.

"Let's go!" Colonel walks to the four-wheelers, and all the Bubbas follow. They all know he's the boss, even if they won't give up their ecstasy.

He keeps us busy collecting, and tells me to hold Mary so the Bubbas can't get a good look at her.

"Ecstasy makes the Bubbas remember what they want." Colonel runs his hand through Mary's hair again and smells his fingers. I put my hand on my six-shooter in case he's remembering, too.

Nothing unusual happens for a while. At least nothing more unusual than everything that's happened since civilization disappeared. Colonel keeps on finding things. The Bubbas keep on following orders. There might be a little more shoving and grumbling than usual, but it's hard to tell while I'm holding a little girl who never talks.

I hold her, and she holds a stuffed animal that might be a mouse with floppy ears or a dog with whiskers, or something that lives in factories in China where stuffed animals used to come from.

"NNNNNAAA!" It's not a word, but it's the closest thing to a word Mary's said since we collected her. She's looking over my shoulder, and wrapping her arms around me so her stuffed animal is pressing into my neck.

I turn around just in time to step away from a dirty hand reaching for us. Black grease highlights every fingernail and every crease in every finger, like a graffiti hand that's somehow been drawn on the end of a Bubba's arm. The fingers close into a fist, as if it's holding an invisible rope that's connected to me and Mary.

"Let me have the little girl."

The Bubba's voice trembles like knuckles running over a washboard. His eyes fill up with big black pupils that completely swallow the irises. Full of hallucinations. Full of desire. Full of unrequited Bubba-love.

"Pretty, pretty, pretty." The hand reaches out and pulls at the air again.

"Three times too pretty for you. Go away." I make a fist of my own and hold it so he can see the pinky ring Colonel gave me.

The Bubba's smile might look friendly except for the missing front tooth, and the stream of tobacco-stained drool running down his chin.

Mary squeezes her arms around my neck so tight, I can barely say the word, "Asshole!"

I draw my pistol and point it at the Bubba's chest.

"You won't shoot," he tells me. "There's no end of shooting once you start." He gestures at the other Bubbas who are moving our direction now, along with Colonel, who's not doing anything to help.

"You won't shoot," the Bubba says again, like a Jedi warrior tricking a stormtrooper with a weak mind.

He takes a giant step forward, like ecstasy has distorted the distance between us. So instead of shooting, I stomp on the foot that's already reached too far.

The instep crumbles like a sand castle, and the Bubba howls like a champion pig caller and tries to keep his balance while he hops around on his good foot.

Mary makes her "NNNAAA!" sound again, which blends perfectly with the Bubba-noise. I take a graceful step forward like a mediocre soccer player from Brazil whose been hired by the Texas Rangers to kick field goals. My foot connects with a part of the Bubba that's so soft it makes me cringe.

He falls onto the ground and cries until bubbles of mucous mix with the tobacco juice on his chin. He tries to get up, but his legs aren't taking orders from his brain.

"Let's move out," Colonel says.

The Bubbas load boxes into the four-wheelers and we ride off without their partner with the broken foot and the swollen testicles.

"What will he do now?" I ask Colonel.

He doesn't tell me, and I don't ask again.

—

COLONEL SAYS WE CAN'T LEAVE the 44th Medical Evacuation compound for three days.

"One for the Father. One for the Son. One for the Holy Ghost."

He makes all his most important orders sound like messages from God. He's not sure how much ecstasy the Bubbas found, but he's pretty sure they'll use it up in three days.

"You and Mary lie doggo." Colonel says that's an expression he read in a science fiction book a long time ago when people thought we'd live on the moon and travel to the stars.

He tries to post a guard or two to keep the Bubbas used to following orders. He warns them about heavily armed lesbian bands who roam the city looking for men who steal little girls. But the Bubbas are too stoned to be afraid, so he locks the gates and tells me to find a place to hide.

"Take Mary with you," he says, like I could go anywhere without her. Mary holds onto me the way baby chimps hold onto their mothers when they swing through the trees. She won't let go even when she eats.

Having a little girl like Mary means always having a little hand on you, even at the most private moments. It means never doing anything without a pair of terrified eyes following every change in expression. It means never lying down without an arm across your chest and a sweaty little body pressed against you.

There are only twelve Bubbas, but ecstasy won't let them sleep and I have to. I take Mary into the enlisted men's quarters, because Colonel says it's too ugly for anyone on ecstasy.

"Men on ecstasy like bright colors, pretty girls, and boys who look like pretty girls," Colonel says. "They don't like cots lined up in a large room with walls the color of body bags."

But Colonel forgot that everything looks the same in the dark.

I start to say a prayer, because Colonel is right about everybody getting religion when the world comes to an end.

It starts with, "Now I lay me down to sleep," but it's mostly about dying before I wake and that makes Mary nervous.

"NNNAAA."

"Just in case," I whisper to Mary. "Just in case there is a God and he's keeping score, you know?"

"NNNAAA," is all Mary has to say about God.

"Help us, please." I look at the ceiling of the enlisted men's quarters so God will know I'm talking to him. "Please, please, please—and thank you." I can't think of anything more to say. If there's a God he'll know what to do without being told, and if there's not. . . "Just get us out of here, okay?"

I don't remember to say, "Amen," and it's too late, because the front door of the enlisted men's quarters swings open and Bubbas stumble in.

The full moon fills up one of the impossibly small windows in the southern wall. There's plenty of light but it makes everything look like shades of silver. The Bubbas turn their flashlights on and point them in all directions, like a game of German Spotlight. Bright circles of light land on plumped pillows and flat matrasses. They dance across Bubba-faces. Some of the men call out "Raj," and some call out, "Mary," as if we're playing Marco Polo. They whistle and cluck their tongues as if we're a pair of puppies who can be tricked with funny sounds.

We roll onto the cement floor, more quietly than Bubba-footsteps, and crawl under one cot after another until we are as far away from Bubbas as the room will let us go. That's against a wall, which cuts off one route of escape, so I crawl back into the center of the enlisted men's quarters with Mary sheltered between my arms.

I wonder how loud prayers have to be to catch God's attention, because I suddenly remember The Lord's Prayer and it might work better than Now I lay me down to sleep.

But it's too late for prayers. The Bubbas bump into each other and shout curses that are part sexual perversion and part racial slander. They trip over cots and roll onto the floor, but they've forgotten how to crawl, or how to search under things, and after a while, they forget about me and Mary too.

Then the shooting starts. Muzzle flashes light the Bubbas up like mannequins in a county fair horror ride, where ticket holders are told to keep their hands and arms inside the car for their own safety.

Mary and I huddle under a cot and try not to watch, but there is so much noise and so many flashes and so much screaming that finally I run toward the door with Mary clinging to my back.

I can't help thinking maybe she will shield me from the bullets. Maybe the little girl will save my life by losing hers. I hate thinking that so much I snatch her around in front of me so I'll die first. Even though things still won't work out for Mary, I can't let it happen the other way around.

Bullets whiz around us. They ricochet off of things like sound effects in a gunfight movie, which makes me remember I have a gun, and maybe it's time to start shooting back.

Twenty paces from the enlisted men's quarters, I stop and kneel. I push Mary behind me. I draw my pistol and hold it in a double-handed grip, like I've seen policemen do on television back when laws and science looked so promising.

A Bubba stands framed in the doorway of the building, illuminated by the insane silver light of the full moon, turning into a werewolf inside—where it really matters.

"Put your fingers in your ears," I tell Mary, as a black mist of blood covers the Bubba's face and floats over his body. He slides down the doorframe as if he is exhausted from a hard day of rape and pillage.

"NNNAAA!" Mary says. She pats my back with her tiny hands.

"Thanks," I say, "But it wasn't me." The muzzle of my pistol hasn't flashed. No explosion in the cylinder. No fingertip-size lead projectile flew out the barrel. I hadn't found the trigger.

"Friendly fire," I tell Mary, but I'm not sure that's the right way to describe what just happened. The friends who killed the Bubba accidentally gather behind him at the door. Their faces don't look sorry in the moonlight. One of them steps over the body. Then another. Then another.

Mary climbs onto my back again. She wraps her arms around my throat and breathes panic into my right ear.

I holster my pistol and back into the shadows while the Bubbas shine their flashlights at the moon. Everything my mother told me about drugs was true.

"Sorry I ever doubted you, Mom." I aim those words at the sky like I'm talking to God again. I wonder if that means I think she's dead. It's hard to tell, with so much going on.

"NNNAAA." Mary bounces up and down to remind me we don't have time to think about our mothers.

High ground sounds like the right place to go, so I climb a steel fire escape ladder to the top of the Central Headquarters. Mary hops off my back, so I know we're safe, at least for the time being.

The Bubbas run around the compound shouting, "Raj," and "Mary," and "Ally ally all come free." I'm afraid they will figure out we're on the roof, but they are too busy chasing ghosts of us between buildings, and whenever they look up, all their attention is captured by the moon.

I pull out my pistol and point it at the Bubbas.

"If I shoot, I'll give away our hiding place," I tell Mary. "Besides, there are still too many." But what I'm thinking is, *There's no end to shooting once you start.*

The roof of Central Headquarters isn't quite flat, but nearly. There's a rim of brick around it, like an old time castle, tall enough to hide all of Mary except for her head.

She runs around the roof the way an ordinary child might do, inspecting the moon's reflection in puddles of water that have collected in the low spots. Lots of puddles, each with its own full moon bouncing light around the roof so our faces are lit from the bottom.

Some of the moon reflections fit around the shapes of empty bottles thrown up here by soldiers during their two days a month of active duty training. Large brown bottles that once held Budweiser, and Stroh's, and Labatt 50. Green bottles that held a dozen varieties of apple wine and muscatel. Clear bottles that held Miller High Life and Country Club Malt Liquor.

I select a green one with a nearly naked woman on the label. She is too fat to be a modern girl and too slutty to be art. She's lying on a bed of block letters that spell out the brand—Sweet Pig. Perfect Bubba bait.

I go to an edge of the Central Headquarters Building where the Bubbas aren't and toss the bottle off. It breaks beside a large gasoline tank truck—maybe the last one in Oklahoma City.

The Bubbas run toward the sound of broken glass, holding pistols in one hand and flashlights in the other. They see people who aren't there and shoot them. They see people who are there and shoot them too.

Screams and the smell of gunpowder and gasoline fill the air, but nothing explodes or even catches fire and the shooting goes on so long, Mary and I fall asleep beside a chimney.

I dream of blood and bullets and little girls who hold on tight.

—

WE ARE AWAKENED BY THE sound of Colonel shouting orders.

"Get those jerry cans positioned. Cap 'em when they're full. Over here, replace this one."

Maybe this is a good sign. Colonel is running things again.

The cement between the buildings is littered with dead Bubbas soaked in gasoline. Gas is spurting out the tank through bullet holes into green metal cans that are almost too heavy to lift when they are full.

I climb down the ladder with Mary on my back and go to stand by Colonel. He kicks a dead Bubba and says, "Look at all the trouble you caused, Raj."

He makes the Bubbas get all the jerry cans, but it's clear there won't be nearly enough.

I start to tell the Colonel none of this was my fault, but he kicks another dead Bubba.

"Wasted men is one thing, Raj, but wasted gasoline. . . Best thing is to give them Mary." He nudges the dead Bubba's nose with the toe of his wingtip shoe. "Trade her for the ecstasy. If there's any left." Colonel walks up to the tank and raps on the side. There's at least three feet of gasoline above the lowest bullet holes. "The boys'll swap their dope for the girl, Raj. Don't you think?"

What I think is, there are only four Bubbas left. Four Bubbas and Colonel—one less than the number of bullets in my pistol.

"Consider the alternatives, Raj. It's an important decision."

I look at the pinky ring Colonel gave me. I feel Mary on my back. I take the pack of Marlboros out of my pocket. One left. Perfect timing.

I put it in my mouth, but I don't light it.

"I don't think Mary wants to go with the Bubbas." I talk around the cigarette the way Clint Eastwood did in spaghetti westerns. I wonder what those words would sound like in Italian.

I pull my pistol out and point it in the general direction of the Bubbas, not threatening Colonel yet, but defying him.

"Keep working," Colonel tells them. "Raj won't shoot. He needs time to think, is all. Are you thinking, Raj?"

I'm thinking, *There's no end to shooting once you start.*

I'm thinking, *Do I really care about Mary all that much?*

I'm thinking, *Stop Colonel!* Because he is walking toward me, with his hands out, the way he forced the Nazi Bubba to give Mary to him.

"Stop, Colonel!" But he doesn't stop until I point the pistol at him and pull the trigger.

Click. The pistol jumps in my hand even though it doesn't fire.

It takes me five clicks more before I understand.

"Did you think I'd give you a gun that worked?"

The Bubbas stop collecting gasoline long enough to laugh at me.

"I guess you've made your decision, Raj." He crosses his arms and stares at me. He's made his decision too.

Mary loosens her grip around my neck, like she might be ready to let go. Like she might be better on her own than with Raj Patel, a Bengali-Okie-Virgin, who's only been a man long enough to smoke nineteen cigarettes.

I spit the twentieth Marlboro on the ground. I holster the pistol. I shine my pinky ring on my pants, and pull my Zippo lighter out.

"Raj. . ."

The sound of a Zippo opening isn't as loud as a pistol shot, but it fills up the air around the gasoline truck. I roll the steel wheel with my thumb and catch the wick on fire. I hold it in above my head for a moment the same way the Statue of Liberty holds her torch.

"Think about this for a minute, Raj."

I toss the Zippo into the gasoline that's pooling around the tank truck. Mary bounces up and down to remind me that we're flammable. I take a step backward, then another, but the Bubbas stand perfectly still. So does Colonel, because they see the almost invisible blue layer of flame that floats knee level for a little while before it lights up the air like a camera flash.

They stand there as I walk away with Mary on my back, watching us get smaller while their lives are sucked into a ball of flame that gathers over the truck and lifts into the sky.

"Quick." Mary's vocabulary comes back as the Central Headquarters Building catches fire.

"*Very* quick. All the really important things happen in an instant."

BOUNCE

RAJ TOLD MARY, "GOT TO get worse before I get better. Got to hit the bottom before I bounce back." Then he sat down in his chair and didn't get up again.

That was two days ago—three, if midnight has come and gone. Mary can't keep track of hours in the dark so she counts her heartbeats and wonders what she'll do if Raj dies.

She tries to slide into a dream where Raj's fever goes away and they both live happily ever after, the way people do in stories about the olden days. Everybody had a last name back then, and a birthday you could circle on the calendar, and parents. They had friends who talked to each other just for fun— taking turns, not interrupting, using inside voices. Like the voices in the living room that are probably part of a dream trying to break into her sleepless night.

In the olden days there were electric lights. You could turn them on with a flick of a finger. Darkness vanished in an instant. The way Raj said his fever would vanish in a day or two or three. After he hit bottom.

But electricity is gone forever, and the fever might be here to stay and the words in the living room are getting louder but still aren't clear enough to understand. First, there's Raj's dad-voice, the one he saves for giving orders like, "Don't go outside after dark, even to look for your favorite cat."

The second voice is full of tears, like Mary's, when she talks about all the things that disappeared before she learned how to remember—her mother, her father, towns where people lived instead of ghosts.

The first voice asks questions. The second answers. Raj, and someone who is not Raj, even though there's nobody else in the whole world.

No one living, anyway.

When footsteps fall between the words, Mary knows she'll have to investigate, because Raj is too weak to leave his chair except for bathroom visits. Unless the fever made him strong again, the way fevers sometimes do.

Maybe a ghost is here to fetch him off to where everybody goes after they're through with living. Where everybody in the world already went, except for Raj and Mary.

"Not yet, please." She runs the words through her lips without any noise behind them. That's all you need when you're asking ghosts for favors. Some ghosts are friendly, some are not. It's all in the diary she found under a loose board in the closet floor—hidden below all the clothes that fit perfectly since her growth spurt.

The diary tells her everything Raj can't—what it's like to get your first period or how to keep your boyfriend happy.

Boyfriends—one more thing that doesn't happen anymore.

The diary-girl didn't have a name, just the letter, *M*, signed under every entry in red ink. Red is the color of the most important diary-things, like how *M* felt when a boy kissed her. Like how boys did everything *M* said because she was so pretty.

Mary is pretty, too. Pretty enough to write in bright red ink, *"I am very pretty,"* if she had a diary.

One side of her face is exactly like the other. Her lips are a perfect cupid's bow. Her hair is glossy black with streaks of gold like people used to pay hairstylists to put in. Blue eyes, long eyelashes, straight teeth, and tall. Tall enough to be fourteen—at least. When her breasts come in she'll be a real hottie, just like *M*. It's good to have an older girlfriend, even if she is a ghost.

"My best friend who never knew me." Mary says that out loud, so *M* will know she really means it. Her fingers tingle when she rubs the letters pressed into the cover of the diary hidden underneath her pillow. Cimarron Girls, embossed in gold. Even Raj doesn't know exactly what that means. And Raj knows almost everything.

He says ghosts are something people made up to pass the time, like the ghost of Christmas Present, or *The Legend of Sleepy Hollow*. But The Cimarron Girls are definitely real. At night, Mary hears them moving through the cabin. Their footsteps and voices blend with noises the cabin makes as it settles into the Arbuckle Mountains. Sometimes the Cimarron Girls show her things with bumps and thumps, like the key to the cellar taped to the back of a picture that fell off the wall and shattered. The Cimarron Girls can whisper if they have to tell you something so important random noises aren't enough. And there's the diary.

—

MARY CAN'T UNDERSTAND WHAT RAJ is saying, but she knows it is a question because the sentence floats up toward the end.

The quiet voice answers too softly to tell if it belongs to a man or a woman. A dead man or a dead woman? She has to know.

Her feet remember every square inch of the hardwood floor. The planks are worn into familiar patterns by her footsteps and Raj's—the million-zillion footsteps since he saved her life when she was too young to remember anything but fear.

A million-zillion and one footsteps, a million-zillion and two. Turn to the left and the yellow kerosene lantern light shows her the rest of the way.

Raj paces in figure eights sputtering words that stick together like the vowels are magnetized. One slur runs into another. He keeps on talking when his breath is all used up. Keeps on talking while he's breathing in. His backward words are filled with whistles, punctuated by slurps. The cats have formed a circle around Raj, hiding under furniture in case ghosts are real. They turn some of their attention Mary's way, trying to decide if it's safer to stay inside or take their chances with coyotes. The kerosene lantern sputters on the mantle beside the pictures of the women who built the cabin. Their eyes flicker with the flame and follow Raj's progress.

He shouts, "Cimarron Girls," as clear and sharp as a thunderclap. The way he finishes stories with surprise endings.

Cats streak across the room in too many directions to follow. They disappear, like the legendary Cimarron Girls who collected everything they needed to survive and left it all for Raj and Mary. And then evaporated, like cats who stay outside too long.

Raj picks up a framed photograph of two older women and a girl who looks like Mary posed underneath a cottonwood tree.

"Who took the photograph?" Raj's eyes find her, but they dance away.

His breathing slows. So do his words. Raj's skin looks yellow in the lantern light, as yellow as a burning wick that's almost out of fuel. His black hair is plastered against his head with sweat. A trickle of blood has dried in a crease at the corner of his lip.

"Someone always takes the photograph." The sentence forms on a stream of air pulled backwards through his lips by lungs that are as empty as the world.

Raj drops the picture a second before his knees fold and lower him onto fragments of non-reflective glass.

"Can't fix things anymore," Raj says. "Broken things stay broken."

He's too heavy for her to carry, so she slides a cushion under his head. She brings him a glass of water and gives him one of the Augmentin tablets the Cimarron Girls left behind. There aren't many, but maybe there are enough to make Raj bounce.

—

THE SUN CLIMBS HIGH ENOUGH to shine into the living room window and cover Raj with a rectangle of yellow light. He sits up part way and drinks chicken noodle soup from a giant coffee cup with the word Halliburton printed on the side.

"Chicken soup and sunlight." Mary smiles, but she can't hold it very long, because even though Raj is better he still looks pretty bad.

"I'll have to use the bathroom soon," he says.

It's already too late, but Mary pretends she hasn't noticed.

"Bad night." She puts another Augmentin tablet in his mouth and watches him struggle to get it down. The ghosts talked with Raj off and on till dawn. Whatever they told him made his fever break. It had to be the ghosts because it takes three days for antibiotics to do anything.

"Eight hundred seventy-five milligrams," she says. "Sounds like a lot, but some of the milligrams are expired."

One of the nameless cats climbs onto Raj's belly and gives him a special happy paws massage.

"You never see cats die," he says. "They go outside. They find a secret place. They evaporate." The cat doesn't mind the smell of urine, or the talk of cats evaporating, or the way Raj's fingers tremble when he strokes her behind the ears.

M says there are pharmacies in Ardmore full of miracle drugs put up on shelves where they last for years. Mary shows Raj the page where *M* wrote this in black longhand letters as loopy and symmetrical as petals on a daisy.

"It's been years already." Raj makes a face like his soup has turned to vinegar.

"*M* wouldn't mention it unless it was important." But *M* wrote the message in black, the color of maybe, the color of doubts in the middle of the night. Only her signature is red.

The cat on Raj's chest opens her eyes. The fur along her spine stands up, like there's a coyote at the door. She leaps away and disappears into a secret cat-place.

"I have to. . . ." Raj's eyes wander in different directions, like a pair of spiders stalking the same butterfly. He blows a stream of air in her face that smells like rotten apples.

"Tell you. . . ." His voice squeaks like a rusty hinge. His head tips back and smashes against the cushions. His arms reach into space while his legs curl in a knot, like an insect dropped onto a burning log.

She tries to hold him, but Raj's body clenches into spasms that shake the room. Just when she thinks the seizure will never stop, it does.

Raj's head droops back. His mouth falls open. Respiratory arrest. Mary read about it in a Red Cross manual the Cimarron Girls left in the cabin in case of emergency—like now.

"Are you okay?"

She shakes him but it does no good.

"Call 911!" Those are the magic numbers in the Red Cross book.

She sweeps Raj's mouth with her fingers, tips his head. She locks her lips over his. The rotten apple taste is almost enough to make her pull away, but not before she fills his lungs with air. She can't remember what comes next, but Raj coughs and sits up.

"Better." The blue in Raj's lips turns scarlet. He stands up on his own, touches the urine stain on his pants. "Got to take a bath."

"Plenty of water in the roof tank," she says. "Do you want me to start a fire and boil some?"

"Cold is good." Raj rubs cramps out of his arms and legs, smiles and stretches. "We'll talk when I come out." His breathing is regular. His voice is strong. "About things I haven't told you." Strong and straight, like the old Raj, who carried Mary on his shoulders when she was young and fussy and too tired to walk.

M says people sometimes get stronger just before they die. That's near the end of the diary, where everything is written in red.

When Mary hears the water running, she counts the Augmentin tablets. Not nearly enough. She tears a blank page out of *M*'s diary and leaves a note for Raj to read when he's clean enough to tell her what she needs to know.

"Gone for antibiotics." She shapes the bright red letters exactly like *M*'s. At the bottom of the note she writes, *"Love Always, Mary."*

—

A GIRL CAN FIT EVERYTHING she needs for Ardmore in a backpack—a compass, a canteen full of water, three days' supply of food, and her best friend's diary. Mary tucks a pistol into the waistband of her M-jeans that fit perfectly. The pistol is a six-shot revolver with a mirror finish and a bone grip. Perfect for scaring away coyotes. There are millions of them now that people are gone. They like to eat cats more than anything.

She doesn't know how many cats will follow her. How many will evaporate before she reaches Ardmore? If the coyotes come around more than six times, the cats are out of luck.

She's a long way from the cabin by the time Raj tries to call her back. Too far to see him stand in the doorway and cup his hands around his mouth so his words will be loud enough to make it through the trees.

"Maaa—rry!" He stretches her name into two long syllables that sound like the beginning of a song.

She puts her fingers in her ears so she won't have to listen. She's disobeying him for his own good, after all, the way heroines do in books the Cimarron Girls left behind—*The Golden Compass, Ella Enchanted, Twilight.* The books Raj taught her to read.

His rotten apple taste is still on her tongue. Strong and fermented, like the jugs of cider in the cellar that make your head spin if you drink too much. She clears her throat and spits on the forest floor. That makes the cats disappear, but after a few minutes they return.

So do the rotten apples.

The Arbuckle Mountains are full of streams and house-size rocks, so it's impossible to walk in a straight line. She remembers the double-rutted path that used to connect the cabin to the outside world, but it is full of trees now, and underbrush and poison ivy. Raj says that is nature's way of hiding them from bad things.

Maybe he'll tell her more about bad things when she comes back with the antibiotics. Ardmore's only one day's walk down I-35, the concrete ribbon that connects old time cities like beads on a string—San Antonio, Dallas, Oklahoma City, Kansas City.

Walking through the trees is difficult when you have an actual destination. Thorn bushes, drop-offs, and walls of stone make her change directions every few minutes. Strange noises in the undergrowth set her nerves on edge, especially when the cats explode in all directions.

Leaf shadows look like jumbled faces on the rocks and dirt, moving their lips as if they're whispering, "She'll never find her way to Ardmore."

Mary touches the bone handle of her six-shooter.

"You guys aren't real," she says to nobody. The cats come closer to the sound of her voice. They don't know about pistols but they know about faces in the shadows.

M says you can whistle ghosts away. That's near the end of the diary after *M* had lots of ghost experience. Mary tries to whistle but her lips are too nervous to make the right shape. She licks them and starts over, but the taste of rotten apples gets stronger and she has to give it up. Her temples throb—not a headache exactly— and her throat feels dry and sticky.

One of the cats rubs against her legs, gives her a reason to be brave. She sings a song about cats and girls walking through the woods to Ardmore. Her voice turns rough and smoky, like the villains in the bedtime stories Raj used to tell her. Her song pulls the cats close enough to count. Six, the same number as the bullets in her pistol.

By the time she runs out of words that rhyme, the leaf faces disappear into bigger shadows. Maybe that's because of the song, but it's probably because clouds are building up in the southwest.

In the olden days people listened to weather reports on radios in their cars. The weather reports are gone but the weather is still here.

So are the cars. Lots of them. Abandoned on I-35 according to *M*. Broken, like almost everything in the world, but they'd still keep out the rain, and only a few will have skeletons inside.

She crosses herself the way Raj says Catholics used to do. It might not help, but it certainly won't hurt. The wind stops turning tree leaves upside down.

A beam of sunlight as straight and shiny as a butter knife breaks through the clouds and she sees I-35 for the first time since she was three years old.

She picks up a large, round stone, as big as a ripe apple, because there's a pack of coyotes—more than she has bullets for—clustered inside a knot of rusty cars.

Eating something.

She throws her rock without aiming. It bounces off a rusty black car and lands in the coyote pack. They look at her, deciding whether to be afraid.

"Go away!" Her voice sounds small and weak and it's pushed out of her mouth by the most powerful rotten apple stench so far. She spits again and draws her pistol the way Raj says cowboys used to do. She's never fired a shot because once all the bullets in the world are gone there won't be any more.

The coyotes form a wall, with the boss coyote in front. He's bigger than the rest, with the best fur and a look in his eyes that means he's smart. The shiny pistol glitters in the beam of sunlight that falls on Mary like old time spotlights used to do with actors on a stage.

She pulls back the hammer on her pistol so the coyotes will understand something is up. Something deadly, so they'd better back off and let the last girl in the world and her cats go in peace.

The big male coyote takes a few jittery steps away. He makes a sound halfway between a growl and a song, then trots into the woods on the opposite side of the highway, away from Mary and her cats and her pistol. All the others follow him.

Except for one.

That coyote is hungrier than the rest. She looks at Mary with big brown girl-coyote eyes and goes back to eating whatever died among the cars on I-35.

Raj says things used to die here all the time, armadillos and rabbits and white tail deer, run down by cars going so fast they didn't even try to stop, but these cars haven't killed anything for years.

Mary circles the hungry girl-coyote, instead of walking down the road toward Ardmore, because the pistol is full of warm, reassuring power that moves from the bone grip into her hand, clear up to her shoulder, which was aching a minute ago but now feels strong.

She swallows saliva that is thicker than it should be, and tastes more like rotten apples than ever, but she doesn't spit, because that might make the girl-coyote think she's weak.

And Mary is *not* weak. She has a pistol in her hand and it would be only the slightest inconvenience to kill this coyote. Revenge for all the cats it might have eaten. Prevention for the cats it hasn't eaten yet.

What is the coyote eating now? A few more steps will tell her. The pistol leads the way. The trigger feels soft and flexible, ready to be squeezed into action, ready to show her what it means to be the top link of the food chain.

Until she sees the coyote's meal.

A man's face looks at her out of a mask of bloody meat. His belly is ripped open. Ribs are broken. An empty corpse without organs but with enough meat left on his bones to prove he used to be a man.

Someone who didn't die in the olden days, like Raj said everybody did.

"Things I haven't told you." Things Raj would have told her if she'd waited.

How did this man die? Why didn't he die a long time ago? Why doesn't someone stop this coyote from eating what's left of him? Someone besides Mary.

Thunder rumbles in the distance. The beam of light that looked so promising a moment ago is gone, replaced by darkness turning black in the southwest and green directly overhead, almost the color of blood drying over pale dead skin.

"Get away!" She waves the gun in case the coyote hasn't noticed it yet. She tries to pull the hammer back a little more, but it's as far as it will go. The firing pin is sharp and ready to strike.

"I'll do it!"

She squeezes the trigger a tiny bit to prove to herself she can still control her fingers. Her pulse throbs in her temples. Her thoughts run in circles. She realizes she's not breathing.

She releases a rotten apple breath and replaces it with air that smells like meat that's only fit for coyote food.

"*Shoo!*" She's never said that word before, but it's exactly the right way to describe a coyote's last chance before Mary fires her first bullet ever.

"*Shoo!*" She almost can't hear that word above the thunderclap that comes without a lightning flash. The pistol jumps in her hand. Hot sparks touch her face. The smell of burned matches fills the air. The girl-coyote falls beside the dead man, who doesn't look nearly as important now as the animal Mary's killed.

Not quite. The girl coyote tries to run away, but her back legs fold like Raj's did. She drags them through a pool of blood then rolls onto her side so Mary can see the coyote's ribcage move, trying to take in enough air to make up for the blood she's lost.

Pregnant!

Why didn't Mary see that before? Almost full term. Raj told her how all that works, even though she doesn't really need to know. Wishes she didn't know about the babies waiting to get out but won't now.

Everything dies exactly the same way, hanging on no matter how it hurts. The coyote's breathing is louder than the thunder. Mary kneels beside her.

"Sorry." She reaches out to stroke the dying animal, but the coyote still has enough strength to show her teeth.

How long does it take for a wounded animal to die? Mary looks at the pistol. Maybe she should finish it. Definitely she should finish it, but her finger won't go around the trigger again.

A new sound competes with the throbbing in her head. A little like a heartbeat. A little like drumsticks on a hardwood floor.

She recognizes the sound from descriptions in *M*'s diary, from sound effects Raj does when he tells cowboy stories. Horse hooves on a solid surface. A horse walking Mary's way up I-35 where horses were never meant to go. She's already on her knees, so it's an easy matter to lie flat—to roll underneath a car and wait until the danger passes. When there's a dying coyote lying beside a dead man on a dead highway clotted with dead automobiles from the olden times, it's better safe than sorry.

She sees the horse and rider from underneath the bumper. Appaloosa—that's what they call horses marked with red and white splotches. And the rider is an Indian.

Native American. Raj told her all about them. How white people took away their land and force-marched them to Oklahoma. That was a long time ago but maybe they still hold a grudge.

This one has a rifle, and a cowboy hat with a feather in the band, and a look on his face that gives nothing away—except danger.

The horse stops beside the dying coyote. She's looking right at Mary now as if to say—there she is, brother. Under the car. Hidden like a dead girl's diary.

The coyote takes a breath so deep it expands her chest to its outer limit. She exhales a bloody mist that smells like popcorn. Her eyes glaze over, still full of blame.

Mary doesn't notice when the horse moves past. Too busy thinking about baby coyotes dying inside their mother. She doesn't realize she is crying until she feels a cat's tongue on her cheek.

Salt. That's why the cat wants her tears. Salt and chemicals that make people feel bad and cats feel good. All six cats join her. She has plenty of tears to go around.

The horse hooves circle the car four times and then move south toward Ardmore, where there are miracle drugs on shelves and other things Raj should have told her about. Like men on horseback.

"Listen to your heart," was *M*'s advice for when you see a guy for the first time. Mary's heart says, "Stay hidden!" in loud, clear, rapid thumps.

The cats purr like there is nothing wrong. Like there isn't a live man patrolling a dead highway. Like it isn't starting to rain, and streams of water aren't going to run underneath the car. Like the dead mother coyote doesn't have her eyes open, hoping to see Mary die on I-35.

A little stomach acid works its way into Mary's mouth. She spits it as far away as she can, but not toward the coyote.

The rain turns to hail for a couple of angry minutes, bouncing ice marbles off the dead man and the dead coyote. Then suddenly the storm is gone, leaving irregular balls of ice behind and a fresh, safe smell in the air.

Mary's headache drifts away with a gust of wind. Her stomach cramps turn into hunger pangs as she crawls out from under the car. Cats rub against her legs as she walks toward the trees, listening to her heart tell her—the forest is safer than the road.

Every step is trouble with six cats in the way, all wanting to be rubbed and fed at the same time.

"Plenty of food in Ardmore." She looks down the road in the direction of cat food and miracle drugs and wonders if she'll have to walk all the way in the forest.

The cats arch their backs and twitch their tails, like the biggest cat fight ever is about to happen and they don't know whether to pick a side or run. They all take off together, tumbling over each other, hissing at the air while they disappear into the trees.

What they're afraid of is behind them. Behind Mary. She turns slowly, as if whatever scared the cats won't be there until she sees it.

Nothing at first, just a jumble of dead cars rusting on the highway where their owners abandoned them in the olden days. A flock of starlings lands on the cars, looking for worms that have crawled onto the highway to keep from drowning. They perch on every car but one and shout insults at the world.

Every car but one. Mary sees it now. How could she have missed the Indian in the driver's seat, behind the steering wheel of the car the starlings have rejected? He tips his hat. He smiles, and she can see immediately he has a plan.

The kind of plan coyotes have for cats. The kind of plan the big bad wolf had for Little Red Riding Hood.

The kind of plan bad men have always had for girls like her.

Pretty girl. The words are in his smile. So are the things he wants to do with pretty girls. *M*'s diary doesn't describe those things and Mary doesn't know exactly what they are, but she doesn't want to know.

When the car door opens, she sprints toward the forest. She shouldn't look behind her, but she can't help herself. The bad man isn't running. Doesn't have to because he'll never stop. He'll keep on chasing her until she is too tired to run, until she falls, until she has to rest, because even though she's never seen a man like this before, Mary knows he won't give up until he gets what he is after.

Pretty girl.

She doesn't realize she's not running anymore until she sees those words take shape on the bad man's lips. And when she starts running again, her legs don't move as fast as they should, because somewhere inside her a decision has been reached—he'll get her in the end.

Branches snap and leaves rustle no matter where she puts her feet. One panicked step after another until she finds the perfect hiding place. The live oak straight ahead. Tall and rambling with lots of branches. Perfect for climbing. Perfect for hiding from a bad man with a wide-brimmed cowboy hat.

The treetop is full of leaves and branches dressed with Virginia creeper and mistletoe. It doesn't look high from the forest floor, but from the top it's different.

Dangerous-different.

Forked branches hold her like a crippled hand that might lose its grip any second. She presses her cheek against bark and prays the limbs will hide her. It has to be enough because there is nowhere left to run.

Birds abandon the live oak as if she is a feral cat on a search for dinner. The bubble of silence surrounds her hiding place like a bull's-eye on a target, but the quiet only lasts until she gets her breathing under control. Then the birds return, complaining about the intruder hiding in the branches from a killer on the ground.

He follows her as if he has a map. Indians can do that, at least in Raj's stories. Indians can talk to the trees and the grass in a silent language no one else understands.

He stops underneath her hiding-branch. He sniffs the air for the scent of a pretty girl whose breath smells like rotten apples.

She peeks around limbs that should be thick enough to hide her but aren't. The bad man has taken off his wide-brimmed hat. He smiles at her as if he sees her clearly through her leaves. He reaches up with a calloused right hand that she can feel even though it's twenty feet below her. A spirit touch, like ticks crawling on her skin, looking for a place to bite.

Images flash behind her eyes. Pictures she doesn't want to see. Things she shouldn't know about but suddenly does.

The man under the tree extends his hand another few inches, as if she is a ripe peach in an orchard from the olden days. When he flexes his fingers she can feel him pulling her toward him. A magical connection. Raj would say it's her imagination.

But it's real. As real as a dead coyote full of babies. As real as the pistol in the waistband of her *M* jeans that are suddenly too tight. She draws the pistol and the pants fit perfectly again. Mary feels the killing power in the pistol grip. She points the weapon at the bad man on the ground who's calling her without saying a word, who's pulling her out of the tree with the force of his desire.

He smiles and flexes his fingers, leaving the decision up to her. Whether he lives or dies. Whether she can kill a man—even a dangerous man—the way she killed a coyote who was only trying to keep her babies alive.

The weapon is heavy in her hand, almost enough to tip her out of the tree. She wraps both arms around the tree trunk, holds the pistol in both hands, and orders her finger to squeeze the trigger.

Now. She waits for the thunderclap, the feel of the pistol bucking in her hands, the smell of burned matches, the guilt. But those things don't happen. The bad man underneath her doesn't drag himself away leaving a blood trail behind. He smiles.

She slides the pistol back into her waistband. She stands on the branch of the live oak tree that wasn't big enough to hide her, pushes herself off from the trunk, and leaps onto a branch of the tree next door.

Every bird in that tree takes flight at once. Hundreds of wings send shockwaves through the air, as if the spirits of the forest are shouting, "Jump some more!"

Mary leaps from tree to tree, like a girl-size squirrel with a backpack and a pistol running from a predator who can kill with magic.

Faster than possible, until she has time to think. To realize things like this can't go on. Until she stops in a red cedar tree she knows is the perfect hiding place because a cat is there already. It's huddled against the tree, so full of fear that everything looks like a coyote.

After a few tender strokes the cat remembers. She purrs. She bumps her face against Mary's. Recoils a little at the rotten apple smell, but then goes at it again. Mary doesn't really think the bad man can hear a cat purring in a cedar tree, but she tries to shush her anyway.

The cat climbs onto the backpack and settles in. Mary edges around the sticky cedar branches looking to see if the danger is gone. No one could follow her through the trees, not even a Native American with magic tracking skills.

The branches are full of sap and needles. They bend but don't break, so Mary's descent is quiet. She steps onto the forest floor, with her cat passenger on her backpack ready to run. Ready to draw the pistol again, maybe even ready enough to pull the trigger this time—if the bad man is far enough away to give her time to draw, take aim and fire.

But he's not that far away. He stands just beyond the branches of the cedar tree, so quiet he hasn't scared the cat on her backpack until now.

Claws bury in her shoulder, piercing *M*'s shirt from L.L. Bean. The claws go deeper when the bad man takes a step closer, smiling the way a coyote smiles at an injured rabbit when he knows it will be over in a minute.

Cat claws keep her from freezing. They hurt too much to ignore, even if she might be hurting a lot more in a minute or two. When the bad man takes another step she knows what to do. She grips the cat by the loose skin on the knap of her neck—the way a mother cat carries her kittens. The cat remembers and lets go.

She flings the cat in the bad man's face, like a mother cat would never do. The claws come out again. They take hold of the first thing they find. While they scratch the smile off of the bad man's face Mary runs back toward the highway.

Toward the rusty cars. Toward the dead coyote and the dead man. No destination but away, until she sees the Appaloosa.

The horse is easy to untie. It's easy to get into the saddle. Not so easy to make him go.

"Geddiyup!" Isn't that what you say? Mary kicks her heels against the horse's sides. She smacks it on the rump, once, twice. Hard enough to hurt her hand. The bad man is out of the forest now, twenty feet in front of her. Cat scratches haven't changed his plans.

She pulls her pistol. Lines the bad man up in front of the sights. Closes her eyes so she won't have the image of a murder in her mind.

Now she squeezes, slow and sure, even if she can't see, even if she's almost sure to miss.

Gunshots are always a surprise. The pistol jumps. Hot particles sting her shooting hand. The Appaloosa lunges forward. Almost too fast to hold on. Way too fast for the bad man to get out of the way.

The pistol clatters to the ground behind her as she grabs hold of the saddle horn and presses her knees against the horse. There's no stopping him. No steering either. Just leaning against the horse's neck. Holding on and looking backward over the horse's rump. Mary didn't feel anything when the Appaloosa ran the bad man down, but there he is, lying on I-35 beside her mirror-finish pistol. Getting smaller and less dangerous every bouncing second.

—

MARY'S STOMACH CLENCHES LIKE A FIST. Nothing inside her but more rotten apples. Her eyes ache with tears that are stuck just below the surface. Lots of bouncing on the back of an Appaloosa that won't stop even when she says, *"Whoa!"*

Maybe this horse only hears thought commands from bad men who track girls by magic. She wants to close her eyes but it's even scarier to be on the back of a wild horse in the dark.

Her legs burn from trying to stretch all the way around the horse. Her arms ache from trying to hold onto the saddle horn. Her brain hurts from trying to erase images she picked up from the bad man, but the images hang on like burs in cat fur. She'll pick them out later one at a time after she's made it to Ardmore and found enough Augmentin to save Raj's life.

If the Appaloosa doesn't run forever. If the bad man doesn't catch her.

Will he track her all the way back to the cabin now that he has her scent? Will Raj be able to save her? Is Raj still alive?

The throbbing in her head synchronizes with the Appaloosa's gallop. In the olden days men raced horses this way. Ran them around tracks for. . .

How long?

One mile. Two miles. She sits up in the saddle like the cowboys used to do. Her knees clamp against the Appaloosa's sides like a vice—so tight it sends a splitting pain to the middle of her belly. Her head throbs in rhythm with the galloping horse so perfectly she will never fall off.

Never, ever. Even though the Appaloosa has run so far and so fast his body is covered with sweat slick as olive oil. Foam gathers around his mouth and flies into her face like snow. Colored snow, tinged in blood. The horse runs so fast it makes everything else in the world slow down—the pulsing in Mary's head, the seconds that used to last exactly long enough to say, *"One Mississippi."*

Slower and slower, like someone pulled a cosmic emergency brake. Everything slows down and stops, as if time catches on a snag.

Everything stops but Mary. She flies over the Appaloosa's head, defying gravity, the way she does in dreams sometimes.

Ballistics. The word comes to her all at once as I-35 rises up to smack her so hard it doesn't hurt. She bounces. You have to hit the bottom before you bounce like that.

She flips, bounces again, and lands on her feet, like an olden days girl gymnast doing a gold medal floor exercise.

A girl's voice tells her, *"Don't look behind you,"* but she looks anyway. The Appaloosa lies dying on I-35. No cars or bad men anywhere around, but there are coyotes. There are always coyotes.

The girl's voice says, *"The horse is not your fault."* Mary knows it's *M*, because the words are accompanied by bright red looping subtitles written on the backs of her eyelids. *M* talks to Mary the only way ghosts can talk to people. Using Mary's lips. Using air pulled in backwards by Mary's empty lungs. The way ghosts talked to Raj as he was getting worse before he could get better.

Inhaling deeply hurts almost as much as the throbbing in her head. A slow burn spreads from her face to her shoulders, running down like a stream of blood pulled by the force of gravity.

She wipes moisture from her face. Not blood. Not the trail an animal leaves behind when she goes looking for her dying place. Mary's face is dripping sweat, like the Appaloosa before he fell.

M says, *"Horses and people fall at exactly the same rate. So does civilization, but you can't worry about things like that."*

Mary has other worries, like Raj's fever. Like his conversation with ghosts, the rotten apples on his breath, his seizure. Fevers kill you. Fevers are contagious.

"Augmentin fixes everything. Keep walking." M gives Mary a gentle push in Ardmore's direction. *"Not much farther now. The bad man is following, but you have a good head start."*

"Best friends forever," Mary says.

"Fever friends." M gives her another gentle push and sings a song about bridges over troubled waters. The kind a mother might have sung to her baby in the olden days.

—

LIVES ARE ONLY A LITTLE LIKE the books left in the cabin by the Cimarron Girls. The end is never satisfying. How can Mary die with pastel colors cutting through her head like kitchen knives with loose handles and chipped blades? How can things go bad so fast after she escaped from the big bad wolf? After she walked all the way from a dead Appaloosa to a dead town?

Maybe Ardmore would look better if her eyes weren't filled with ground glass and blurry images. If her head didn't throb, and her ears didn't ring, and a ghost wasn't prodding her along.

"Fever friend," M tells her. *"Walk around the cars. Stay in the middle of the street. Feral dogs own everything now."*

M makes perfect sense, or she would make perfect sense if she weren't dead. A figment of Mary's imagination like Santa Claus, and the Easter Bunny, and boys who bring you corsages and take you to the prom.

Are there any boys left in the world, except for bad ones who want to kill you? Mary has a lot of questions but her tongue has turned to cotton and there are lumps of concentrated pain in her throat that would make it hard to swallow if she had any saliva.

She finds her reflection in a store window the looters overlooked back in the olden days when they tore Ardmore apart. She's still pretty in a used up, dying sort of way. She tries to smile but can't get it exactly right, and she doesn't want to smile when she sees the reflection of people and cars in an orderly city all around her.

When she turns around to check it out, everything is gone. Ardmore is rusted hulks of cars and burned out buildings and scattered bones that used to be people. Augmentin won't fix that, but maybe it will make her fever go away, and maybe it will save Raj's life.

The ringing in her ears turns into voices. *"Not so bad. Not so bad to be a ghost."*

"Whistle them away." M nudges her around a corner toward a Walgreens that advertises twenty-four hour service on a rusty sign over the door.

She can't whistle, but the effort makes the voices stop. The pastel colors intensify into primaries that change with every passing second.

One one-thousand, two one-thousand. This is what it's like to die.

M shoves her into the store, past the skeletal remains of looters, past the sounds of animals rustling through the aisles, until she can't walk another step. She sits on the floor in the back of a twenty-four hour Walgreens that stays open, true to its pledge, even after the world has come to an end.

She closes her eyes and when she opens them again a bottle of water is in one hand. A bottle of pills is in the other.

Augmentin.

Does it really fix everything like they say? How many of the 875 milligrams are still working? She swallows two just in case and waits to see what happens after intermission.

—

THERE'S A WET SPOT BETWEEN MARY'S legs. Her eyes won't open right away—stuck closed with a glue that feels like sticky sand when she rubs it. Her skin burns every place it's touched by clothing, or grime, or even a stray breeze, but the ringing in her ears is gone.

So are the voices and the colors.

M is still around, prodding her to wake up. *"Take another Augmentin."*

Everybody knows it takes three days for antibiotics to work, but she feels better. She remembers things from the olden days. Her mother, her father, an RV trip to see dinosaur footprints.

And things from yesterday. Was it yesterday when she killed a mother coyote and a horse and threw a cat into a bad man's face and saw a city full of ghosts in the reflection of the last unbroken window in Ardmore?

Take another Augmentin. Sometimes you get better right before you die."

So many ways to die. She swallows the pill and thinks about how far it is back to the cabin where there is running water, and clean clothes, and Raj.

Rats poke their twitching noses out of dark places under shelves and sample the air to see if she is weak enough to eat.

Not yet. Maybe never. Augmentin fixes everything. She is almost strong enough to stand on her own now, to walk away from the smell of sweat and urine and a fever that has almost burned itself out.

A flash of heat and a chill reminds her the antibiotics have only started.

Another flash of heat accompanied by the sound of footsteps in the front of the store. So many ways to die. Ways much worse than fevers.

Rats scatter when the bad man finds her.

He tips his hat to her, polite to the very end. He doesn't hate her any more than a hunter hates the animals he kills. He needs her. Has to have a girl like her every now and then and there are so few. Surely she understands.

He tells her everything about himself with a twitch of his lips, a tilt of his head, a subtle shift in posture. No point in talking, because there is no one left to listen—except Mary, and she won't be around for long.

M says, *"Men like this want a certain kind of girl—young, powerless, afraid."*

Filth and foul odors won't matter if he's hungry, and Mary knows he's hungry. The bad man's eyes sample her body through her clothes. He's not worried about the fever that is coming back so fast it's making the world spin into nausea. He's not worried about the taste of rotten apples coming up in hot surges. He doesn't hear the ringing in her ears, or *M* telling her things are about to happen really fast. She's about to get a present from her fever friend.

The bad man kneels beside her, puts his hand where her breasts have barely gotten started. He leans in close, as if he's about to tell her something she has to hear before she dies.

"Now!" M shouts.

Bright red letters explode though Mary's mind retelling every passage in *M*'s diary. There's a shriek from the back of her throat, filling the world with rotten apple mist. Her arms and legs and head and body thrash and flail like a marionette in an earthquake.

For a few ticks of the cosmic clock she isn't there—but then she's back. Looking into the wide eyes of a bad man who's seen his first seizure. He wants to step back, but his mind is running in a circle trying to figure out what happens next.

"Let me help you make up your mind." She puts her arms around the killer and kisses him on the lips. A French kiss. The kind of kiss *M*'s diary said would drive men wild. Lots of tongue and her salivary glands are working again. Hot and deadly, because Augmentin hasn't had time to fix everything.

The killer pushes her away. Backs out of the room where the miracle drugs are stacked safe and dry on shelves.

"It won't take long," she tells him. "Better start looking for your dying place." Then all she can hear are his footsteps running off to join the ghosts of Ardmore.

"Take another Augmentin," M tells her.

And Mary does. She always listens to her fever friend.

—

M ISN'T TALKING ANYMORE, BUT she hasn't gone away. She never will, not completely, now that Mary got as bad as she could get and then got better.

"Is it too late for Raj?" She knows M isn't real enough to answer. Ghosts don't talk to you unless you're dying. But she talks to M, anyway, because there's nobody else. Not even one of the six cats who followed her as far as I-35, but couldn't run as fast as a wild horse.

So many cats have disappeared since Raj brought her to the Cimarron Girls' cabin. They evaporate, like puddles of water you can't find anymore. You don't have to cry for evaporated cats because they might come back. The way she is coming back to the cabin with a backpack full of Augmentin and a 9mm Glock looted from the glove compartment of an abandoned car, and a magazine full of bullets. Enough to kill ten coyotes. Enough to kill ten bad men that Raj never told her about.

She weaves through the trees stepping on rocks and bare stretches of dirt, almost floating above the forest floor. Without leaving tracks. Quiet enough to sneak up on a ghost.

Mary circles the cabin, because she's careful now. She heard voices deep in the woods not ten miles away. Male voices—maybe something left over from the fever, but they sounded real enough. Loud and cheerful. Young men making too much noise because no one's tried to kill them yet. She will check that out after she makes Raj well again. After she saves him the way he saved her when the olden days came to an end and not quite everybody died.

Three cats run out of the cabin when she opens the front door.

"Raj!" She can feel the emptiness inside. Nothing here except the space left behind by the three frightened cats.

"Anybody home?" Raj's impression remains in his chair. His Halliburton coffee cup sits on the floor, a crust of chicken soup dried at the bottom.

She sits in the chair hoping to feel warmth, but that evaporated along with the chicken soup and Raj. She waits for tears, but they don't come, because you can't cry for a cat that might come back.

And if Raj doesn't come back, what then?

"I'll bounce," Mary removes the 9mm Glock from her waistband and sets it on the floor beside the Halliburton cup.

"Got to hit bottom before you bounce."

CROSSING

WHO'D HAVE THOUGHT THERE'D BE so many wrecked cars on the Oklahoma River Bridge? Rusted out hulks, left over from the riots when people didn't know which way to run. Mary makes the sign of the cross, the way old time Catholics did when things might go terribly wrong.

"In the name of the Father and the Son and the Holy Ghost." She synchronizes the words with the motion of her hand—exactly like Raj showed her before he went away.

It feels good to be in control of something, even if the something is a ritual from the olden times. There'll be so many things she can't control when she starts across the bridge. Every wreck is a hiding place for something deadly—a wild dog, a coyote, a man left over from the olden times.

A bad man. Is there any other kind, now that Raj is gone? She crosses herself one more time, sucking up to God just in case he's real. She whispers a silent prayer that there are men like Raj on the other side of the bridge. Exactly like him, only less dad-like. Men the right age for her. Good looking men who aren't solitary killers or members of misogynist boy-gangs who give a whole new meaning to the idea of one-night stands.

Misogynist. She likes to say that word. It sounds smart—college educated, sophisticated. It's a library word. There'll be libraries in Oklahoma City. There'll be bullets too, and maybe something special, like the 9mm Glock she found in Ardmore, or the switchblade knife she found in Seminole. Everything in the world is finders-keepers now.

"Mis-o-gyn-ist." Mary stretches that word into a whole conversation. Works so hard on pronunciation that she almost doesn't see the flicker of movement beside the overturned UPS truck halfway across the bridge.

A man's shoulder moves beyond the rusty brown truck as slow and steady as the sun edging from behind the moon at the end of a total eclipse. Careful, like a new cat introducing herself into a household full of cats that doesn't really need one more. Quiet as a ghost. Raj said there's no such thing as ghosts but she's not so sure. There are ghost-books in the libraries. That's proof, isn't it? Maybe she even saw a couple of ghosts when she was sick to the point of death before Raj went away forever.

Instead of drawing her 9mm, Mary whistles "Bridge Over Troubled Waters" because everybody knows ghosts can't stand whistling. She doesn't get the tune quite right and the apparition beside the UPS truck keeps on being there. But he doesn't charge her, and pointing a gun at him doesn't seem like the thing to do.

She changes her tune to "Happy Birthday." Whistles it twice, which is exactly the right amount of time to wash your hands according to Raj. The ghost is still there, looking less ghostly by the second. Spirits don't have dirty blond dreadlocks or bad teeth. His eyes start out polite but that fades into a creepy glint like Raj got sometimes when he looked at pictures in the magazines he didn't think she knew about.

Not creepy enough to shoot—not yet, anyway—but this guy definitely isn't the ghost of some long dead riot victim whose bones have been carried away by wild dogs. He's very much alive. Alive and dirty.

Mary wraps her fingers around the grip of her 9mm, but she doesn't engage her trigger finger yet, because Glocks don't have a safety and it's stuck in the waistband of her pants and she can draw and fire really fast if it comes to that. She walks toward the man like she isn't afraid at all, the way cowgirls did in the Wild West stories Raj used to tell her. Like Calamity Jane, and Belle Starr, and Annie Oakley. Mary has the attitude if not the marksmanship, and the man beside the UPS truck doesn't know about her pathetic shooting skills.

Two more steps and she's close enough to see the pimples on his skin. The rotten places in his front teeth where he hasn't brushed since the world came to an end.

His tongue slides over his lips, like a snake sampling the air for Mary molecules. Not quite dangerous enough to shoot, but maybe dangerous enough to show him her pistol.

Two more steps, then she will be close enough to put a bullet into him even if she shuts her eyes at the exact moment she pulls the trigger. But by the time she's ready it's already one step too late. He pulls a coal black revolver with an exceptionally large barrel from behind him and points it at her chest.

"Pardon me, miss."

A polite killer. Mary freezes like she used to do when she and Raj played German Spotlight. When there were still batteries and flashlights and she didn't know about all the bad men in the world who wanted to do things to her Raj wouldn't talk about.

The gunman's fingernails are caked in black grease, the kind a man gets from scratching his unwashed body while he thinks about all the nasty things he'd like to do with the last few girls in the world. She's not sure what this man wants to do with her, but she's very sure it won't be pleasant.

Less pleasant than a bullet at close range? Wait and see. Still plenty of time to die quickly if she can't escape. She has her secret ways. Ways she's read about in library books.

Plan A was her pistol, but she still has plan B ready to go—and this dirty, dreadlocked, bad-skinned boy hasn't got a clue.

The important thing is not letting fear paralyze her.

The important thing is being ready when the time is right.

The important thing is getting close enough—and Mary figures she'll be close enough before long. Getting close is what a man has in mind when he points a revolver at a girl and says, "Pardon me, miss."

"You sure are pretty." He keeps the pistol pointed at her chest but his eyes explore every part of her.

"Turn around."

She can feel his eyes on her back now, moving lower.

"Sure are pretty."

In a second he's taken her Glock. In two seconds he has her switchblade. He pats her down with his free hand as if she has weapons hidden in all the girl places he's been thinking about but hasn't gotten to touch for a very long time.

"What's your name, sweetheart?" He pokes her back with the barrel of his pistol. Nudges her across the bridge into the city full of ghosts on the other side.

Before she can answer, he sings a little snippet of a song about love and marijuana and racial harmony. A reggae song—Raj told her about those. It doesn't make sense, a song like that coming from a dirty white boy with a gun. She hears a kitchen match strike on a rusty car. Hears the gunman inhale deeply and hold it. Raj told her about smoking dope too, but she hadn't thought people still did it.

"My name is Mary." She works the words around the single-edged razor blade hidden under her tongue—plan B. She moves her hips a little more than usual so her captor won't notice the lisp. Would the dope make escape easier or harder?

"You can call me Bob." The gunman's voice is full of phlegm and smoke. "Just like Bob Marley—you know, the reggae king from the old days."

—

BOB THE GUNMAN KNOWS A LOT of reggae songs and he sings them all to Mary while he marches her through the city.

"To the garden of Eden," he tells her. "Used to be the old Oklahoma City Botanical Garden back in the day."

He isn't worried about dogs or ghosts or even feral men, because according to Bob, the Marleys have this part of Oklahoma City, "All sewed up." They have guns and tents and crops of the best dope in the world.

"Rolling papers is scarce. And matches. Girls is even scarcer." Every now and then Bob gets close enough to touch her. Usually that comes between songs, and she thinks maybe if she times it right, she can spit her plan B razor blade into her hand and swing around at exactly the right moment to change her captor's attitude about women.

"You sure are pretty." Bob keeps coming back to that and his touches are getting much more frequent. Mary figures it won't be too much longer until he confuses her passivity with compliance and decides to steal a kiss or two— and maybe a little more—before they get back to all the other Marley Men.

"Only six of us right now, so it shouldn't be too bad. And you can smoke all the weed you want to make things go easier." His voice goes up a notch when he talks about weed. "Aurora Indica's harvested and aged. Seeds came all the way from Afghanistan before the world went to hell."

According to Bob, the Marley Men have a good supply of dope of every description. "White Widow, Northern Lights, Hindu Kush, and my personal all-time favorite, Jack Horror. Good for headaches, toothaches, stomach aches, whatever aches there is. My you are a pretty girl." The gunman's mind is on a single track with three stops, drugs, reggae songs, and pretty girls.

"Want a hit?"

She stops at the sound of smoke being pulled into his lungs.

"Sure." She does a slow about face, brushes one hand over her breasts, which bounce in a way that's sure to please. She walks toward her captor the way slutty girls do in romance novels, and she's pleased to see it works just like the instructions say.

Bob has a mouth full of joint, and a mind full of Mary, and at that moment he believes she is totally blown away by his charm. He's not too sure what he should do with the pistol, because he's sure he's going to be enjoying his share of this pretty girl before any of the other Marley Men even get a taste.

Mary gives him a soul gaze, like the ones that usually come around page sixty in young adult romances. She's pleased to see Bob can't figure out how to smoke his joint and hold his pistol while he gropes her.

The air makes a little whistling sound as he breathes around the joint. His Adam's apple dances as he swallows his inhibitions. His eyes jerk back and forth as he sorts through all the nasty things he wants to do as soon as he figures out how to manage the pistol and the joint and her at the same time.

He puts the pistol in his waistband beside hers, even though it's pretty clear his pants will be coming off soon. It's a real dilemma until she takes a running step and kicks him in the testicles.

She stands in front of him watching him choke on the joint and double over. No point in using her plan B razor blade, but it sure would be nice to get her pistol back.

She kicks him again—a little refresher—and reaches for the pistol, but Bob is already bent over as much as he can go, so the kick doesn't do much good.

He grabs her by the wrist as she reaches for his waistband, hard enough to hold her—not for long, but long enough. He turns his body sideways so he can catch her future kicks on his legs. Bob isn't very smart. He doesn't know much about girls. Especially girls like Mary. She drives the heel of her free hand into his nose.

Once, twice, three times, until he lets go and lies sprawled on his back like a mangy dog that desperately wants its belly rubbed.

Her pistol has disappeared inside Bob's pants but his cowboy gun is clearly visible. No time to be choosey. Footsteps approach her from behind—two men, close but not as close as the revolver. She snatches it from Bob's waistband and points it in the general direction of the men. Dirty men with dreadlocks just like Bob's, stepping apart so they'll make a harder target. Five yards and closing. She cocks the hammer back, shuts her eyes, and points a few feet above the sound of running feet.

Click.

Mary recognizes the sound of a hammer falling onto an empty cylinder. Two more clicks and she has to face the facts. Bob took her prisoner with an empty gun.

The two Marleys point revolvers at her from a few feet away. Close enough for her to see bullets in the cylinders. Mary already knows the first thing one of them is going to say.

"Pardon me, Miss."

The other one says, "You sure are pretty," just like Mary thought he would.

"I'll bet you guys are Marley Men." She hardly lisps at all around her plan B razor blade.

—

THE THREE MARLEY MEN CARRY on a banter about Bob's testicles and how the pain won't go away until he takes the girl-cure.

Bob smiles at the jokes while he waddles and inhales clouds of Jack Horror smoke. He holds his hand up like an old time Boy Scout swearing to do his best to do his duty, only Bob is swearing to never let another girl get close enough to kick him.

"Not unless she's tied up proper."

Marijuana dulls the pain, but he walks so slowly that the sun is setting by the time they reach the Garden of Eden—at least two acres of cultivated marijuana growing among decorative grasses run wild and exotic trees in need of trimming.

They tie Mary's wrists in front so she'd be comfortable while she waits to die. The knots aren't very good—nobody knows how to tie them anymore—but they might hold her until sunrise. The Marleys start a fire with fresh books from the library so she'll be warm and well illuminated.

"Everything is kindling but the Bible and the Quran." Bob stands bow-legged in front of the fire and tosses in the remnants of civilization. "Anything that don't have God in the title."

Jack Horror makes it hard to stay angry, but Bob keeps his distance.

"This here's *Encyclopedia Britannica*." He holds a volume close enough for Mary to read *Compton's Encyclopedia* on the spine. She wonders how many religious books are thrown into the flames by mistake.

The Marleys are all white boys, except for a black man so thin he looks as if a sheet of brown rubber has been stretched over a skeleton. His legs and arms are bent in places that are supposed to be straight as if they'd been broken and allowed to heal without being set. His face is a mass of keloid scars that run in parallel lines across his cheeks and forehead. The injuries make him look powerful, even mystical. Mary tries to make the sign of the cross, but her bindings rob the ritual of its power.

"That's Stick Man," Bob holds a *World Atlas* beside his face, shielding his voice from the black man. "Don't look at him direct."

None of the white boys look at him direct. They glance Stick Man's way just long enough to make sure they aren't on intersecting paths. A quick check before they remember something important on the other side of the camp, as far away as possible.

The boys all wear their hair in dreadlocks. They greet each other with elaborate handshakes, and reggae dialect. Silly, dangerous white boys pretending to be Jamaicans—disorganized, moderately violent, and thoroughly high. Saint Robert Nesta Marley told them to smoke herb, stay in touch with Ja, and watch out for no good women, so they do.

Mary looks away from Stick Man as he searches her for weapons Bob might have missed. His twisted fingers are especially thorough around her breasts.

This is her first encounter with a real live African American. Was he injured in the troubles, after the electricity went off and everybody started going crazy? It's hard to guess the age of a man who looks more like an Egyptian artifact than a human being. He's forty at least. Maybe even older—fifty, sixty, seventy. Mary's only seen pictures of people that old in books like the ones the Marley Men throw in the fire.

Stick Man holds his arms out like wings as he limps in a circle with her at the center. His dreadlocks swing like snakes with every lurching step. A male, African American Medusa. She feels her face turning to stone.

"You gonna cry to me, yeah!" Stick Man follows those words with a string of sing-song lyrics that sort of rhyme and sort of have a tune. Probably one of the old reggae songs that used to be on iPods and radios before the world went down the drain. Maybe the skeletal brother is channeling Bob Marley.

The few words she understands make women sound pretty bad. Why not? Women have been causing trouble ever since Adam and Eve. Just ask the Christians and the Jews and the Muslims if there are any left. Just ask the boy gangs who use women up and toss them onto the fire like so many copies of *Encyclopedia Britannica*.

"Sorry for your troubles, sister." Stick Man tells her he's powerless against the will of Saint Robert Nesta Marley. She can button up her shirt any time she wants, but it's understood that everything will be ripped off for the sunrise ceremony.

"Ain't personal." Stick Man looks at a gold Rolex watch that flops around his wrist like a bangle. There are still plenty of watches in the world, but no batteries to run them. The wind-up kind would still keep time but nobody cares about hours and minutes any more.

"Men still got their needs." He stumbles. Leans like a balanced rock that's been perched at the top of a mountain for a thousand years and is just getting ready to fall. He lowers himself to his knees in front of her. Puts his face so close to hers his yellow teeth are all she sees.

"Killin' you afterward makes it pure." His breath smells like something inside him is dying.

The white boys stand outside of Stick Man's visual field discussing how they'll use Mary when their turns come around. It's understood the black man will go first.

"Ja don't want no more propagation." Stick Man uses the loudest outside voice she has ever heard. "Man done spoil't the world." When he raises both arms in supplication, he loses his balance. Still powerful, still dignified in spite of falling on his butt. "Everybody guilty." He raises the volume a little more to make up for his vulnerable seated position. "Women guiltiest of all."

The white dreadlocked boys light up their joints with looted butane lighters. There must be billions of those still in the world. There'd probably still be billions when the last man on earth murdered the last woman.

Once God wipes the slate clean, he'll start all over again. That's the Gospel according to Stick Man. Now that the Marleys have used up their own women, they hunt for the wild girls like Mary who live by their girl-wits without men or marijuana or rhyming poems written before the collapse.

She wants to tell Stick Man she's not given up on the world. Hasn't given up on men either—not entirely. But there's no reasoning with a man who wants to rape you and kill you afterward because that's what God told him to do.

She wants to tell Stick Man lots of things, but that would mean she has to talk, and that would mean she might reveal the secret hiding underneath her tongue. The secret that will set her free, so she can collect her guns and bullets and library books and however many years she might have left to live.

So she doesn't say anything, because she knows it won't do any good, and because it's hard to talk around a single-sided razor blade.

—

THE SUN ALWAYS LOOKS BRAND NEW in the morning, even though it's older than everything in the world. Older than Oklahoma City. Older than America. Older than the olden times when people built the botanical garden and never imagined it would belong to Marley Men.

Everybody's tired and stoned but Mary. No White Widow or Jack Horror for her. Too much to do when the sun shines through the tall empty buildings that used to be the pride of Oklahoma City and now are nesting habitats for eagles. Nothing lasts long in the cosmic scheme of things, not people, or politics, or the trappings of civilization. And most certainly not a girl like Mary, tied up and ready to take the blame for everything that went so wrong.

Stick Man checks his gold Rolex again. An old habit from the time when people used gears and batteries to count minutes. The sun still keeps perfect time, an unbreakable cosmic wristwatch. It measures every remaining second of her life with skyscraper shadows that stretch across the Garden of Eden like hangmen's ropes.

"Time to get the business done." Stick Man's accent was all Jamaican last night, but now it's fifty percent Okie. He's too tired to fake it this early in the morning. Worn out from smoking dope, and singing reggae songs, and planning details of the ceremonial rape.

Too tired to notice when she spits the single-edged razor blade into her hands and starts working on her ropes.

She leaves a few strands intact so the bindings won't fall away until the time is right. Then the blade will become a weapon and prove the Marley Men have been right all along about the treachery of women.

Stick Man taps his Rolex. "Are you feelin' irie?"

Mary won't stick around long enough to find out what *irie* means, and the last Reggae-English dictionary in the world has probably been burned in the ritual campfire.

Stick Man hobbles around the dying fire three times, a long way on bowed legs with atrophied muscles. He sings a few low energy verses of a song about sexual violence. Every Marley Man had a mother. They had sisters and girl-friends before the world they knew broke in a million pieces. Maybe they'll remember later, after the ceremony is over and her body is fertilizer for Jack Horror. Maybe they'll be sorry later on when it is too late to do any good.

Maybe she will make them sorry sooner.

Stick Man kneels in front of her, a few inches taller because she's sitting down. He tells her, "Ja want no more babies to be made."

She folds her legs underneath her the way she folds over the corners of library book pages to mark her place. This is a place in her life she'll revisit later on—if things work according to plan. She'll sit around her own campfire with guns and ammunition looted from Oklahoma City. Maybe she'll have friends. Maybe even a tame, civilized boyfriend to entertain with stories about the time she fooled the Marley Men and narrowly escaped with her life.

"Ja want all of us to die in our time."

She smiles and nods in agreement. Something this crowd has never seen a captured wild girl do. Their eyes stay on her face, away from her hands, while she stretches the rope until the last strands gave way. She holds the razor blade between the thumb and middle finger of her right hand, her index finger, poised on the protected edge like she is taking the pulse of the surgical grade stainless steel.

"But Ja want some of us to suffer."

She pushes herself up and forward, like a sprinter on an olden times track team. She rakes the edge of the razor blade across the side of Stick Man's face, not deep, just enough to lay open a wound that must be tended immediately.

He shouts as she jumps the campfire and runs into the old overgrown botanical garden.

Three sets of footsteps follow her. Two fall away before she's gone ten yards. But the remaining Marley Man is stronger, faster than the others. His footfalls grow louder, closer with each passing second. The pressure of his hatred fills the air between them with electricity that makes the tiny hairs along her spine stand up. His breath is deep and steady, like he's used to running in spite of his smoke-damaged lungs and his dope-damaged coordination.

Looking back would slow her down, so she sprints harder, desperate to pull ahead. Her pursuer is five yards back, maybe ten. She'll be out of the park in another few seconds, over the berm that once spared visitors from street noise, but now makes her escape route blind. Waist-high grass and creeper slows her down. The long-legged Marley Man gains a few critical feet. She feels his breath on her back as she reaches the top of the berm and jumps.

Her left foot tangles in a creeper vine as she pushes off. Not enough to send her tumbling, but she pitches forward as she hits the pavement. She dives into a roll, so she can change direction, charge at her attacker and cut his throat before he figures out she's not running anymore.

Murdered by a girl. Will that make him an outcast in reggae Heaven? She tumbles twice, bounces to her feet—blade ready. But the Marley man is face down on the cracked concrete, an arrow protruding from his back.

She drops to the ground. No one around that she can see, and there's little cover outside of the park. A few abandoned cars. Some bus stop shelters with broken panels. The shooter must have taken aim from the top of the berm. He could get her any time he wanted, and he hadn't.

"Show yourself." When that doesn't happen, she walks slowly to the body. She's never seen an arrow shaft like this one. Nothing any sporting goods store had ever carried. It's wooden, with an uneven surface, as if carved with a sharp edged tool. Imperfectly straightened, but obviously straight enough to kill.

Fletched with real feathers glued into slots in the arrow shaft's end with something that looks like dried blood. The arrow found its way between two ribs, pierced a lung, and probably a major artery or two.

A fluid ounce of blood leaks out as she pulls the arrow free. Not a stainless steel razor arrowhead as she expected. This one is made of flint. Pressure-flaked, thin with graceful lines, a deadly point and an edge sharp enough to cut hair. The kind of arrowhead Indians used to make back in the oldest olden times.

She drops the arrow beside its victim. The archer hasn't killed her yet. Maybe he doesn't intend to. She wipes her razor blade on her shirt, and slips it into her mouth. Stick Man's blood tastes sweeter than she had imagined.

Now plan B is all Mary has, until she finds something better. Oklahoma

City was full of guns and bullets in the olden times. More guns than people according to Raj, and he lived in Oklahoma City before the fall so he should know.

Too bad Raj didn't bring more guns and bullets with him when he escaped. When he saved her life. She crosses herself, like she always does when she thinks about him. So far it hasn't done much good, but you never know when ghosts are watching.

—

Styrofoam cups rattle against cracked curbing. Faded happy meal boxes flop along the pavement. Plastic grocery bags fly in circular currents between buildings. The same trash has roamed Oklahoma City since the troubles.

Mary stays in the middle of the streets as much as possible, away from the empty buildings with broken glass fronts and occasional mysterious noises in their dark interiors. Feral dogs and cats have taken up residence inside, staying close to home in case their people come back. How many generations will it take until they turn completely wild?

Everything she needs to survive will be inside the legendary Bass Pro Shop somewhere along the Oklahoma River. Built by Oklahomans at the pinnacle of civilization when people believed the world would never end if they had enough guns, ammunition, and Meals, Ready to Eat.

Beef stroganoff, lentil soup, Thai red curry chicken, honey glazed ham, stored in aluminum foil packets that keep them fresh for years after the people who made them turned to dust. Food she doesn't have to stalk and kill. Thoughts of a full belly crowd fear and curiosity out of her mind, even curiosity about old time Indian arrow sprouting between the ribs of a Marley killer.

The wind stops and the city goes dead quiet, like the few seconds of peace that come before a thunderstorm. Fragments of glass fall from a nearby building. They pick out a xylophone melody as they shatter on the pavement. Troubling sounds, almost hiding other sounds that are even more troubling, like claws skittering across the pavement somewhere behind her.

Three dogs, at least. She can't be sure, because of all the cars giving them cover. They stop when she stops, waiting to catch her in an open space. The philosophy of the pack.

Dogs can't open car doors, and the ones in the street might be unlocked. She must have ridden in a car a long time ago. Everyone did, once upon a time when there was gasoline. That had run out by the time she was three, according to Raj. There was still enough for motorcycles and Molotov cocktails for a few years after that.

The first door she tries is locked. No problem. The dogs hang back, in case she is bait in a complicated human trap. The second car is also locked, but the passenger side window is partially rolled down. Enough for her to put her hand inside and change her fate.

She's safe inside with the door pulled shut before the dogs can reach her. Well, not exactly safe. The heap of bones and rotted clothing behind the steering wheel is proof of that. Ants have stripped the flesh and tendons, probably the marrow too, but the indigestible minerals are still there. The skull with its empty eyes and permanent smile.

Her scream scares the dogs away, but not far enough to allow her out of the car. She opens the door but slams it shut again when the dogs come back. They don't know about the MREs in foil pouches. All they know about is Mary-ready-to-eat inside a rusty car that will open of its own accord if they wait long enough.

The pile of bones doesn't look so scary after all. Friendly, once she is used to it. A lot more friendly than the dogs that circle the car, whining and scratching at the doors, like olden times pets who want to be taken for a ride. One of them jumps onto the hood. He lies down, panting, hungry, patient, no reason to be anywhere else.

Is this how the previous occupant of the car died, waiting to be eaten by wild dogs? Probably not. The skull wears a plastic retainer with a silver wire around the front teeth. The pants are unisex, the shirt in tatters, but the shoes have heels and pointed, uncomfortable looking toes. Women's shoes. There's a purse in the back seat. Some kind of simulated reptile hide. Everything was simulated before the world went to hell.

Women carried guns in their purses sometimes. Mary dumps the contents on the seat, but there's no gun. No weapon of any kind, just a cell phone, and some makeup. There's a wallet with credit cards, a driver's license and a student ID. The dead girl's name was Sharon Winslow.

"What would you do?" Mary asks the picture on the driver's license. "Just between us girls."

She can see what Sharon Winslow did. There's a bullet hole in Sharon Winslow's temple, barely large enough to let the soul escape. A gunshot wound inside a locked car. Suicide.

Mary crosses herself and says, "In the name of the Father the Son and the Holy Ghost," before she sorts through Sharon Winslow's bones. She looks in the floorboard. She searches the space between the driver's seat and the driver's side door.

There it is. Not much as weapons go. A .22-caliber revolver, what people called a Saturday Night Special back when days had names. A fine patina of rust covers all the metal. The hammer makes a crunching noise as she pulls it back. She points the weapon at the dog on the hood, pulls the trigger, and waits while the hammer doesn't fall.

The dog licks the windshield, smiles a friendly predator smile. In better times this dog would be her faithful companion, but now he wants to eat her. He's willing to wait and he's not afraid of the pistol.

Maybe he shouldn't be afraid, but she keeps it pointed at him anyway. She pounds the handle on the dashboard trying to shake the hammer loose so it will fall on the percussion cap and prove to this pack of dogs that girls are more dangerous than they look. The dog presses its nose against the safety glass, investigates how his next meal is spending her last hour.

She pounds the pistol against the dashboard again and again, holding her finger on the trigger, until she hears a pop, like the last fluorescent light in the world just fell on the floor. Not nearly loud enough to be deadly but the safety glass breaks in a perfect black widow spider web pattern. The dog tumbles backward, leaving a trail of red splatters behind him. He limps along the pavement away from the car for a few feet and falls onto his side. The other two members of the pack sniff at him and lap his blood off the pavement.

Mary cocks the pistol. She steps out of the car and aims. The dogs flinch backward, but reconsider when the hammer doesn't fall. They move toward her with their heads down.

Back in the car. One dog down and two to go. She pounds the pistol grip on the dashboard again, but this time the hammer doesn't move. Even suicide is out of the question.

Inside Sharon Winslow's car is an ice scraper, an owner's manual, registration, insurance verification, an inexpensive handbag, a broken pistol, a pile of bones, and Mary. The two wild dogs have forgotten how things didn't work out for the first dog on the hood of the car. They take turns sniffing at the bullet hole in the windshield, picking up just enough scent to be sure she is terrified and edible.

"Got any ideas, sister?" She holds Sharon Winslow's skull up to the windshield so she can assess the situation. The dogs pull back—afraid of a dry skull even if they have no fear of the one Mary wears behind her face. Perhaps a pile of human bones can be useful after all.

She picks through Sharon Winslow's bones the way she's seen coyotes do. The upper leg bone is the longest and the strongest. One end is shaped like a ballpeen hammer. Not as scary as a skull, but more useful as a weapon.

Femur, she remembers. Olden times people gave dead things names from a dead language. Femur sounds a little like female, and that's what Mary is. She'll show these wild Oklahoma City dogs how girls take care of business.

She opens the car door, bowls Sharon Winslow's skull between the dogs, and charges the bigger one. She swings the femur like an axe, strikes the dog square in the side of the head, sends it yipping and running for cover.

Dogs' heads are a lot harder than Mary thought they'd be. The hip joint end of the leg bone separates with the impact. It leaves a sharp broken point behind that reminds her of the flint arrowhead she pulled out of the Marley Man.

The second dog considers his options for a moment, and then decides rats are a better dietary choice.

Mary whispers a silent prayer of thanks to Sharon Winslow. She climbs into dead girl's automobile to retrieve the pistol. Looters can't be choosers.

Should she take Sharon Winslow's keys, search her trunk for something useful? Should she confiscate Sharon Winslow's other leg, in case the dogs come back? In case there are more predators waiting between her and better weapons? There are always more predators. Always something bigger waiting to ambush her. Waiting to eat her or worse.

Sometimes not even waiting patiently.

—

FOOTSTEPS STAND OUT IN A DEAD CITY. Four shuffling men, if Mary's count is right, and one hard rubber wheel rolling along the pavement. She steps out of the car holding the gun at her side. Not a threat, exactly, but not friendly either.

The Marley Men form a semi-circle, trapping her between them and Sharon Winslow's car—four of them, all right, with Stick Man riding in a wheelbarrow. They want the same thing from her as the dogs, but the Marley Men have guns.

Stick Man tells her, "Throw the pistol down, or we kill you now instead of later." Not a trace of Jamaica in his voice, only hate and left over pain.

She shows the Marley Men her rusty pistol with its hammer frozen back, useless, but they don't know that yet. She tosses it toward Stick Man, under-handed, the way girls pitched softballs in the olden times. The Marley Men watch the rusty pistol spin through a graceful parabolic arc and strike the pavement. They continue watching while the hammer falls and the gun discharges with another deceptively ineffective pop. They look to Stick Man for instructions now that the girl has been disarmed more easily than they expected, and only then do they realize the .22 bullet has pierced their leader's throat.

She thanks the ghost of Sharon Winslow again before she takes off running, because that bullet might have gone anywhere but it had gone exactly where she needed it. Like it was planned by a higher power who liked Mary but didn't care much for Stick Man.

She runs between two buildings before the Marley Men remember they have guns and numbers on their side. One of them fires as she turns a corner. They won't expect her to double back, and they'll be afraid of her, because it must look like St. Robert Nesta Marley is on Mary's side. One more corner and she's back, almost where she started.

The Marley Men aren't chasing her. They can't. They're lying in the street surrounding Stick Man, all dead with arrows sprouting from their chests. As silent as the viruses that killed millions of riot survivors, as quick as the mass suicides that emptied cities.

The archer steps out of an abandoned shop with broken picture windows and no door, a bronze-skinned man with long black hair tied in a ponytail. Taller than her, but not by much. Better looking than Raj, and maybe a little younger. He carries a compound bow, and wears a quiver of homemade arrows on his shoulder.

"Been watching you." He moves to the nearest body and uses a hunting knife to dislodge his arrow. He moves to the next man and the next without a word, harvesting his arrows the way Marley Men gathered Jack Horror plants from their gardens. He adds the arrows to his quiver, stands a dozen feet away looking at her as if she were the eighth natural wonder of the olden times world.

"Something special." No emotion colors the archer's words. No wasted words. No wasted energy.

"You're something special too." Her voice isn't as calm as his, partly because her life had been at risk twice in the last ten minutes, but mostly because this is the first man since Raj who didn't want to kill her.

Safe to stand close to him. Safe to talk to him. Safe to flirt with him. She smiles the way olden times girls smiled on posters advertising beer. She picks at his body with her eyes, one XY particle at a time, until she's memorized every detail.

Prettier than a switchblade knife. Prettier than a 9mm pistol full of bullets. Prettier than a crate of MREs.

A finders-keepers kind of man.

THE DREAMING
MOON

MY ALMOST MOTHER-IN-LAW brushes a hint of red onto her cheeks while she recites a poem about lost youth and dying flowers. That jar of blush might be the only one left in the world, and Mona is careful to make it last. Sunscreen went stale long ago. Moisturizer turned to dust. People never considered the cosmetic implications of worldwide disaster.

Mona stumbles over a few more lines of her poem but stops when the meter goes wrong. "Really Karma. What are you and Joseph waiting for?"

Lipstick lesbians like Mona are full of advice for heterosexual girls, but we have to deal with men—sexually supercharged creatures with penises and facial hair and attitudes that have made women's lives miserable since the Garden of Eden. I shrug instead of telling Mona her only son is completely impossible. He's smug and impatient and pretends he doesn't understand what I am hinting at so clearly. Especially lately. Especially right before he left on one of Mona's missions.

She practices her mystical look in the mirror and tells me to grab the Ouija board. "Governor Anotubby will meet us in the Oracle Cave for a reading." She's wearing red Capezios and a designer dress looted from a store in Tulsa right after civilization collapsed. A short skirt and a runway walk will make the most important Choctaw in the world a true believer. She brushes concealer over a blemish on her chin and checks the lacquer on her nails.

"A girl has to maximize her assets."

I don't say, "You haven't been a girl for a long time."

I don't ask, "What will you do when the last makeup in America is gone?"

She sent her only son all the way to Oklahoma City on a quest for wrinkle cream and lip-gloss, "As well as other necessities." He was happy to go, even though I didn't want him to. Even though it was a very bad time, for reasons that I didn't want to discuss quite yet. But now I wish I had.

"Maybe Joseph will find something for you, Karma," Mona says, as if she knows he's on my mind. "Maybe something that will lift your spirits and your. . . ." She places the palms of her hands under her breasts and gives them a microscopic lift. "You've been looking a little down—you know?"

I know. Mona is the fairest woman in the land, even if she is past forty now. Too bad her boy Joseph is stuck with poor plain Karma, who doesn't even have a pleasing personality.

Mona smiles, and then remembers the cavity in her central incisor and tones it down. She pictures Mona Lisa in her mind. Mona Beaver is a lot prettier than that frumpy old Italian but she hasn't quite mastered the enigmatic smile.

"It will all work out, Karma." She kisses me on the cheek, softly, so her lipstick won't smear. "A mother knows these things, you'll see."

I'll see. For a second I feel like crying, but the tears never make it to the surface. Exactly what kind of things does a mother know?

—

AFTER THE SUN HAS SET behind the Ouachita Mountains, Mona perches on her special rock in the Oracle Cave with a Ouija board on her way-too-pretty legs and tells the Governor what he wants to hear—"A spirit fog covers the calendar but Joseph will return before the Dreaming Moon. He's found. . . ."

She squints into the great unknown, not quite hard enough to deepen the lines around her eyes, and ponders the Great Mystery. Everybody knows how stingy spirits are with details, but Joseph's quest is a success. As usual.

Governor Anotubby listens while he peeks at Mona's hemline. I sit across from her with my fingers poised on the plastic pointer and nudge it in the right direction so she doesn't misspell important words like Chief, or Pusmataha, or, God forbid, Anotubby.

Mona gives the Governor a smile that barely shows the brown spot on her front tooth. "Any questions?"

"We're short on drugs," he tells her. "Especially antibiotics."

All the pharmaceuticals in the world reached their expiration date years ago, but most of them still work—of course they might work like Mona's readings. They might just give us something to do while we either get well or die.

My almost mother-in-law and I sit facing each other, pretending we're not pushing the heart shaped stylus around the gothic letters on the board. We used to have scientists to tell us what to do, but now all we have is Mona Beaver, Oracle of Wilburton.

She mumbles a list of all the great Choctaw chiefs she can remember and pauses while I guide the stylus around the board. She does pretty well with Tuscaloosa and Taboca, but slurs Apuckshunubee. Who can blame her?

Mona moistens her lips when she calls on Pushmataha, the greatest Choctaw Chief and her favorite spirit messenger. She whispers his name like it's an offer of sexual favors and turns her gaze on the Governor. He doesn't notice I'm the one steering the heart shaped plastic pointer across the appropriate letters. Mona makes me fade into the scenery.

Governor Anobtubby is perfectly willing to believe a lipstick lesbian like Mona suddenly sees the attraction of heterosexuality. If she plays it well enough, he won't remember what everybody knows—that Mona Beaver has never been with a man, that her son Joseph is the product of artificial insemination.

Men find that whole virgin thing a turn on—don't ask me why—but virgin birth scares the hell out of them. That's why Mona is the Oracle. She's a beautiful, mysterious virgin mother—like another one I could name if it wasn't sacrilegious.

"*Pushmataha*," she says again, putting an edge on the consonants to sharpen the Governor's attention.

Votive candles light the cave, salvaged from a religious warehouse in McAlester. The flickering light makes rock shadows flutter like owl's wings. According to legend, Jesse James spent time in this cave. So did Belle Star, and other less famous outlaws of the Indian Territory. It's not a proper cave at all. Just a pile of rocks crowded into a shelter for homeless spirits. Geologists probably had an explanation for it, but they're all gone.

Names and dates are carved into the rock along with hearts and plus signs—the mathematics of romance. Joseph loves Karma is written in quarter-inch deep scratches above Mona's head. A gray patina covers the rock, but the scratches cut through the oxidized layer into the heart of the golden stone, exposing flecks of silica that sparkle like stars in the postindustrial sky. Jennifer loves Jake now and forever is engraved below our names in letters that are rounder, smaller, more feminine. Forever has come and gone, but their profession of love is still here, frozen in time like the memory of a first kiss.

Pushmataha speaks to the Governor using Mona's seductive voice. "Patience is the measure of a leader."

The greatest Choctaw Chief gazes at Governor Anotubby through Mona's eyes like foreplay is next on the agenda. Pushmataha-Mona is full of compliments and vague advice, but after a while there's no more spirit small talk. A deep breath followed by a meaningful pause. My signal to produce the gold-plated pocket watch that belonged to my father back when hours mattered.

"My, look at the time." The hands have been stuck at five o'clock for a decade.

"Yes," Mona runs her fingers through her recently colored hair that doesn't show any gray after sunset. The hot dead chief is gone and the lesbian oracle is back, still looking good but out of reach.

"So Joseph will be back with the antibiotics?" The Governor makes the statement into a question by running it uphill.

Mona lets the question hang in the air until I show her the watch again.

"Indications are positive," she says as if she's reading answers on the crystal.

Mona's butch girlfriend, Chris, walks into the cave as if on cue.

"Pardon me." She gives Governor Anotubby a modified salute, as if she's a soldier in his army. "Joseph is back."

She looks like she wants to say something else, but instead she turns and walks out of the cave.

—

THE CIVILIAN CONSERVATION CORPS BUILT the Oracle's Lodge in 1939 from native stone and cedar, so it fits well with post-apocalyptic conditions. No air conditioning. No central heat. No electricity. None of the things that made a mockery of roughing it in the good old days of excess and luxury.

Torchlight fills the room with dancing shadows, so it's not much different from the cave. Joseph looks like a pre-Columbian warrior in the flickering light, with his braided hair, his bronze skin, and his black eyes that reflect the torch flames like signal fires.

Those eyes are locked on the two large booty bags he's brought from Oklahoma City. He studies them as if they are prehistoric chrysalises about to break open and release extinct monster butterflies. He doesn't look at me, or Mona, or Governor Anotubby, and he most certainly does not look at the teenage girl with her arm laced through his.

But she looks at each of us in turn, saving me for the last. She and I stare at each other, figuring things out.

She's younger than I am and prettier. We both know it. Her hair is the lustrous black color Mona's used to be before the world ran out of conditioner. Mine must look like a stack of dirty blond hay by comparison.

Her eyes are the color of the turquoise ring Joseph gave me after his last quest. I explore the stone with my thumb while the teenager works her arm around Joseph's waist and pulls herself so close I think she might be laying eggs inside him like a parasitic wasp.

She makes sure she is the center of attention by shifting her hip, like an old time prima ballerina executing a perfect seduction scene. Her flawless skin glows with the warmth of sexual invitation smoldering inside her perfectly proportioned chest that rises and falls in the rhythm of a bolero. Even I want to touch her.

She says, "Joseph saved my life."

Joseph finally looks my way. He shrugs with his eyebrows. What choice did I have?

The girl shows us a smile so dazzling it makes the room turn darker. "My name is Mary." She has the voice of a country and western singer who knows exactly how to steal your man. Funny how I never thought of Joseph as my property until this moment.

I move toward them like a coyote on the trail of an injured rabbit. I put my arms around Joseph—pulling him away from Mary. There's a little tug of war, but it's over in a second. I press my breasts against him, even though they've been a little sore lately.

I whisper, "I'm so glad to see you," my words as full of moisture as jungle air. Like I have something special planned for later. Something that would stain my reputation if anyone found out. Something so delicious that no beautiful teenager would know anything about it.

"Hey there." Mary pokes my shoulder. She's found a place where no muscle covers the bone so it hurts a little. "You must be Karma. Joseph told me all about you."

I want to say, "Has he, now?" but I know I won't be able to get the proper offended tone quite right, so I step back and take a look at her.

Lovely, ingenuous. I didn't realize that word was part of my vocabulary. Mary glows like a religious icon, with an inner light that displays her like a neon advertisement for the Goddess of Love. She's as ripe and ready to consume as an October apple.

It's October now and I'm a piece of fruit that's fallen to the ground, hoping someone gathers me before I rot. I'm standing in front of a tiny teenage girl—maybe five feet two inches tall. Goliath vs. David. She doesn't need a sling. Mary's body is shaped like a three-minute egg timer, exactly the amount of time it took Joseph to achieve his last orgasm—the last one I know about, anyway. She extends her elfin hand for an old fashioned businessman's handshake, as if she's offering me a deal. Her fingers are exquisitely shaped, but there is a layer of black grime beneath one nail. Thank God for that. Otherwise she'd be perfect.

Mary walks over to Mona, who is speechless for the first time since I've known her.

"Are you Mona or Chris?" she asks as if there is no significant difference between the beautiful Oracle of Wilburton and her low-estrogen girlfriend.

Chris is nowhere around. She's never needed to compare herself to beautiful teenage girls. For the first time in my life, I wish I was a lesbian, although it doesn't seem to be helping Mona.

Mary turns to Joseph. "You could—you know—introduce me." Her movements look like choreography, but her words don't match. The content is simple, even ignorant, and the tone is filled to the brim with disrespect. Pretty and unlikable—but so pretty that unlikable doesn't matter to the two men in the room.

I can't blame Joseph for losing the power of speech, or the Governor, who hasn't said a word since he entered the Oracle's Lodge. Their minds are occupied by thoughts of Mary naked.

"This is Mona," I tell her.

"Guess I should have known." Mary taps her forehead with her fingertips. "Joseph said she was really pretty."

I wonder what Joseph said about *me*.

—

"AMOXICILLIN, CLINDAMYCIN, CIPROFLOXACIN." JOSEPH STACKS the boxes of expired generic antibiotics at Governor Anotubby's feet. Enough to cure a gonorrhea epidemic.

He's brought cosmetics for Mona, and ammunition for Chris. For everybody else he's brought sewing kits, sutures, hunting knives, scalpel blades, compasses, bundles of athletic socks and underwear.

I see things he's brought especially for me in the bottom of one bag, things he won't show to anyone else. A gross of Trojan condoms, still unopened—that's a good sign. A Victoria's Secret chemise, still in the package—just what every girl needs to keep her warm now that central heat is gone forever.

Joseph is so full of wants and needs he can barely tell the difference between his desires and mine. That's the way men are. He winks at me, forgetting the fight we had before his Mona-quest. The fight that wasn't really about anything except that I feel like fighting lately, when I don't feel like crying.

Feelings change, like when I don't like being touched by anyone, especially Joseph. Like how the taste of blackberries drizzled in honey makes me nauseated, even though they used to be the best thing ever. Like how my favorite pair of pants are too tight now and my ankles are bigger than they used to be and all the colors in the world are a little bit too bright, and all the odors are too strong.

Joseph reaches into the bag and draws out a gold chain one inch at a time. When he's sure everybody's watching he says, "Ta da," and pulls the necklace all the way out so I can see the amber pendant shaped like a heart.

He says, "Ta da," again, in case nobody noticed what a clever thing it was.

He puts the necklace around my neck as if I just won the gold medal at the love Olympics. I pretend to be interested in the prehistoric gnats trapped inside the petrified tree sap so I won't have to look at the identical necklaces he's brought for Mona and Mary.

Men are so stupid, and there are so few to choose from.

———

"WHO COUNTS YEARS ANYMORE?" Mary puts her hands on her hips the way Shirley Temple used to do in old time black-and-white movies. "It's not like there's voting anymore, or legal drinking age, or driver's licenses."

"Or statutory rape," I tell her, as if I might know a secret law that still applies even after the law books have all disappeared.

She looks younger in daylight, especially when she makes a point of ignoring me and scrambles up the rocks outside the Oracle Cave looking for signs left behind by the *"olden days people."* Everything is *"olden days"* to Mary. She's too young to remember cars speeding down highways or cable television. She thinks Cher and Elvis are characters from the Bible. She thinks they came from Oklahoma.

"So how old are you, Mary?"

She runs her finger over a backward swastika carved into the rock by some young man whose great-great grandfather probably went to war with the Nazis. She tells me how she was on a quest, looting the remnants of civilization for useful things.

"You know." She turns her head so I can see the tears forming at the bottom rim of her eyes. "Like Joseph." Mary looks at the sky when she says his name, and collapses her upper body against the boulders as if she's a rock climbing marionette and God has just released the strings.

"The Marley men captured me." Her voice is thick with the memory of something bad that almost happened. "A scruffy old black man was the leader. He had dreadlocks and scars and he knew all the words to every reggae song ever written." Her tears run down her cheeks and dribble off of her chin. She wipes them away with one hand and nearly loses her balance. "Joseph killed him. Just for me, and it's kind of sad because he might be the last black man in the whole wide world. Like an endangered species, you know. Like dinosaurs and dodo birds and Democrats and Republicans—gone forever." She sacrifices her handholds on the rock for the sake of a dramatic gesture and slides a foot or two before she finds another.

"Lots of African Americans live with the Choctaw in Durant," I tell her. "You could go back there with Governor Anotubby. He'll introduce you."

"No way." Mary talks exactly like middle school girls did back when there was such a thing as junior high and adolescence. She wants to be my, "Best friend forever." She also wants to steal Joseph from me. She doesn't see how both things can't work out.

"How old are you, Mary?" I have her trapped on a pointed rock covered with Scotts and Heathers, two vandal lovers who came here five years in a row with a sharp knife and a can of red spray paint. Their relationship spanned from 2006 through 2011, but in 2012, Scott wrote Rachael's name next to his own inside a heart.

Below the declaration of love he printed *"HEATHER IS A WHORE"* in two-inch block letters.

That's how you end an argument in stone.

"How old?" I stand in her only egress so she'll have to stay up there until one of us dies of starvation or has to go to the bathroom. Now Mary understands we are rivals in a war of love, and I am a product of the devious ancient times that tore apart the love of Scott and Heather.

"How old?" I consult my father's pocket watch—still five o'clock. "I have all the time in the world."

"Okay! I'm thirteen. Are you happy now?"

—

EVEN JOSEPH THINKS MARY LOOKS like a little girl now that he knows how old she is, but she's still a very cute little girl, and men have a way of forgetting things like age.

"Way too young for you," Mona reminds him, "Thirteen is the most irresponsible age ever."

Joseph pretends he hasn't got the slightest idea what Mona is talking about. His eyes light up for a moment, like he's just thought of some clever way to change the subject. He starts to speak but Mona beats him to it.

"Sexual awakening." She looks at me as if this is something all girls know about, but the world ended before my sexual alarm clock woke me up. Joseph is the only boy I ever really liked, and I was his first and only girlfriend and suddenly we were holding onto each other really tight because people get lost so easily when civilization slips away. Before we knew it Joseph was carving my name and his in the Oracle Cave with the word love in between.

"Joseph loves Karma," I say out loud without meaning too.

His face turns red and he chews on his lower lip hard enough to make it swell.

Mona pretends she doesn't notice. "Thirteen-year-old girls want boys to like them, but they're not sure what that involves."

I wonder how she knows this because—except for Joseph—Mona never wanted boys to like her.

"Thirteen-year-old girls make promises they don't want to keep," Mona says. "And men always believe them because they're men—bless their little testosterone-soaked hearts."

Joseph looks even more embarrassed when she says this, but he also looks like he knows it's absolutely true.

"Mary needs a mother." It's pretty clear that Mona wants the job, as if being the Oracle of Wilburton isn't enough. "Someone who knows exactly how to put her on the right track." Mona looks at Joseph when she says this, because he is the wrong track Mary is currently on. "Someone who can show her how to mend a broken heart."

I remind her, "Mary doesn't have a broken heart."

"She will, when the Dreaming Moon is full."

Now that calendars are gone all the moons have names, like the Green Apple Moon, and the Hunters Moon, and the Dreaming Moon that waxes halfway through the old-time month of October. The moon of first frosts, and nightmares, and coyotes singing songs to spirits.

"It'll be easy," Mona says. "Mary's so impressionable."

"Impressionable." Joseph is all dreamy-eyed, like the word has something to do with touching thirteen-year-old cream-colored skin in places no man has ever touched before. He reaches out with one hand and caresses my neck. He kisses me and wipes his lips with his fingers.

Comparing me with Mary, I realize, even if he doesn't. Figuring out who is softer, who is sweeter, which one thinks he is the most important man in the whole world.

"Joseph." I whisper his name to bring him back from dreamland. I put my lips over his and explore his mouth with the tip of my tongue. I look into his eyes and make my breath tremble, faking an orgasm perfectly.

This won't go anywhere, because Mona is in the room, but Joseph knows without a doubt, *"Karma loves him best of all."*

Mary isn't the only one with an impressionable mind.

—

MARY DOESN'T KNOW SHE'S THE CENTER of attention. She takes turns looking at Joseph and Mona and me as we sit on our rocks inside the Oracle Cave and wait for something special to happen. Everything is special to a girl like Mary, even ceremonies Mona made up to trick her.

The cave is lit by candles arranged in a circle around the four of us so we're a target for the spirits. According to Mona this is the night the Dreaming

Moon turns full. We can't see it from inside the cave, but there are holes in the rocks that let in moonlight and starlight.

The rock walls press against each other like gravity is stronger when the sun goes down. Everything looks solid and dark outside the reach of the candlelight, pushing us toward the center of the magic circle.

Mary doesn't remember a time when there was no Oracle of Wilburton. She doesn't remember Facebook or McDonald's, or the latest and greatest Apple smartphone with a thousand useful applications. No Wikipedia or Google. No MTV or Netflix, or rap songs about hos. The history of the world is thirteen years of gossip to Mary, just words written in books she never read.

The truth is whatever Mona tells her—isn't it? And miracles happen all the time—don't they?

Joseph sits close to me but he can't keep from checking Mary out with not-so-discrete glances every few seconds. She looks so pretty in the candlelight, so ready to make an impulsive decision that will change everyone's life forever.

"Listen." Mona looks taller than the rest of us from her seat on the Oracle Rock, like she is the only adult in the room. It's easy for Mary to do what Mona says, easy for Joseph too, because he's been doing what she says since he learned to talk.

Not so easy for me, because Mona isn't my mother, and the rock I'm sitting on is digging into my bottom and sending a burning sensation all the way to my ankle. But I hear coyotes singing their song in the surrounding hills, calling to each other, and to the spirits who walk the earth under the influence of the Dreaming Moon.

"It's starting," Mona tells us, and we are all a little bit afraid. Even me, and I know there's nothing magic about Mona.

She seems to know exactly where trickery stops and mysticism starts. Mona rises from her seat, and extinguishes the candles one at a time, plunging us into darkness incrementally, making the stars and moonlight shining through cracks in the rock seem brighter and more important.

"It's time." She blows the last candle out as every coyote in the hills sings the same note.

The Dreaming Moon drifts on the coyote song over a space between rocks and captures Joseph and me in a silver rectangle of light. Mona and Mary are invisible. The rock walls are invisible. There's only Joseph and me, and the Dreaming Moon accompanied by coyote songs.

The rectangle moves off of us, across the floor of the cave and up the wall illuminating hearts and initials and plus signs until it stretches around my name and Joseph's and part of the inscription directly below it.

Joseph loves Karma
Now and forever

Then the moonlight rectangle vanishes, leaving only the darkness and the coyote songs until Mona lights a candle.

Joseph and I are locked in an embrace, and Mary is covering Mona's shoulder with tears.

Joseph belongs to me, the Dreaming Moon has chosen.

Mona whispers mother-words in Mary's ear. She kisses the tear streaks on her face, and promises better times to come.

I feel an almost imperceptible movement inside me. Then another. I guide Joseph's hand so he can feel it too. He smiles at me the way men have smiled at their wives since this happened for the very first time.

"It'll all work out," I say, loud enough for Mary to hear. "A mother knows these things."

The author and publisher wish to thank the organizations and publications in which parts of Sacred Alarm Clock *have appeared previously.*

End Times Confusion was published in *Constellations a Journal of Poetry and Fiction, Vol. 3,* December 18, 2013.

An Inconclusive Girl was published in Kansas City Voices, Col. 11, September 2013.

Sacred Alarm Clock was published in the online magazine *Open Road Review,* issue 4, Feb. 2, 2013.

A Different Kind of Indian was published in *Eleventh Transmission,* Oct. 2014.

Manning Up published by Chupa Cabra House in *Small Town Futures,* October, 2014.

The Most Mysterious Way Possible was published by the print and digital magazine, *Pravic,* issue 3, June 2013.

Following Footprints was published in the on line flash fiction site, *Lightning Cake,* April 3, 2013.

Messages was published as a *Max Avalon* short by Zahrmae Publishing Press, February 15, 2014.

In an Instant was published in *Urban Fantasy,* an anthology by KY Stories, August, 2013.

Bounce was published in *Alban Lakes Frostfire Worlds,* May, 2014.

Crossing was published by Deepwood Publishing in the *Ruined Cities* anthology, November 27, 2013.

Dreaming Moon was published in *Clerics, Charlatans, and Cultists,* by Gothic City Press, July, 2013.

EVERYTHING JOHN T. BIGGS WRITES IS so full of Oklahoma that once you read it, you'll never get the red dirt stains washed out of your mind. The tribes play a significant role. No authentic discussion of the state is possible without them. Traditional Native American legends are reworked and set in the modern era, the way oral historians always intended.

One of John's stories, "Boy Witch" took grand prize in the 80th annual Writer's Digest Competition in 2011. Another won third prize in the 2011 Lorian Hemingway short story contest. Sixty of his short stories have been published in one form or another, along with several of his novels—*Owl Dreams, Popsicle Styx, Cherokee Ice,* and *Sliders.*

Facebook: John T. Biggs
Twitter: @biggspirit

www.johnbiggsoklahomawriter.com

www.ingramcontent.com/pod-product-compliance
Lightning Source LLC
Chambersburg PA
CBHW020906180626
46816CB00007BA/2274